To Lydia
Happy 2020
hugs LOliver

# Get Off My Case
## Book One: Stockton Wolves Series
### By
### Lisa Oliver

Get Off My Case is a work of fiction. Names, characters, places and incidents are either the product of the author's imagination or are used fictitiously and any resemblance to any actual persons, living or dead, events or locales is entirely coincidental.

**Warning:**

This book contains material that maybe offensive to some people including graphic language, cursing, explicit sex between males, male-male sex, anal intercourse, oral, rimming.

The author acknowledges the trademarked status and trademark owners of the following trademarks mentioned in this work of fiction:

Armani Suits, from the Armani range.

Clive Christian's X Factor

Ferrari F12 Berlinetta

Mt Diablo State park

California Penal Code 647(b) PC

Two naked men lying on a bed; the smaller one on top of the bigger one, his head resting on the other man's chest. The man underneath has his arms up around his lover. There is the hint of a white fluffy rug covering them from the hips down. The two are obviously lovers and are at peace with each other.

Genre: Paranormal Romance

Tags: Paranormal, Detectives, wolf shifters, gay-for-you, enemies to lovers, HEA

Content Warnings: None

**TITLE: GET OFF MY CASE**

By Lisa Oliver

Read and edited by my beta reader

Proofread by my writing group

## Dedication

*Thank you to the MMRomanceGroup at Goodreads for putting this event together. A huge thank you also to Isla for her lovely letter and to Stephanie for her skills as beta reader and editor.*

# Prologue

*Eight years ago*

Shane was running as fast as he could, the sound of his pursuers' feet ringing in his ears. He was sweating bullets, his heart was pounding and his lungs felt as though they were going to burst right out of his rib cage. But he didn't stop. He knew if he could get through to the school's cafeteria he would be safe, at least from a physical beating. Sure, the taunts and name calling would still continue and he would probably be humiliated in front of the entire school, but he wouldn't be touched. All he had to do was duck down the alley way coming up, run about another 100 meters or so after that and the cafeteria building would be in sight. Shane ran faster.

As soon as he turned into the alley he realized his mistake. There, leaning against the wall, was his biggest nemesis - Dimitri Polst. Tall, dark, and too fucking good looking for his own good, he had been tormenting Shane for as long as Shane could remember. Shane had heard that Dimitri had gone through his first shift on the last full moon so had actually thought the male had left school already. Seems Shane couldn't be so lucky especially as he saw the narrowed glare of pure hatred in the other shifter's eyes.

"There you are little pretty boy," Dimitri snarled, "I was hoping to get one more crack at you before I left."

Shane skidded to a halt and looked behind him. Three of Dimitri's friends, humans but big jocks all the same, were blocking the entrance to the alley. The only way out for Shane was past Dimitri. If Shane had shifted before he would have probably taken on his human predators, but Shane was two years younger than Dimitri and although his shift could come at any time, it wasn't likely to happen in the next five minutes. Besides, it was against pack law to shift in front of humans. Much like it was against his pack's law to be gay, or apparently, to look gay.

Taking a deep breath Shane adjusted his weight on his feet and then without warning took off running again - his plan simply to get past Dimitri and hopefully to safety. Shane was a fast runner, one of the fastest in the pack, but Dimitri had quick reflexes on his side and before he even had a chance to get away, Dimitri had grabbed him, snagging him around the waist with one strong arm and pulling him towards his chest. Shane cringed and raised his arms above his head in the hopes of forestalling the inevitable blow.

The blow never came.

Daring to peek at his attacker Shane could see an absolutely stunned look on Dimitri's face. It was like he was seeing Shane for the first time. Then without warning Dimitri pushed his face into Shane's neck and sniffed him, really sniffed him. Shane thought he imagined a little groan escape Dimitri's mouth although it was more likely to be a growl, but before he could process what was happening Shane heard the catcalling from Dimitri's friend.

"What you trying to do, D? Trying to snog the faggot? Gonna give him a hickey?"

Shane felt Dimitri push him away with a snarl and he landed in a heap on the ground.

"Course not. I'm more inclined to rip his throat out with my teeth," Shane heard Dimitri say, "But I can't be bothered with this shit. Don't want to get blood on my jacket. Come on, let's get a beer," and with that Dimitri walked away, gathering his friends as they left Shane alone in the alley.

What the fuck had just happened? Had Dimitri Polst just saved him from a beating? Why on earth would he do that?

Dimitri had been Shane's worst enemy since Shane had started kindergarten. It seemed wherever Shane went, Dimitri and his inevitable gang of friends were always there - calling him names, stealing his lunch money, making him cry, stuffing him in lockers, throwing his shoes in the dumpster.

As Shane got older the threats became more physically violent and many times Shane had gone home from school with a black eye and worse. While his mother fussed over him, his father refused to say anything to the Alpha about it. In his father's opinion Shane just needed to toughen up and cut his hair. Shane lived for the day when he would go through his first shift, because the first thing he was going to do once he knew he could access his wolf form successfully, was get the hell out of his pack and as far away from Dimitri Polst and the others like him as possible.

And that is what he did. When Shane was seventeen he went through his first shift and became a full wolf. He went home, packed his bag, told his mom and dad he was gay and walked out of the house as the shouting started. He had never been back.

## Chapter One

"So did you have a hot date last night?"

Shane heard his very pregnant partner's whispered comment even as he tried to slip unobtrusively into his seat. The regular Monday morning meeting had already started and Shane was more than five minutes late. He had been out in the park the night before having a well-needed run in his wolf form. There had been hares, and rabbits and well, time got away from him and he hadn't crawled home until well after three in the morning. The last place Shane wanted to be was at an early morning meeting listening to his Lieutenant drone on about statistics and the need for the police to present a caring face to the public.

Handing a large cup of hot chocolate to his partner, Ruby, Shane waggled his eyebrows at her, but didn't say anything. He was too busy trying to inhale his own jumbo cup of coffee. That was the only thing he needed - well that and a couple of cigarettes but as smoking had been banned in the precinct building for a while now that would have to wait until after the meeting had finished.

Leaning back in his chair, Shane half closed his eyes and let the drone of his Lieutenant's voice wash over him. Really the man never said anything new and Shane was sure the only reason for these mandatory meetings was so that the Lieutenant could hear the sound of his own voice. He was almost asleep when he heard a loud brusque voice yell out, "Listen up people."

Shit, when had Captain Reynolds come into the investigations room - the Captain never attended these meetings. Dimitri sat up a bit straighter in his chair and took another long sip of his coffee. He looked up over his cup to see what the Captain was doing, and stared straight into the eyes of Dimitri Polst.

Hell no, what was that man doing here?

Vaguely Shane heard the Captain introduce Dimitri as a new detective to the precinct, starting immediately. He registered that the Captain was waffling on about making the man feel welcome and all of that shit. But his mind couldn't get past the fact that after eight years, Dimitri Polst was not only in his fucking precinct, but he was coming here to work. Shane was just gob-smacked.

"Hey, you look like you've seen a ghost," Ruby smacked his arm and Shane looked around noting that the meeting was over.

"Yeah, it's nothing," Shane mumbled, "late night last night and all that, you know."

"I don't know, pretty boy, I'm pregnant haven't you noticed and haven't done anything exciting for months - so tell me did you have a date?"

Shane laughed and shook his head. Ruby Pearl was a fine Detective and a really good partner. She was a short little thing and perps often underestimated her fighting ability, her smart mouth and quick wit. Before she had gotten pregnant she could almost outrun Shane and that was saying something. Shane was going to miss her when she went on leave at the end of the week.

"You know I don't date, Rubes. I just fuck, often," he commented wryly, opening his drawer and pulling out his case files. They currently had three open homicides and Shane wanted to go over the material to see if he could come up with anymore leads. All three of the victims were young gay men who had all been out clubbing when they were apparently intercepted on their way home, strangled and their faces slashed by some kind of knife.

Despite the amount of carnage on the bodies, so far not one drop of evidence pointing to a possible killer had been found and while Shane wanted the cases brought together as a possible serial killer, so far the department, or rather his Lieutenant had been reluctant to do it. But as Shane went over his files again he realized what he actually wanted to do was anything he could in the hopes he would forget that Dimitri fucking Polst was going to be working in his department.

"Come on pretty boy," Ruby coaxed, "you can tell me. You know I live vicariously through your exploits."

"I can't think why," Shane replied as he started reading, "You know darn well I'm gay. Not as though you would be doing any of the things I like to do anyway."

"I'm not doing much of anything lately," Ruby said with a pout in her voice. The phone beside her rang and she picked it up. Seconds later she put the phone down and tapped on Shane's arm.

"Come on pretty boy, the boss wants to see us."

"Who, the Lieutenant?"

"Nope, you'd better put your jacket on, 'cos it's the Captain that wants to see us both, right away. What have you done this time, Shane?"

"I haven't done anything," Shane hissed, even as he ran his mind over his recent busts. Because his senses were that much sharper than humans, Shane would usually scent out more in a scene than humans could, normally. Unfortunately that also meant there had been occasions where Shane hadn't wanted to wait for back up, or he had taken what some might consider unacceptable risks when collaring a perp. Those occasions had seen Shane and Ruby pulled up in front of the Captain for a lecture on team work and acting in a responsible manner.

Shane knew it was only because of his exemplary arrest record that he hadn't been fired before today although he had been suspended on full pay a few times. He always made sure the Captain knew that Ruby wasn't responsible for his actions, but as his partner she still had to suffer through any lecture they might get. Following his partner out through the Investigations unit and down the corridor to the Captain's office Shane was certain there wasn't anything he had done lately to cause his boss to have another go at him.

Maybe the Captain wanted an update on the three open cases he and Ruby had. No, that couldn't be it. All updates had to go through the Lieutenant first. That's why no-one had recognized the fact that a serial killer was on the loose. But as Shane and Ruby went into the Captain's office, Shane was surprised to see the Lieutenant was in the office as well. That was unusual.

Shane turned to close the door behind him and all of a sudden his senses were bombarded by the most amazing smell - Jasmine, rain on a summer day, a hint of citrus and the underlying throb of wolf. Forcing himself NOT to groan out loud even as his cock rose and throbbed in his pants and he was hit with the overwhelming urge to just find the source of that scent and wallow in it, Shane resisted banging his head on the door he was closing and instead turned to face the others in the room. Captain Reynolds, the Lieutenant, Ruby of course and Dimitri Polst.

For a moment all Shane could do was stand there, staring at the man who had been the source of so much of the bullying that Shane endured growing up. Dimitri hadn't changed much since Shane had met him in that alley all those years ago. He still had dark hair, now cut short enough at the back to conform to police policies but long enough on the top for Shane to fist if he ever got to fuck the man's delicious mouth. A man who could well be the central character in Shane's wet dreams from now on with his height, his well-formed chest and shoulders, trim waist, long legs and edible ass. Dimitri, who had the face of an angel with his dark eyes, straight nose, sinfully full lips, and a scent that Shane knew was going to drive him to hell, every single day. Dimitri - the straight man who should be his fucking mate! Oh hell no.

As Shane looked into those deep chocolate eyes he could see the amusement in the man's face. The sneaky fucking wolf already knew. He knew that Shane was his mate and he obviously thought the whole situation was hilarious. Well Shane didn't think it was funny at all. He was so angry he could spit.

What the hell was the man doing here, and how in hell did a straight homophobe become his mate? Were the Fates having an off day or something?

Shane didn't have time to consider those questions, although he would as soon as he could get some time to himself, but he noticed the Captain and Ruby looking at him with concerned expressions on their faces. Shane drew on the years of experience he had of keeping his feelings to himself and slapped a questioning look on his face saying quietly, "You wanted to see us Captain?"

"Yes, West, I want you to meet your new partner. Polst here will be taking over from Ruby at the end of the week and I thought it would be a good idea for the three of you to work together this week so that Polst is up to speed with your cases and how we do things here before he starts his job officially on Friday."

The captain looked as professional and calm as ever. The man had no idea he had just officially thrown Shane's life into a living hell.

Refusing to look at Dimitri's smug face Shane concentrated on Captain Reynolds.

"Respectfully, Sir, I thought we had agreed that the department couldn't afford to replace Ruby while she was on leave, and that I would be working my cases solo from now on. I have no problem doing that, as I explained at the time. I totally understand the department's need to make budget cuts," Shane added the last bit because he knew that would appeal to the Lieutenant who so far hadn't said a word.

The same Lieutenant who was now looking more than a little bit uncomfortable. "I understand what you are saying, West, and I appreciate your concern about the department's budget" he said curtly. The Lieutenant was one of the few men in the Investigations unit who blatantly didn't approve of Shane's sexual orientation and he made his distaste for Shane abundantly clear. The feeling was mutual.

"However," the Lieutenant went on, "I have been informed that taking Polst here into the Department will be a positive move given his skills and as he specifically requested a transfer here, we would be foolish not to take him up on his offer."

In other words, Dimitri was prepared to work cheap. But Shane's head was reeling - what skills? Since when was Dimitri even a Detective? And why the hell did he request a transfer to the very station where Shane had established himself? Totally unsure about what was going on, Shane decided the best defense was a good offense and he decided to fight with the one weapon he knew would put Dimitri off - the gay card. There was absolutely no fucking way he wanted to work with Dimitri and once Dimitri was aware that he was out at work, then Dimitri wouldn't want to work with him either.

"Sirs," Shane included the Captain and the Lieutenant in his sweeping gaze, although he steadfastly refused to acknowledge Dimitri. "You are aware of my sexual orientation and the fact that many of the cases I work on and the informants I deal with are mostly related to the gay community. I remember Polst from school and I think it would be unfair to put a man like him, with the skills you tell me he has, in a situation that he might find difficult or unpleasant to handle. Ruby, here" Shane nodded to his partner who was looking at him like he had grown three heads in the past five minutes, "has never had a problem working with me, the cases we deal with, or the informants and places we go to chase leads. I doubt I would be able to have the same sort of working relationship with a man like Polst given his *conservative* views."

Captain Reynolds glared at Shane. "There is nothing in this man's resume to suggest that he has a problem with homosexuals. I am sure, regardless of his personal viewpoint on the subject, that Polst is capable of conducting himself in a professional manner regardless of the environment. Isn't that right Polst?" Both the Captain and Shane turned to look at Dimitri who still had that smirk on his face.

"I have to confess I don't have a lot of experience in that type of lifestyle choice, Captain," Dimitri said in a deep sexy drawl. "We don't have many gay people in Jacobs Lake. However I am confident that I can work with West here without any problems. I am sure he can show me the ropes."

When the fuck did that man's voice get so deep and downright sexy? All Shane could ever remember about Dimitri's voice in the past had been his snarling and the hate that poured off that delectable tongue. Damn it, Shane thought his cock would just explode and he needed to get out of the office and away from Dimitri fucking Polst as quickly as possible.

It was that need that made Shane swallow his pride and accept the inevitable. There was no way he was going to point out what a homophobic bully Dimitri was because to do that would mean admitting his own past weaknesses. "My apologies, Captain, Polst. I had no right to judge a person without assessing their experience in an environment in person. Is that all now, Captain," Shane spoke directly to Reynolds, "Only if it is, I do have some leads I need to follow up. I am sure Polst won't mind if Ruby shows him our case files and gets him set up on the computer. I can fill in both Ruby and Polst on any information I get later today."

Captain Reynolds looked at Shane with that knowing bloody stare of his that always made Shane feel about ten inches tall. It was that look that suggested that Reynolds knew every single thing that was going on in Shane's head and it took all of

Shane's willpower not to flinch. Reynolds knew that Shane had never played the gay card in the office before. Sure everyone knew of his sexual orientation but Shane never spoke about it, never complained that most of the cases he dealt with were gay related, and never did he bring it up as a means of trying to get out of what was essentially a direct order from his boss. Shane had a sinking feeling that he was going to be called into the Captain's office again before the week was over.

But for now Reynolds simply nodded his head. Shane leaned down close to Ruby's ear and said, "I'll call you for your lunch order, okay?"

Ruby looked confused but she said, "Yes, sure, see you at lunch."

Shane nodded curtly at Polst and then fled the office. He grabbed his keys from his desk along with his notepad - he always preferred to write things down rather than record them on any of the plethora of electronic devices available, and headed out. He needed fresh air in his lungs and fast if he had a hope in hell of getting his cock under control.

Back in the office Captain Reynolds looked at Dimitri. "Is West going to have a problem with you, Polst, only I have to tell you he is one of our best Detectives and he does have innumerable contacts in the gay community that have been invaluable to our office."

"No Sir, no problem at all," Dimitri said firmly. "I am sure West and I will get along just fine."

Of course at the moment the Captain had no idea just how fine the two of them would be getting along. But Dimitri hadn't left his home, his pack and his job for nothing. He was going to get Shane in his bed and in his life if it was the last thing he did. Of course at the moment he didn't have a clue what he would do with him once he got him there, but hey that was what the internet was for and if there was one thing Dimitri was really good at doing it was research. So he plastered a smile on his face and decided that for now he would make an ally out of Ruby, his erstwhile mate's partner.  He had waited eight years to claim his mate - he could wait a little longer.

## Chapter Two

"I'm just not making any headway," Dimitri whined down the phone line.

"Well what did you expect, sweetie? You made the man's life a living hell while he was at school. He's not going to come running just because you have turned up, is he?" Angela's laughing voice mocked him over the phone.

"But he should," Dimitri persisted. "This 'thing' between us should make him want to be around me, not run out of the office every time I show up."

Dimitri was as frustrated as all get out. For an entire week Shane had flitted in and out of the office, leaving Dimitri with Ruby to go over case notes, files, office procedures and a host of other stuff that not only bored the hell out of Dimitri but made him more and more agitated. Every time Shane came near him, Dimitri felt his body respond. It didn't matter how many times he beat off in the shower or in bed at night, one whiff of Shane's scent was enough to set his cock off again - hard, leaking and so damn needy.

"Well, have you told him you want to go out on some of his enquiries with him?" Angela asked. "You know, do some interviewing yourself, meet some of the local informants; that type of thing?"

"Yes, I've suggested it - every freaking day. But he always has some excuse and takes off on his own."

"Well why don't you do your wolf thingy and track him down at night?"

"Grrr…" Dimitri said, "Because he reckons he works at night as well. He comes in for morning roll call, then goes out. Comes back at lunch and fills me and Ruby in on anything he has found. Then he goes off and says he needs to rest so that he can hit the streets at night. Ruby tells me that has been his routine for like, forever, and until she got too pregnant, she used to do the same thing."

"And he goes out at night without backup? Didn't you tell me he was a pretty little thing?"

Dimitri sighed. Angela knew all about Shane because Shane was the reason that he couldn't commit to Angela in the first place. The two of them had gone out for three years but when Angela said she wanted more, Dimitri was forced to tell her he actually had a mate and it wasn't of the female persuasion.

After laughing her head off, Angela made it her mission to get the two men together. Although she was human she knew all about Dimitri's wolf side and the whole concept of mates - thanks to Dimitri getting really drunk one night and telling her. Now Dimitri considered Angela one of his very best friends - she was definitely the only person he had told about his male mate.

His parents, his brother and sister, his pack and his other human friends that he had grown up with, all thought that Dimitri was off in Stockton being the same womanizing asshole he used to be before he met Angela. None of them knew that Shane was in Stockton either. It seems that when Shane had shifted and then left the pack, he left them entirely and no-one in the pack ever spoke of him.

Dimitri had heard a few unsubstantiated rumors that Shane had come out to his parents before he left, and that could account for the fact that the man was no longer welcome in the pack. Dimitri had used Social Security and DMV records to find out where the man had gone.

"Yes he was a pretty little thing, but damn Angela he has grown up to be a fine looking man. He has lost weight and packed on the muscle. There is not an ounce of fat on him. His long hair is now short as fuck but that just highlights his amazing green eyes - and cheek bones to die for. Oh shit, I'm mooning over him again, aren't I?" It wasn't the first time in the past week that Dimitri had waxed lyrical about how awesome he thought Shane looked now that he had grown up.

"Yup," Angela said without a trace of rancor in her voice.

"It's not just his looks. He smells like sex. All. The. Time. It's driving me nuts and I have the worst case of blue balls I've ever had."

"Do you even know what you are going to do with him when you do get him in bed?"

"Well," Dimitri drawled out, "not exactly. I...er...watched some porn but it didn't do anything for me. I think I know the mechanics, but watching two guys get off on each other really doesn't get me hot or anything. I simply tried to view it like an academic exercise and took notes."

"You took notes," Angela was laughing so hard Dimitri thought she would have a coronary.

"I'm not gay, okay? I don't know how I'm meant to learn about this shit." Now Dimitri was getting pissed off. He had been a sexually confident straight man since he was fourteen. He didn't need to be mocked because he didn't have a freaking clue what he was going to do with his male mate.

"Dimitri, hon, are you doing the right thing here?" Angela's voice had softened now. "If you get together with Shane, mate or whatever you call it, then people are going to think you are gay even if you only get hard for the one man. If you can't handle that then maybe you would be better to come back here and marry some female. She won't be your special one, but you stayed with me long enough for me to know you can fake it."

"Shit, Ang, I'm sorry. How many times do I have to tell you I'm sorry? If it was going to work with any woman, then it would have been you," Dimitri's voice was tinged with regret. He did love Angela in his own way and for the longest time he thought he could marry her and have the kids his parents were expecting. But the closer he got to making that commitment, the more he remembered the absolutely delicious way that Shane had smelt when he had tackled him that last time in the alley back at school.

After eight years apart from Shane the memory was still fresh in his mind and it got to the point where he avoided having sex with Angela because it felt *wrong*. Dimitri knew it was his wolf signaling him that it was time go to get his mate. The fact that Shane was totally the wrong gender, at least from Dimitri's human perspective, was nothing to his wolf. His wolf didn't care about discrimination or labels about sexuality. His wolf knew his mate existed. His wolf had smelt him and damn near tasted him and the older Dimitri got, the stronger that urge to claim his mate became.

"I'm not worrying about that now," Dimitri said forcefully. "I don't care what other people call me - that's their labeling system, not mine. Shane copes with it, and anything he can do I can do as well."

Angela sighed down the phone. "Okay then sweetie, where is Shane supposed to be tonight? You said that

Ruby left today so you are now *officially* the man's partner. Why don't you head off, find him and offer him some backup?"

Dimitri thought about what Shane had said at lunchtime. Shane was convinced the three unsolved homicide cases they had were the result of a serial killer and Shane mentioned going to a gay club in town to do some looking around and talk to some people he knew. He did mention the name of the club and Dimitri had written it down somewhere so that he could do some research on the place.

"Thanks Ang, you're the best, you know," he said to his friend fondly. "I guess I'm off to a gay club."

"Don't forget to wear tight jeans, and phone me tomorrow to let me know how you get on." Angela laughed as she hung up.

## Chapter Three

Shane couldn't decide if he was in heaven or hell. On the one hand dancing at Club Trucker was heaven. Surrounded by hot, sleek, masculine bodies; feeling and moving to a thumping beat; being caressed and stroked by more than one interested hand. Yep, this was gay heaven. But it was also hell in a big way. Because no matter who stroked him, or who pressed a solid cock against his back, Shane automatically moved away. His wolf knew he had a mate and he didn't want anyone touching the human side of Shane unless it was said mate.

Which, Shane figured as he danced and kept an eye out for his contact, actually put him in a type of purgatory. A sexual limbo and one that he would probably continue to be in for the rest of his life unless his mate had a change of heart and decided to embrace the rainbow side of life. Like that was ever going to happen. Fuck, Shane thought, his life couldn't get any worse.

Every day bought delicious torment. Every day Shane's wolf pined to see his mate - Shane refused to consider that his human side might want to as well. Every day for the past week Shane had gone into the office, made small talk with Dimitri and Ruby. He filled them in on what he was doing and set them routine tasks to follow up on any leads that he had found. Dimitri seemed good at that sort of thing and he had solid research skills. Not that Shane had noticed. Well maybe a little.

Every afternoon had found Shane desperately doing chores around his small house - anything to get rid of the tension that came from having a perpetually hard cock. Yes, he was supposed to be getting some sleep because he had been out at the clubs and on the street every night for the past week. But he couldn't sleep, was having trouble eating and he was feeling so strung out he was starting to think he wouldn't be able to wait until Sunday night to have his weekly run.

And as from today he really couldn't stop Dimitri from coming out with him as he went about his work. Ruby had phoned him a couple of times through the week going on about how unusual it was for him to go out alone. Shane and Ruby had been almost inseparable at work, going everywhere together. Ruby had a good instinct for people and she was invaluable in talking to people that might be nervous around Shane. His wolf nature, although hidden, seemed to leak out sometimes and humans, especially those trying to hide something seemed to pick up on it. Her perky nature combined with her small stature encouraged interview subjects to trust her and they often let on more than they might have simply because of her charm.

So, as from Monday, Shane was going to be in permanent purgatory, because how the hell was he going to be able to keep his hands off his mate when the guy would be in his car, walking with him on the streets, and coming with him to clubs just like this one. Okay, well that might be amusing. Shane couldn't imagine that Dimitri had ever been in a club like Truckers and it would be kinda funny to see just how professional the homophobe could be faced with so much blatant male sexuality.

Shane spotted his informant on the edge of the dance floor and quickly wove his way through the throbbing bodies to meet him. CJ was a cute little twink with bright blond hair and sweet blue eyes. Shane had met him when the young guy was homeless on the streets. After stopping CJ from getting a hell of a beating from a couple of much larger men, CJ had become a type of friend. He was also an incurable gossip and seemed to know everything that was going on in the streets, even though he was no longer homeless, having quickly taken up the offer of help with an apartment when Shane offered it to him.

"Hey CJ, how's it going?" Shane asked quietly as he quickly slipped the young man into his arms and pressed into him, much as he would if he was looking for a hookup.

"All good, boss man," CJ breathed in his ear as he slid his body along the Detective's muscled frame. "Got some news, if you're interested."

"Always interested little man." Shane glanced around. There were too many people around for them to talk in private. For a second he frowned. He could have sworn he had seen Dimitri's head across the room, but then Shane shook himself. There was no way that wolf would be in a gay club unless he had to be.

"Want to head out the back?" CJ cupped his hand suggestively over Shane's cock, which of course was hard again, because he had been thinking about Dimitri. "Looks like you might have something there for me to work with."

Shane gritted his teeth to stop the urge to bat CJ's hand away from his crotch. This was a game they played when they were at the club. Shane had never and would never take CJ up on his sexual offers, even if he hadn't met Dimitri. The boy was too young, too pretty and he was a friend

- not a fuck buddy. But he had never reacted so negatively to having his cock stroked before. Damn mating bond.

"You know that's not on the table, blondie, but let's just play it like it is until we get out of here, okay?" Shane whispered in CJ's ear as he led him through the club and down a hallway to the back entrance. The door was supposed to be alarmed but it never was. Too many people used the alley beyond for their quick blow jobs and even full fledged fucks.

Shane found a spot on the wall, deep in the shadows and leaned against the bricks, encouraging CJ to climb his body. CJ wrapped his legs around Shane's waist and buried his face in Shane's neck. To any casual onlooker it would look like the two men were necking, but Shane had found it was one of the most effective ways of getting information without making CJ out to be an informant.

CJ rubbed his hard little cock against Shane's abs and groaned appreciatively into Shane's neck.

"I could get off on this, you know," he whispered.

"Don't you fucking dare," Shane growled. "Tell me what you've got and let's get this over and done with as quickly as possible. I have other people to see tonight."

"Ever impatient aren't you big boy," CJ mumbled even as he continued to rub himself against Shane. "Okay, here's what I heard..."

\*\*\*\*

Dimitri had found Shane at the second club he went into. He hadn't been able to find the piece of paper he had written the name of the club on, so he did a Google search for gay clubs in the area and found three possible venues. As he entered the club, Dimitri spotted the wolf dancing in the middle of the dance floor, but from where Dimitri was watching he could see that Shane was keeping an eye out for someone. Just a few minutes later - just enough time to appreciate how well Shane filled out his tight black jeans, Dimitri saw Shane cross the dance floor and latch onto a small, pretty, young man with a shock of blond hair. The way the blond was clinging onto Shane made it clear that they were more than casual acquaintances and when Dimitri's enhanced eyesight picked out the way the little blond brazenly cupped Shane's cock through his jeans, his anger started to burn. It only increased when he saw Shane lead the smaller man out the back of the club.

"No fucking way," Dimitri snarled to himself as he forced his way through the Friday night crowds. The look on his face was enough to make most people get out of his way, although it might have also had something to do with the fact that he couldn't stop growling. He might not have claimed Shane yet, hell, he hadn't even really talked to him about their mating bond or the issues between them, but that didn't mean that Shane could just go off and let any young blond thing play with what belonged to his mate.

By the time Dimitri had got to the back door of the club he knew his wolf was close to the surface. He could feel his eyes changing and the hair on his arms start to tingle. It was only through sheer force of will that he stopped the change completely. Must not shift in front of humans, he tried to remind himself as he searched the dark alley, sniffing for his mate's unique scent. There, deep in the shadows. The young blond was wrapped around Shane's waist and neck like he belonged there.

Growling loudly Dimitri strode over to where the two men where hidden, his hands changing into claws as he itched to grab the little interloper and tear his body to inch sized bloody pieces. He couldn't and wouldn't hurt his mate, but he could and definitely would shred the little blond until he wasn't a threat to Dimitri's mating again.

"Dimitri, stop damn it!" Shane called out in a low voice as he carefully wound the young blond's arms from his neck. "This is not what you think."

Dimitri stopped himself, just, and watched as Shane spoke in a low voice in CJ's ear and then gave him some money. CJ looked up at Dimitri and scowled at him and then took off back into the club. Shane flung out his arm and grabbed Dimitri by his belt loops and smashed him into the same wall he had been leaning on while he was entangled in his blond. But Shane's eyes weren't full of passion, Dimitri noticed. His mate was pissed off with him, big time.

"You just cost me some valuable information, fuck wit. Now what the hell did you think you were doing?" Shane snarled at him in a low voice.

"Is that how you get all of your information, detective," Dimitri snarled right back. "By giving sexual favors to your tipsters?" Fuck, with Shane so close Dimitri could barely breathe. His cock was so hard in his jeans that it hurt and he couldn't break his stare with his mate. Man, this guy was awesome when he was angry.

Shane tipped his head to the side and then took in a deep breath, obviously smelling Dimitri's arousal. For a moment he looked confused, but that expression was gone in an instant and Shane's angry gaze was back again. He leaned in flush against Dimitri's body and growled softly in his ear, "CJ is an informant of mine. He's been beaten before for talking to the wrong people and I don't want to see my friend in hospital. We act like a hookup so he will be safe, asshole. So don't go judging what you don't understand."

"But you've fucked him, right?" Dimitri regretted the words the instant they came out of his mouth as he watched a flash of pure murderous intent race across his mate's hard face.

"Not that it's any of your business, fuckwit, but I have never done anything sexually with CJ or any of my informants. Unlike you, I have standards." Dimitri knew Shane was referring to the fact that when Dimitri was still in school he used to fuck anything in a skirt regardless of who it was. With his jock reputation and good looks he never lacked for girls willing to lift those skirts and give him what he wanted.

But right now Dimitri didn't care that Shane was angry with him, or that he might have fucked up an investigation. Shane was leaning on him, chest to chest, but had kept his groin area away from Dimitri. And Dimitri was so turned on he couldn't think. He needed friction on his cock and he needed it now. He reached out and grabbed Shane by his hips and pulled the man's groin into his. Both men groaned as their dual erections nudged each other and Dimitri rocked into Shane looking for more.

"What the fuck do you think you are doing?" Shane snarled. Dimitri could see Shane's eyes were blown with lust and the man was panting softly. Against his cock, Shane's sizable erection nudged his and for the first time in his life Dimitri wanted to see another man's cock. But not just any cock - Shane's.

"I haven't got a clue," Dimitri said honestly, his own deep voice raspy with lust, "But I know I like it."

## Chapter Four

Shane decided his brain was on the fritz. In one respect this was his dream, his mate wanting him as badly as he wanted his mate. But this was Dimitri, someone who Shane had pegged a long time ago as a bullying homophobe. The fact that this man was now rubbing his hard dick into Shane's like a cat in heat would be laughable, if it wasn't for the fact that Shane was so damned aroused he could barely keep his control.

Looking up at Dimitri's face, Shane thought he had never seen anything so beautiful. Even in the dark of the alley Shane's eyes could pick out the lust in Dimitri's shining gaze, the flared nostrils and the smell of arousal that was threatening to overwhelm the pair of them. Dimitri hadn't lied, he did like this, and if the rubbing was any indication he wanted a lot more.

Without a thought for consequences, Shane did what he had wanted to do since the first time he had seen Dimitri in his Captain's office. He ran a hand up to Dimitri's neck and pulled the man closer, crushing the man's lips beneath his own. Oh fuck, sweet heaven, one taste and Shane knew he was never going to be able to get enough of this man.

****

Dimitri didn't know what to think when Shane's lips hit his, but he quickly decided it didn't matter. Kissing Shane, because yes damn it, he was going to kiss the man back while he had the chance, was nothing like the thousands of kisses he had shared with girls. Shane's lips were soft but they were applied with precision and confidence. The man knew what he was doing and he played Dimitri's lips like a finely tuned instrument.

As the kiss went on, Dimitri noticed other subtle differences. There was no gooey lip gloss for one thing, which was a nice change. And stubble. Who would have thought that the faint rasp of Shane's stubble against his chin would feel so erotic? Every rasp sent tingles down Dimitri's spine and reverberated through his cock.

It wasn't just the facial thing that was different. Shane's body was plastered against Dimitri's and there wasn't anything soft about the man, at all. Shane's chest pushed into Dimitri's in a way Dimitri found intoxicating. The hips that Dimitri still held in his large hands just fit, perfectly. Taut with controlled power as Shane rocked against him, their erections urgently seeking release as the kiss started, blossomed and then swiftly moved both men to the point of no return.

Shane had forced his lips from Dimitri's and was nibbling up the man's neck. "What do you want?" He rasped quietly against Dimitri's ear and Dimitri shuddered.

"You. Everything." It was all he could say and he knew it to be true. Whatever misgivings Dimitri might have had about mating with a man were gone the moment Shane's lips touched his - his need for his mate was so intense and Shane's body against his felt so perfect that he didn't want the man to ever stop. If that made him gay then who cared. No one had ever made him feel this good, so alive and so full of want. The Fates weren't wrong - Shane was perfect for him.

"Have you ever done anything with a man," Shane asked quietly as his assault on Dimitri's neck and chin continued. Dimitri shook his head. There was no way he would have ever considered doing anything remotely sexual with anyone from Jacobs Lake - that would have been enough to get him shot, beaten, or at the very least expelled from the pack.

"So you've never known what it's like to have another man handle your cock." It wasn't a question this time but Shane's hand was working its way between their bodies and seconds later Dimitri felt Shane's quick hands deftly undo Dimitri's jeans. The cold air hitting his cock was a relief and Dimitri groaned as his hard length was wrapped firmly in Shane's grasp.

Shane's hand explored Dimitri's length before gathering the pre-come and using it to smooth his way up and down over Dimitri's shaft. Unable to help himself, Dimitri groaned again as he thrust himself up into the channel created by his mate's hand. The tension was so perfect. The calluses on Shane's hand added to the friction and Dimitri knew he had never felt anything so exquisite in his life.

"I bet you taste delicious. When I get you in my bed," Shane promised as his hand continued their magic, "I am going to strip you down and take you apart. My mouth will be the first man's mouth you've shot your spunk down the throat of. I will lick you, and suck you and drive you to distraction before I roll you over and rim the hell out of your ass. I'm going to tongue you, finger fuck you and spread you wide to get you ready for my big cock."

Dimitri groaned as he pictured the things that Shane was saying. He had never been so turned on in his life. Shane's hand pressure and speed on his cock had increased and Dimitri knew he was close to coming.

"And then, when you are positively begging for it, and you will beg," Shane continued in his ear, "I am going to slide my fat cock straight in your willing hole. I am going to fill you up so far you will feel me in your throat. I am going to pound into you so hard, so deeply that you won't be able to think of anything but me and the way I am making you feel. You're going to feel what it's like to be possessed, to be owned, and when I shoot my spunk deep into your ass I'm going to make you *mine."*

Shane growled his last words and it was that growl, combined with the vivid imagery that Shane had given him that drove Dimitri over the edge. He came groaning Shane's name as his semen pulsed out of his cock as it never had before. Shane kept working him until he was done, kissing his neck softly and nipping at the joint between his neck and shoulder.

Dimitri slowly came down from his orgasmic high. He became aware of the fact that they were still in the dark alley and Shane's covered erection was still pressed against his thigh. Dimitri thought he should offer to do something about that, but all of a sudden he felt strangely shy and unsure of himself.

He looked at Shane who had a small smile on his face.

"What do we do now?" He rumbled quietly as he gave into the temptation of touching Shane's face. Damn, the man had perfect cheek bones.

"Now," said Shane as he tucked Dimitri's cock back into his jeans and zipped him up, "you go home and I go back to work. I'm still on the clock you know."

"Can I come with you?" Dimitri asked unwilling to let Shane out of his sight just now. His nerves felt jumbled and he knew he was tired. He also assumed he had a lot of thinking to do about this whole gay sex thing, but right now he needed the reassurance of Shane's presence. Shane made him feel complete, both man and wolf, and Dimitri knew this was what he had been missing his whole life.

Shane looked at him in the darkness and Dimitri couldn't read the look on his face. Then he nodded and stepped back and headed out of the alley, indicating for Dimitri to follow him. As Dimitri watched Shane's tight ass rolling in the man's jeans, he couldn't help but note to himself that if he felt this amazing after one hand job, how on earth was he going to feel after Shane had fucked him.

## Chapter Five

Shane let himself into his small house a little after four am. After he had dropped Dimitri back at his car he had driven around to see if he could catch sight of CJ but he couldn't find the little man and could only presume that his friend had got lucky. Which was more than could be said for him, he thought wryly. Dimitri might have gotten off in a spectacular fashion but Shane's cock was still rock solid in his jeans and Shane quickly made his way to the shower, dropping his clothes as he went.

Once the water was piping hot, Shane stepped in and allowed himself to get completely soaked. The hot water pounding away at his muscles helped him to relax for the first time in days. As he soaked himself and started to get himself clean, his mind drifted until he was thinking about Dimitri again. Like he could ever stop thinking about him.

The man had looked amazing in that alley. First his jealous anger when he caught Shane with CJ and then the way the man had been so open and honest. Dimitri hadn't been with any man before, that was clearly obvious, but the way he had kissed Shane back, after just one small moment's of hesitation, and then responded to Shane's touch - the memory was enough to make Shane groan.

And when Shane was talking dirty to him. Spelling out how he was going to go down on him, rim his ass and then fuck him. Dimitri didn't falter, didn't look shocked. In fact if anything he got more aroused, if the solidness of his cock and the increased thrust of his hips was anything to go by. But for Shane, the most spectacular part was when he had growled the word "mine" and Dimitri flew apart.

Dimitri's face as he threw himself into his orgasm was a joy to behold. The scrunched eyes, the flared nostrils, the slack jaw and the way he said Shane's name as though it was a benediction. Shane had loved every minute of it and the only thing he would have changed was their location. Because if they had been in Shane's bed, then Shane wouldn't have stopped there.

Shane's hand dropped to his own cock as he thought about the muscles Dimitri hid under his shirt. Dimitri was solid, like most wolves, and Shane had caught a hint of a definite 8-pack as he had trailed his hand down Dimitri's chest and abs, hell bent on getting to the man's zipper. What would it be like to be clasped in those big arms, to be allowed to run his hands, fuck that, his mouth, over all of those muscles and warm skin. Shane's hand on his cock sped up as he dreamed of exploring Dimitri's body from one end to the other.

As he reached the point, in his mind, where he had circled his lips over that divine cock, Shane came with a roar, his come showering the walls until he had to lean on the tiles to catch his breath. Fucking hell. If thinking about being with Dimitri in a bed made him come so hard, the real event would probably kill him.

But, as it does when you have had a spectacular orgasm on your own, when the endorphins slow down and the heart rate goes back to normal, reality sets in. Rinsing himself off, Shane shut off the water and stepped out, grabbing a towel. If he thought about it logically, Dimitri was probably just impacted by the double blow of jealousy and the mating bond. As the two men had gone around and seen a couple of Shane's other contacts, and checked on a couple of gay prostitutes who worked on the streets, Dimitri had been professional and polite. He hadn't touched Shane in any way, nor said anything inappropriate for an office.

Shane was pleased that Dimitri seemed to agree on the serial killer theory for the murders - that was supportive in its own way. But Shane didn't think that Dimitri was doing it to be supportive. He just had a good eye for details and there were too many similarities between the three murders for it to be coincidence. Of course the biggest problem with trying to solve the murders is that there was not one shred of physical evidence at any of the crime scenes that could be used against anyone they might bring in for the crime. Basically, unless they caught the guy in the act, or a person confessed during a police interview, they were screwed.

And as for Dimitri and him being mates? Yes, well if they didn't consummate their affair soon the pair of them were going to be really snappy wolves. Unclaimed mates could end up going feral if the situation got bad enough, and given that Shane and Dimitri worked together their attraction cycle would heat up, fast. It was Fate's way of ensuring that a matched pair became a matched pair in every sense of the word. But what happens if one of the pair wants but can't trust, and the other part of the pair isn't even gay? Fuck it all, Dimitri had called the gay lifestyle a "choice" back in Reynolds' office, and anyone who knew they were gay, knew it was anything but.

Tossing his towel on the floor, Shane climbed into bed naked. He was just too tired to think about any of this now - he'd worry about his serial killer, and why Dimitri had actively sought Shane out after all of this time apart, in the morning.

****

Dimitri woke up with a hard on from hell and his nose filled with the scent of his mate, thanks to his shirt that he had dropped by his pillow the night before. He groaned as he rolled over onto his back and stared at the ceiling of his motel room. Thoughts of the night before ran through his brain like a slide show along with a gamut of emotions.

The jealousy, the anger, the kiss, the passion, and man oh man, the orgasm. They were all really positive things. But afterwards, when Shane had walked out of the alley and the two of them entered the real world, so to speak, Dimitri just couldn't shut off his fear of being exposed as gay. The deep rooted hatred his father had for gay men had been as much a part of Dimitri's upbringing as his mother's apple pies.

Taking a deep breath, Dimitri calmed his nerves as he thought about what his father would say if he knew that his son had taken a gay mate. If, no when, Dimitri went through with this then he would have to leave his family and his pack forever - just like Shane had done. From watching Shane as he grew up, Dimitri knew the man didn't have a good relationship with his family, although as a boy Shane had been close to his mother. How Shane had the strength to walk away after his first shift amazed Dimitri.

Unable to think clearly, Dimitri reached over and picked up his phone, calling Angela. She was the only one who could help him think about this with a cool head.

"Hey lover boy," Angela's happy voice rang out over the phone, "how did your night mission go?"

"It had its good points and its bad points," Dimitri said cryptically.

"Oh goody, tell me the good points first and don't leave out any details."

Dimitri explained about the night's events - finding Shane, the anger about CJ, the kiss and the hand job. Okay, he skimped on the details about how amazing the hand job had felt, but he did allude to sexual activity and how he and Shane had then gone on to speak to some informants before Shane dropped him back at the club car park so he could get his car.

"Wait, wait," Angela said when he was finished, "there's some holes in your story. You did get the guy off in return, right? And you did at least kiss him goodnight when he dropped you off, yes?"

"Er...that would be a no, on both counts."

"Well, aren't you a selfish date," Angela spat out. "If you had treated me like that I wouldn't go out with you a second time."

"Well what was I expected to do? I've never touched a guy sexually before. Should I have just undone his pants and pulled his cock out?" Dimitri was getting angry because he was feeling defensive.

"What did Shane do to you?"

Thinking for a moment, Dimitri got it. "He...er...opened my pants and pulled my cock out."

"Right, well that doesn't sound that hard to me. You know how the zipper on a pair of jeans works and I'm sure you've given yourself enough hand jobs to know what feels good. So you really slacked off there. Why didn't you kiss him when he dropped you off? You had already kissed him by that point."

"We were in a car park for goodness sake."

"So?"

"Someone could have seen us."

To his surprise Angela started to laugh and at that moment Dimitri was really starting to hate his best friend.

"Er, Dimitri sweetie, don't you remember the last game of the season? In the car park? In the back of your car to be precise? I don't remember you being worried about people seeing us then."

Okay it was official - he did hate his best friend. He did remember that evening. Dimitri had been playing and had scored a winning touchdown. He was flush with success and had taken Angela rather roughly in the back of the car without any thought to who might have seen them. It wasn't the first time he and Angela had engaged in risqué sex activities and even before Angela, Dimitri hadn't cared if people had seen him when he kissed and fondled the girl of the week.

"But if I had done that, and someone had seen us, then they would have thought..."

"They would have thought that you were gay," Angela finished for him. "Which you are."

"You know I can't be gay. I mean, shit, I watched all that gay porn and that didn't do anything for me at all."

"Yet you are sexually attracted to Shane. You can't stop thinking about him. You think he's amazing to look at. You can obviously get off from what he does to you. That, my friend, makes you gay, at least with Shane."

"I can't be. I've never been attracted to any guy, only Shane." Dimitri could be stubborn when he wanted to be.

"Listen to me, Dimitri. If an alcoholic goes six years without a drink and then has just one, then he is an alcoholic. Okay, not the best analogy because once an alcoholic, always an alcoholic. If a smoker gives up and doesn't smoke for a year, but then has a cigarette then he is still a smoker. If you think about Shane all the time, are sexually attracted to him, want to go to bed with the man and spend your life with him, then, given that he is the same sex as you, you are gay."

"I don't think either of your analogies work. Maybe my wolf is gay," Dimitri said sullenly.

"Or maybe your wolf doesn't care," Angela shot back. "From what you've told me about mating, the animal side of you doesn't care what your mate is actually like. He just knows what he wants, who he is drawn to, and gets on with it. Besides didn't you hash over all of this stuff before you up sticks and moved and made your decision to be with him?"

Dimitri said, "Yeah, you're right. I did and I do want to be with him." Dimitri heard a ping to indicate he had a text message. "Hey, look Ang, I've got to go, I've got someone trying to get in touch with me."

"Okay, sweets, phone me when you can," and with that Angela rang off.

Checking his text messages Dimitri saw it was from Shane. *There's been another murder, will pick you up as soon as you text me your address.*

Quickly Dimitri text back the details of the motel and jumped out of bed. He didn't have time for a shower or for coffee for that matter, and as he pulled on his suit pants and buttoned his shirt, he hoped that he could convince Shane to pull into a drive thru so he could get the coffee at least. Because as much as he wanted to see Shane again, Dimitri could feel the flutter of butterflies in his stomach. Hopefully the coffee would help calm his nerves at seeing his mate again.

# Chapter Six

Shane was surprised that Dimitri had given his address as a motel complex, but as he pulled into the parking lot besides the unit, he reasoned with himself that the man had not long been in town, and probably hadn't had the time to find a place of his own yet. Of course, if he and Dimitri completed the mating bond, the pair of them would live together. Shane allowed one brief image of what it would be like to wake up with Dimitri every day, before he firmly squashed that notion on its head. Dimitri didn't want forever with a man; he was just caught up in the mating bond.

Sitting in his car, Shane flicked off a quick text to Dimitri to let him know he had arrived. Yes, he could have gone to the unit. Yes, he could have gone inside the unit if Dimitri had asked him to, but he didn't. Because if he did that, then he would want to kiss the man senseless and Dimitri wouldn't want that in the cold light of day. So Shane kept his face neutral and stayed in the car. And if he groaned at the sight of Dimitri opening the door to his place and stepping out into the cool sun washed day, then only Shane would know about it.

"Did you sleep well?" Dimitri asked as Shane navigated the car out of the motel lot and headed into town.

"Nope," Shane replied shortly. Then realizing he must sound like maybe he couldn't sleep because of Dimitri, he added, "I went looking for CJ after I dropped you off, but couldn't find him. I'm a bit worried about him."

Dimitri sat and stared out of the window and didn't seem to have any response to what Shane had said. The look on his face suggested the man had plenty to say and Shane quickly realized that maybe Dimitri was still jealous. After all, Shane didn't get off the night before, so maybe Dimitri thought he went looking for a hookup. Shane decided it was too much fun to not disabuse the man of his thoughts and left Dimitri to sit in silence.

"Any chance of getting coffee before we get to the scene? I didn't have a chance to grab any before you texted me," Dimitri said suddenly, his voice jolting Shane out of his own thoughts about the night before.

"It's the first thing I do every morning when I head out," Shane said, "I can't live without my coffee."

"I'm the same," Dimitri replied, but he didn't say anything more.

God, the tension in the car was unbearable. It wasn't just the sexual angst, although that was there in spades, but there was something else there. Dimitri had something to say, Shane could sense it. But whatever it was, Dimitri wasn't talking. Reminding himself he had a job to do, Shane resolutely put all thoughts of mating, relationships and all that other shit in the back of his head as he got them coffee and then headed to the crime scene. Apart from thanking him for his coffee, black, Shane noted, Dimitri didn't say a word.

The crime scene was a lot like the others Shane had been to. Yellow tape protecting the area across both ends of a darkened alley. A body was still lying on the hard ground, partially covered by a tarp. Nodding to the two officers waiting for him, Shane bypassed the tape and headed straight for the body, a feeling of dread settling in his bones. As he got closer all Shane could see was a mop of blond hair and even as he prayed, *fuck no,* his fingers twitched aside the tarp to reveal CJ's battered face.

Forcing himself upright, Shane moved to the edge of the alley. Behind him he could hear Dimitri make enquiries of the two officers at the scene and Shane knew he had a job to do. But right now he wanted to remember how amazing his little friend had been. CJ, with his bright hair and flashing smile. The sexy body and the outrageous personality. The man who had been beaten more than once for being gay, and for knowing too much, talking to the wrong people. The man didn't deserve this type of end. He deserved to be happy, with someone to love him and care for him for the rest of a long life. Now CJ would never have any of that and it was up to Shane to find this killer once and for all and put him down. This was more than a job now, this was personal.

Had CJ known more about the killer than Shane had realized? Is that what he was going to tell Shane before Dimitri interrupted them? Had someone seen CJ with Shane at the club and taken out CJ before he could reveal what he knew? If that was the case then that person had to have been following them, and Shane couldn't think of anyone who had been in the alley with them the night before, except Dimitri. Shane briefly considered the idea that Dimitri could have killed CJ but quickly dismissed it. The markings on CJ's face, the way he had been killed in the alley, were all the hallmarks of the same man who had murdered the previous three victims, and Dimitri hadn't been in town during that time.

Lost in his thoughts Shane didn't hear Dimitri approach and as his smell tantalized Shane's nose, Shane stifled a groan. He couldn't deal with the man right now. He had to get his shit together. Find this killer and stop him before any more innocent lives were being taken purely and simply because they were gay.

"Hey Shane, are you okay?" Dimitri asked softly.

Shane nodded.

"That's the guy, isn't it? Your friend, CJ?"

Shane nodded again. He felt if he spoke he would just explode. He was so angry and yet he was on the verge of tears. He knew as long as he lived, he would never forget the sight of CJ's cut up face.

"Could you smell anything?" Dimitri said, stepping even closer and dropping his voice so they wouldn't be overheard.

Shane shook his head, embarrassed that he hadn't even thought to sniff for clues. Usually the victims weren't found until they had been dead for a few days and there hadn't been anything for Shane to find. But CJ had been alive the night before so even without time of death, Shane knew this kill was recent. It was also the first time the killer had left the victim out somewhere where the body would be found quickly. The other three victims had been found in dumpsters.

Looking around quickly, Shane noted two dumpsters lined along the alley. The leaving of the body out in the open had to be deliberate because CJ's body could have been stashed in either one of the open garbage containers.

"I think I might have found something," Dimitri said. "Or smelt it at least. Come over here."

He led Shane to the corner of the alley, beside one of the uncovered dumpsters. The two men stood in a huddle like they were still talking while Shane took a surreptitious sniff. Decay, rotten food, garbage and yes, there amongst the stench. The tiniest hint of expensive cologne. Shane recognized it immediately. He had treated himself to a bottle of the stuff the Christmas before.

"Clive Christian's X Factor," he said quietly.

"What?" Dimitri looked stunned.

"It's a men's cologne. I bought myself some last Christmas as a treat." Shane explained hurriedly. "Real expensive and totally out of place in this alley. I barely ever wear it because my wolf doesn't like it much even though I do."

"So a clue for us, then, even if it's not something we can use officially," Dimitri said.

"Yes," Shane said. "Did you find out anything else from the..." he took a deep breath, "body."

Dimitri shook his head. "Nothing I could see. From what I'd read about the other killings I am guessing this is the same MO except CJ wasn't put in the dumpster. Someone wanted this one to be found quickly."

"My thoughts exactly. The question is why?"

By this time the two men were walking back up to where the body was now being looked over by the medical examiner and his team. Shane and Dimitri would wait for the preliminary findings and then start looking for clues. For Shane that meant finding out what CJ had done after he went back into the Truckers Club. Looking around the alley, Shane saw the huge sign advertising the club just a few blocks over. CJ hadn't gone very far at all.

His thoughts were derailed by the over-the-top entrance of his Lieutenant. The man's car came flying down the road and stopped with a squealing flourish and the man himself got out, flanked by two other men from the precinct. Shane recognized Jones and Parker from the Internal Affairs department. What were they doing here - at a murder scene no less? The Lieutenant never came out into the field, not for anything.

Lieutenant Anthony Green was a big man, but most of it was fat. At six foot tall and appearing just as wide the man, was the picture of over indulgence. His face, currently wearing a sneer, was podgy and without form. Shane would have hated him even if the man didn't make his position on Shane's sexuality abundantly clear every chance he got. The man personified a mean spirit and a narrow minded attitude.

Ignoring Dimitri, the Lieutenant spoke to Shane. "West, I understand you knew the victim, is that right?"

Frowning, Shane stood taller as he answered, "Yes, CJ was a friend." What the hell did the man want, or more to the point what was he trying to imply? He found out soon enough.

"We received a tip that you were seen leaving with the victim from the Truckers Club last night. I'm here to take you in for questioning." The man positively gloated as he spoke the words almost guaranteed to drum Shane straight out of the police force.

"You have got to be kidding me," Shane was stunned. He didn't realize the Lieutenant hated him quite that much.

"Now, Detective, it's just routine, you know that. Can anyone verify that CJ was alive after you left him? After you had finished your sordid little interlude?"

Shane felt Dimitri stiffen beside him. Yes, of course, Dimitri could certainly clear Shane with one well-placed word, but the Lieutenant obviously didn't know that Dimitri had even been in the area. And Shane wasn't going to give the Lieutenant any ammunition on Dimitri. Dimitri wasn't gay. He could play at being straight with the best of them, even after he had come apart in Shane's hands. And no matter how Shane might feel about Dimitri's presence in his life, the man was his mate and must be protected at all costs. That protection wasn't just from rogue wolves and fights. It meant protecting his integrity and honor as well. The Lieutenant was on a gay vendetta and

Shane wasn't going to have Dimitri caught up in it.

"No, Sir," he said even it twisted his gut to say the words.

Smirking at him, the Lieutenant indicated to the two men beside him to handcuff Shane and lead him to the car. Shane got in without a fight and steadfastly refused to look at Dimitri. He didn't want to know what his mate thought about him protecting his ass. He needed to find a way to protect his own without giving up anything about Dimitri.

****

Standing in the alley Dimitri was stunned beyond belief. He couldn't understand why Shane hadn't said anything about him being in the alley at the same time as CJ and Shane. He could tell the Lieutenant hated Shane with a vengeance, and he guessed from the Lieutenant's comment that it was because Shane was openly gay.

For one brief second Dimitri considered the idea that Shane was the killer. After all, Shane had said that he owned a bottle of the cologne that the two men had smelt in the alley. Shane had also told him that he had gone looking for CJ after he had dropped Dimitri back at his car. But just as quickly, Dimitri dismissed the idea. Shane had done his best to protect CJ from Dimitri when he had threatened to go all wolfy in anger. Plus which Shane was gay - openly so. There is just no way he would kill other gay men. He had no reason to.

Shane wasn't a killer. Dimitri knew he didn't know his mate very well, but he knew that about the man. Shane was decent and honest and he worked bloody hard to do his job in an unfriendly environment. Aside from a couple of men in the department who obviously had a problem with Shane being gay, most of the department treated Shane with friendliness and respect.

Okay, so why didn't Shane clear himself before he was taken away in handcuffs? Dimitri kept thinking to himself even as he cleared the scene, took the ME's report and headed out to Shane's truck. Shane had left the keys in it, which was a good thing because Dimitri hadn't thought to ask him for them before the man was taken away.

When the answer came to him, as he was sitting in the truck wondering what the hell he was going to do, he hit his head on the steering wheel to punish himself for his stupidity. Shane was protecting his mate. This slur on Shane's character could cost him his job, even if the police couldn't prove that Shane was the killer. Simply being a suspect was bad enough unless he was cleared outright. If the police came up with enough circumstantial evidence against Shane and Shane was actually booked for the crime, his life as a Detective would be over the moment he hit the cell block. Dimitri had to do something and fast.

Driving into the precinct, Dimitri didn't have a definite plan in mind. He knew there was a possibility that he would have to lie and there was also a strong possibility that even if he didn't out himself as gay, the suggestion would be enough to tar him with that brush for life. At least in the eyes of the police force. That was what Shane was protecting him from. If anyone knew how hard it was to be a gay officer, it was Shane. And Shane worked hard every single day just to prove he was as good as the next man.

All of a sudden Dimitri was hit with how unfair the situation was for Shane and men like him. Sure Dimitri had been one of the bullies that had made Shane's life hell at school. But no-one knew for sure then that the man was gay. Dimitri probably knew before Shane did, when he realized Shane was his mate all those years before. Shane hadn't shifted, and as a wolf didn't get a handle on their sexuality until after they had their first shift, Shane couldn't have known for sure. Shane had been picked on at school because he *looked* gay. He had been small with long hair and a beautiful face. A natural target for bullies like Dimitri and his friends.

Not for the first time, Dimitri regretted his actions as a youth. He could have protected Shane the way a mate should, as soon as he realized that was what Shane was to him. But instead, Dimitri had left school and gone to work at the local police department because that was what his family wanted him to do. It was a sheer fluke that when Dimitri had decided to search for Shane, the man had taken the same career path. Or maybe the Fates were working behind the scenes after all.

Regardless, Dimitri knew now was the time to either put up or shut up. Arriving at the precinct, Dimitri strode straight to the Captain's office. Knocking once, he entered without waiting for the Captain's invitation. Reynolds was sitting behind his desk and looked up in surprise when Dimitri just marched in.

"What do you want, Polst?"

"West is innocent, Sir, and I can prove it," Dimitri said in a rush.

Captain Reynolds raised an eyebrow at Dimitri's words, but he stood up nonetheless, picked up a piece of paper from his desk and grabbed his jacket off the back of his chair.

"Come on then, let's go and see what this is all about. The ME's report has just come through giving time of death as between 4.30 am and 5.30 am. Well after West was seen with the victim."

"I see, well I can still clear him" Dimitri said. "Sir, what's your policy on people in a relationship working together in the department?"

****

Reynolds led Dimitri down to the first interview room and entered without knocking, Dimitri hard behind him. Shane was sitting on one side of a table, still in handcuffs, while the Lieutenant and the two men from the IA department were on the other. Dimitri's heart broke over the dejected look on Shane's face. The man was prepared to give up his career, damn near his whole life to protect Dimitri. And Dimitri hadn't even claimed him as a mate yet.

"Why is this man in cuffs?" Captain Reynolds barked. "He is a material witness, not a bloody suspect."

"Sir," the Lieutenant said, obviously surprised to see both Reynolds and Dimitri in the room. "We have a witness statement that shows that West here was probably the last man to see the victim alive. That means he is a suspect until he's cleared."

"I was with West and the victim," Dimitri blurted out, "And I can vouch that the victim was alive when he left the alley."

## Chapter Seven

As Shane was being driven back to the station, he figured the best thing he could do for himself and Dimitri was to say as little as possible. Shane knew it could be easily proven that he was in the Truckers Club - the place had excellent video surveillance. The video may or may not show that Shane had gone out the back with CJ, but there would have been enough people in the club that night, who knew both Shane and CJ, that it wouldn't be hard to confirm that they left together.

The fact that they left by the back door did imply a sexual liaison. That is why Shane and CJ had established that very system of passing information about a year before. CJ had been beaten by a couple of gang members that he had offered to testify against. He had been seen talking to the police and it had damn near cost him his life.

So Shane and CJ pretended to hook up every time CJ had information to pass on. They had done it before countless times and never had any trouble. Shane was known at the clubs in town as a man who liked a quick rough fuck or a blow job, and it was nearly always in some alley behind the establishment he was in. The fact that Shane was good at pleasuring the men he hooked up with meant he never had a shortage of partners, despite the fact that most of the patrons knew he was a Detective. As far as anyone was concerned, CJ was one of those hookups.

If the time of death came back to the time when he and Dimitri were interviewing other informants then he could be cleared of the murder. There was no way he could hide Dimitri's involvement there, because too many people saw them together, but the two of them had maintained professional standards from the moment they left the alley. It was perfectly plausible that Shane had called Dimitri in after he had seen CJ, and that they had interviewed informants together. That wouldn't do anything to blow Dimitri's cover as a straight man.

Unfortunately determining the exact time of death would take a little bit of time given that it was over the weekend. Shane knew the ME would put in a preliminary report before the end of the day which would establish time and possible cause of death. So all he had to do was stall the bozos who would be questioning him long enough for that report to come through. The less information he offered, the better it would be for both him and Dimitri.

As expected, once he was put in an interview room after being paraded right through the investigations department, the taunts began. The Lieutenant refused to take the handcuffs off Shane's wrists which were starting to hurt, but he refused to be goaded. All he would admit to was that yes, he had been at Truckers. Yes, he had seen CJ and yes, he did leave with CJ by the back entrance of the club.

"And what were you doing in the alley behind the club, West?  Exchanging crochet tips?"

"What do you think I was doing, Green?" Said Shane, refusing to give the repugnant piece of shit any respect whatsoever.  If he was going to be treated like a criminal, then he wasn't going to make it easy on the man.

"I imagine you were having sex with the victim, West, so I don't see why you won't admit it.  I am sure the ME's report will show evidence of anal intercourse when it's done."

Shane certainly hoped not.  Not because he had sex with CJ, but because it would mean that the man was probably raped as well as murdered, and that was just too horrific to think about.  Keeping a bland look on his face he said smartly, "Not if he gave me a blow job."

"What?" Lieutenant Green looked outraged.  His face was so red that Shane thought he might have a coronary. "So you admit you were having sexual relations with the victim?"

"No," Shane said quietly. "I said that if CJ had given me a blow job there would be no indication of anal assault. Likewise if he had fucked me there would be little, if no evidence of that, in CJ's autopsy report. I didn't say that he had done any of those things. I was simply pointing out a flaw in your logic. You were the one who admitted to imagining me having sexual relations with the victim."

Shane thought he saw Parker hide a grin behind his hand, but he couldn't be sure. He was too busy watching the Lieutenant getting closer to his heart attack.

The Lieutenant leaned over the desk and sneered at Shane. "What were you doing in the alley with the victim," he snarled, flicking spittle all over Shane's face. Shane leaned back in his chair and made no secret of wiping his hands over his face.

"I was talking to him, Green. He was a friend of mine. I talked to him. He talked to me. He left. End of story."

"I don't believe you," the Lieutenant sneered.

"Look Green," Shane said with an exaggerated patience he didn't feel, "Just because two gay men get together doesn't mean they are having sex. Gay men are just like straight men. We have friends. We talk to each other. Being gay isn't all about sex. It's also about being supportive of each other when someone is having problems."

The Lieutenant shook his head and pulled out a piece of paper that was in a folder on the table. "The eye witness we spoke to said, and I quote, 'the victim was all over the Cop in the club, rubbing on him, groping his crotch and whispering to him. It seemed the Cop enjoyed it. Then they left the club together out the back door," end of quote."

"CJ was affectionate," Shane said.

The pudgy piece of shit had the audacity to laugh and Shane fumed silently, although none of it showed on his face.

"I can be affectionate also, West, but I don't go around groping men's crotch area," the Lieutenant said, the sneer in his tone evident.

"No, I imagine you don't," Shane said, "but then you don't know what you're missing. CJ was just appreciating the package. Didn't mean he planned on doing anything about it, nor does it mean that I would have let him." Shane sat up, he'd had enough of this already and he really hoped the ME's report came through soon. Shane didn't want to share anything else about his night until he knew time of death.

"Face it Green, you have nothing except that I was seen with the victim before his death. But I wasn't the last person to see him alive. The killer was. Now give me the time of death. I will tell you where I was and this can all be cleared up," Shane said with more strength than he felt. If CJ was killed anytime after 3 am when he dropped Dimitri off at his car, then Shane was screwed. He'd spent an hour driving around looking for CJ before going home and there was no-one to verify his whereabouts during that time.

"The time of death hasn't come through yet, West, and you know it. And if you think I'm going to believe a fairy tale like two gay men just talking in a dark alley, then you are ridiculing the years I've spent as a police officer. I know what you perverts get up to," the Lieutenant said with a smug look on his face.

Shane raised a single eyebrow at the man, but didn't say anything. Instead he slumped back in his chair, determined to say nothing more until he had more information. He knew the Lieutenant was fishing, and Shane couldn't stop him. But Shane wasn't going to oust his partner and he would just put up with the shit that Green threw at him until more details came to hand.

The door to the interview room opened and in walked Captain Reynolds, with Dimitri behind him. Shane barely heard the Captain's comments about his handcuffs, although he was happy when Parker came forward and took them off. He was too busy trying to catch Dimitri's eye. God the man was infuriating, especially when Shane was working so hard to protect him.

Then he heard it. Dimitri's statement, "I was with West and the victim and I can vouch that the victim was alive when he left us."

"You weren't in the club," the Lieutenant blustered.

"Check the video surveillance tapes," Dimitri said. "West called me and said he was meeting a friend at the Club. I got there a bit late and saw West and his friend head out the back. I followed them out, was introduced to CJ, and was there during the conversation. CJ left after about ten minutes and headed off back into the club."

"What were you all talking about, Polst? West here seems to think it was personal and doesn't want to share," the Lieutenant said.

Dimitri smirked, and Shane couldn't believe the bolt of lust that shot through to his groin. He didn't know what his mate was doing, but damn he looked real good doing it.

"Penis size," Dimitri lied with a straight face. Parker and Jones weren't being as professional and were both hiding their grins behind their hands, while Captain Reynolds laughed outright.

"It seems…" Dimitri made as if to go on but Captain Reynolds stopped him.

"That's quite alright Polst, we get the gist. It was a personal conversation."

"Yes, Sir."

"Unfortunately," the captain said, "I'm still going to need to know your whereabouts for the rest of the evening, West. The victim was killed between 4.30 am and 5.30 am this morning. So what happened after you left the alley."

Fuck, now Shane knew for a fact he was screwed. He had no verifiable alibi for that time of day and with the Lieutenant hell bent on reaming his ass one way or the other, he knew he wasn't going anywhere anytime soon except a jail cell. Shane didn't have a clue what he was going to say.

But it seemed that Dimitri did. "He was with me, Sir."

"What, all night?" The Lieutenant again.

"Yes, Sir," Dimitri lied. "After CJ went back in the club, we went and spoke to some informants. We checked on a couple of gay prostitutes who work the streets and then West took me around and showed me some of the town hot spots. After that we went back to pick up my car from the Trucker's car park and I followed him back to his place. I've been staying in a motel and it is not very comfortable. We were there from about 3 am until we got the call about the murder this morning. We dropped my car back at the motel and then headed out to the crime scene."

Now everyone was looking at the Lieutenant who had gone purple in the face and there was a large vein pulsing in the top of his head. The man was obviously thinking hard enough to generate steam.

"It doesn't mean that West didn't do it," he said triumphantly. "You weren't actually together in the same room all night and West could have sneaked out, found the victim, killed him and got back before you noticed."

The idea was plausible although really weak by anybody's standards. Shane looked at Dimitri pleading with him not to say any more.

Dimitri just shook his head slightly and said, "nope, Lieutenant, that wouldn't have been possible at all. You see," and he leaned down and whispered in the Lieutenant's ear. The Lieutenant's eyes just got bigger and bigger and then all of a sudden he pushed away from Dimitri and hurried out of the door. "You're freaks," he yelled back through the door, "You and West both, freaks."

The Captain frowned at the sight of the Lieutenant's back heading down the hall, but then he shrugged and turned looked at Parker and Jones. "As far as I am concerned this interview is over. Did you two have anything else you need to know?"

"No, Captain, we didn't think that Detective West here had anything to do with the murder of his friend in the first place. But the Lieutenant was rather insistent," Jones said.

"Good," said the Captain, "Then let's get out of here. It's the weekend and I'm sure you guys have other things you would rather be doing. West, I can't have you investigating your friend's murder, you know that. But I'll put Trent and Mace on it so that they can keep you in the loop, unofficially of course. And on Monday I want to see what evidence you have connecting this murder to your other three outstanding cases."

The Captain smiled at Shane's look of shock. "Yes, West. The Lieutenant did tell me your theory, but he was extremely unflattering about it and I have to confess I did dismiss the idea at the time. But if there is a serial killer in our city then I want him found. So I will expect you and Polst in my office after the Monday morning meeting." Nodding at Parker and Jones, Captain Reynolds left the room.

Parker and Jones went to leave to, but at the door, Jones turned back and said, "You know, West, that Green really has it in for you. I'd watch your back if I were you."

"Yeah, I know, Jones. That's why I didn't want my partner involved in all of this," Shane said. All of a sudden he felt dead tired.

"It seems your partner can take care of himself," Jones laughed. "Hey Polst, what did you tell the Lieutenant to make him run out of the room like that?"

"Not telling you, Jones," Dimitri drawled. "I'm not the kiss and tell type." Jones and Parker were still laughing as they went out the door.

Shane looked up at Dimitri who was still standing by the door, looking so fine in his grey suit and the smirk on his face.

"Why'd you do it, Dimitri?" Shane asked softly. "I know you aren't gay, and I don't want you tarred with the same brush I am. I was trying to protect you from the likes of the Lieutenant."

"You are mine," Dimitri said firmly. "Yes, you are my partner, but you are also my mate and I guess in the eyes of the department that means you are going to be my boyfriend until we can get married. I checked with the Captain before I spoke up, about interoffice relationships and he said he was fine with it so long as it doesn't interfere with our work, and we both know it won't. I figured I was going to have to come out sooner or later, and given what you were going through, sooner seemed better."

Shane shook his head, and got up from the table. He wandered over to Dimitri and leaned on his chest, saying softly, "I'm never going to be able to thank you enough. You know that, right?"

"Oh yes, you will," Dimitri said confidently as he led them out of the room, down the hall and out to the car. As he went to get into the truck Shane said, "So are you going to tell me what you said that freaked the Lieutenant out so much?"

"Nope," said Dimitri, "I'm going to take you out for lunch and then home to rest. And when you have been fed for the second time, I'm going to get you to show me what I said in graphic detail. I don't want you making a liar out of me." The grin he gave Shane over the top of the truck was positively feral and Shane felt a shiver of excitement run down his spine and lodge firmly in his groin. Somehow he didn't feel so tired anymore.

## Chapter Eight

Lunch was excellent. Shane directed Dimitri to a small diner he knew of on the edge of town where they could eat good food in relative private. After they had ordered, Dimitri looked down at his hands, and then up at Shane.

"You know I never did apologize for the way I treated you growing up," he said quietly.

"There's nothing to apologize for," Shane said, "You were doing what you were programmed to do by your parents, the school social system and the pack. I know I was small and too pretty for my own good." He smiled. "If it hadn't been you and your friends, it would have been someone else."

"How can you not be upset about it?"

Shane shrugged. "It happened a long time ago as far as I'm concerned. Once I 'grew up' I got the hell out of town and I don't plan to ever go back. The negative thoughts and any hurt I might have felt at the time have long gone. You know, in a way, you guys did me a favor. I mean, look at me now. I'm bigger, stronger and a lot less pretty. I doubt I would have made those changes, which incidentally have worked really well for me especially with the men I attract, if it hadn't been for what I went through at school. So don't worry about it, okay?"

"There's more," Dimitri admitted.

"What more can there be?" Shane said. Then his face darkened. "You didn't tell anybody I was out here, did you? Anyone back at Jacobs Lake?"

Dimitri shook his head. "No, Shane, I wouldn't do that to you, although I may have to tell my mother when I let her know you and I are mated. I owe her a phone call at least."

"How did you leave things with your pack and your family?" Shane asked.

"I didn't really tell them anything," Dimitri said as he fiddled with his napkin. "Look, I knew you were my mate that last time we met up in the alley at school and I admit it, I ran for it.  I couldn't get away from you fast enough.  I kinda figured you wouldn't have felt the same pull because you hadn't shifted yet, but I did and I freaked the fuck out.  I feel bloody awful about it now, but at the time all I could think was about fitting in with the pack, living up to the expectations of my family and getting a job."

"You knew and you left?"  Shane couldn't begin to describe the hurt that punctured his heart at the moment.  He struggled to put things into perspective.  He had only been 16 years old at the time, while Dimitri had been 18 years old.  They both would have been too young to cope with the pressures of mating, even if same-sex partnerships were accepted in their pack.  But the fact that Dimitri knew they were mates, and had left him to the mercies of school bullies for the next almost two years was really hard to take.  A mate was to be cherished and protected - not abandoned.

Shane could feel Dimitri watching his face which no doubt betrayed the range of emotions he was feeling. Taking a deep breath he deliberately configured his face into the bland, professional expression he used at work.

"That would have included getting married and having kids then," he said calmly.

"Yes or at least it would have, if I had gone through with it," Dimitri admitted. "I was with this girl, Angela. She was human but she had accepted my wolf. We were together for three years. She was pushing for a commitment, but I just couldn't do it."

Dimitri looked Shane straight in the eye. "Angela is the only one who knows about you, what you mean to me, and why I sought you out after all of these years. In fact she encouraged me to come here. My parents simply think I got offered a better job and they expect me back for pack meetings and holidays. Of course, once I tell my mom we're mated, I will be as cut off from my family and the pack as you are. But I know that and I accept it."

Now the pain Shane was feeling was for his mate. Dimitri was going to lose everything just like he had. But this was something he had actively chosen for himself. No matter what had happened in the past, Dimitri cared enough about them being mates to give up his whole life and move to a new place, without even knowing what type of a welcome he would get.

It really wasn't easy for a wolf to give up his pack. Shane had been able to do it relatively easily because he had never been 100% accepted by the other pack members. But even despite his problems with the pack, his wolf still missed the company and sense of belonging that any wolf craves. Dimitri had been with the pack a lot longer, and unlike Shane, he had been an accepted member. He had friends and colleagues and he could have had a mate, if not a true mate. But anyone of the single female wolves in the pack would have taken Dimitri in a shot.

"Why didn't you try for a pack female? Surely that would have been easier for you, rather than a human and the pack would have been more accepting," Shane asked.

"I couldn't do it," Dimitri admitted. "I did try with a couple after I found out about you, but my wolf just wouldn't let another wolf close to me. He was kinda accepting of Angela, in that I didn't get an instant droop every time I went near her, but as I got older and she got more insistent about a commitment from me, my wolf got more and more adamant that he wanted his mate."

"So this wasn't really a choice you wanted then," Shane persisted although he really didn't know why he was saying these things. Especially not when Dimitri looked a damn sight more edible than the food on his plate.

Dimitri shocked him by putting his hand over Shane's as it sat on the table. There, out in the open for anyone to see.

"I do want you Shane," Dimitri said, his voice low and ringing with honesty. "I want you more than you could ever know. Not just in my bed, or up my ass, but in my life, forever. You have all of the qualities I want in a mate - honesty, integrity, strength, not to mention the desire to protect me. You work hard and you care about your job and the people you serve. You're a good man and one I will be proud to call mine. I know you might have doubts and I know it might take you some time to trust me after what I put you through in the past. But I will wait as long as it takes for you to be my mate."

Wow, okay, Shane could safely say he never expected anything like that to come out of Dimitri's mouth. He knew the wolf was pulled by the mating bond, but Dimitri's little speech showed that the man had thought long and hard about what it meant to take a mate like Shane.

Suddenly the past really didn't matter anymore. Sure, Shane had been hurt by his past but through the years he had been determined not to let his past dictate his future actions. If Dimitri could go out of his way to give up everything just to be with his mate, then Shane could let down the walls in his heart and give this man his forever.

Dimitri had grown up as well. Yes, he had become even better looking, but that wasn't the main selling point for Shane. By his actions that very day, Dimitri had shown that he could be counted on. He could be trusted. Hell, he could even be counted on to lie to anyone just to save his mate. That took a lot of guts and a commitment that Shane had never experienced from another person before in his life.

Shane looked up into those steely eyes that had captivated him from that day, just a week ago in the Captain's office.

"I have been so mixed up this week," he confessed shakily. "Wanting you and telling myself time and time again it could never happen between us. I needed you to show me that you wanted me before I could trust you. And today..."

Shane couldn't speak for a moment. He was so overwhelmed. First, CJ's death, and now Dimitri accepting him as his mate. He wanted to laugh, and cry, but most of all he wanted Dimitri in his bed with his teeth firmly embedded in his mate's neck as he fucked the man who had haunted his dreams for the last week. Once mated the two men would be together forever. Dimitri would never be able to lie to him, would never hurt him and would always be there, just for him. Faced with all that, the past really didn't matter at all. They would face whatever the future brings together.

"Today you gave me every reason to trust again," he continued. "Every barrier I have put up to this, you have torn down, without even trying. By being yourself. I have never wanted anyone the way I want you. And like you, it's not just in my bed, although I want that really badly. You are a decent man, Dimitri. You gave up everything to come here and be with me. How could I not want you? I don't need to wait. I don't need anything else to be sure. I want you in my bed and in my life. But being gay is not easy, and no matter if you and I both know the only man you will ever get hot for is me, those who don't know about us, and about what being mates is all about, will assume that you are gay. Are you really sure about this?"

"I've had eight years to think about this, Shane. I have never been surer about anything in my life," Dimitri said simply.

And when it came down to it, for wolves it really was that simple. Mates wanted each other regardless of the labels outsiders might put on their relationship. That want, that desire and that passion would never die. And when life was put into perspective like that - where one man would remain steadfast to another regardless of what life threw at them, then there honestly wasn't any reason not to jump right in and hold on tight.

"You know I'm not going to want to rest when we get home, don't you," Shane said quietly.

"I'm counting on it," Dimitri growled as he signaled the waitress for the check.

## Chapter Nine

Shane didn't know how he managed to contain himself on the drive back to his place, but he did, barely. But the moment the two men were inside his door, he turned and had Dimitri up against the door. Reaching up, he cupped Dimitri's neck and pulled the man down so that he could fasten his lips on the mouth that had plagued his thoughts throughout their meal.

Dimitri didn't hold back either. The moment their mouths touched Dimitri kissed right back, his big arms coming around and cradling Shane as though he was the most precious person in the world. Lost in their passion for each other time stopped. Together they stood, their bodies perfectly fitted to each other, their mouths fused as the kiss went from sheer relief in coming together, to soft and searching and then as the need between them grew, the passion returned with vengeance as both men dueled for dominance. Hands flew as both men tried to touch as much of each other as they could reach, clothes frustrating their way.

His hands fisted in the top of Dimitri's hair, Shane pulled the man off his mouth so he could speak.

"I need you in my bed and naked, Dimitri. I'm not having your first time in a bloody doorway."

His eyes blown with lust and his lips swollen, Dimitri simply nodded and he let Shane lead him upstairs to a large open bedroom. All Dimitri had a chance to notice was the head and foot boards were both solid wood and the linens were white. There was a shaggy, faux fur throw on the foot of the bed, also in white and Dimitri longed to see what his mate would look like stretched out on it. But then his brain turned to mush again as Shane skillfully pulled off his jacket and started working on the buttons of his shirt. Suddenly it became more important that Shane be as naked as he was about to be and he reached out impatiently to tug at Shane's clothing.

Of course they both got in the way of each other; clothes do not magically fall off. By unspoken accord both men stepped back and worked on their own clothes, stripping down without any embarrassment. Shifters were used to nudity, but this was something more. Something far more powerful and intimate.

When they were both naked, Shane stepped forward and pushed Dimitri on the bed. Scooting along the bed until he was in the center of it, Dimitri settled back and let Shane look at him, his gaze possessive and full of lust.

Shit, Shane thought, he is so beautiful. Shane had never seen Dimitri naked. He hadn't shifted when Dimitri had, and the first time he had shifted himself he was on his family's land, not on the pack grounds. Now Shane was really glad he hadn't set eyes on Dimitri at that time. His lust for the man would have been really hard to hide. The man was all broad shoulders, lean muscle lines and tattoos. When the hell had Dimitri got those tattoos?

There was a yin/yang symbol on one shoulder, with a gorgeous wolf head beneath it. Underneath that was a tribal cuff and down his forearms Dimitri wore a combination of Chinese characters. There were two more tattoos on his pectoral muscles and damn Shane just wanted to take the time to trace every single one with his tongue. The only tattoo he had ever got was a series of paw prints that he wore as a cuff around his bicep - a reminder to him of the fact that he had walked away from his pack. One day he would get Dimitri to tell the story of his tattoos, but that could wait, because aside from the fascinating ink, the man had the most amazing body.

Growling his appreciation Shane stalked toward the bed. Grabbing a bottle of lube off the side dresser, he climbed up and straddled Dimitri's slim hips, the man's hard cock pulsating under his balls as he sat. Dropping the lube on the bed beside him, he leaned forward, grabbing Dimitri's hands with his and holding them fast on the bed.

"You need to tell me what you want," He said softly as he watched a play of emotions run over his mate's face.

****

Dimitri had never been so turned on in all his life. His cock was so hard it hurt, and looking at his mate, so self-assured and sexy sitting above him, it was all he could do not to flip Shane over and plunge his cock deep into the nearest orifice he could reach.

But he wasn't going to do that, although he couldn't help but rock up into where Shane was pressed down over his hips. Hmm, the friction on his cock felt so good, so he did it again. He groaned at the sensation of Shane's balls rolling over his cock as he considered his answer.

In most situations during the mating the more dominant wolf would fuck the lesser one. Dimitri was the stronger and bigger wolf. But as far as male-on-male sex went he was also the least experienced, hell he was a virgin, and Dimitri didn't want to hurt his mate by doing the wrong thing. He figured it would be better to let Shane be the top. He could learn by following what Shane was doing and hopefully get to be the giver the next time.

Besides, if anything was going to test this whole gay thing in Dimitri's mind, then getting fucked was the right way to do it. Although Dimitri didn't have any doubts in his head that he could tell, he had no way of knowing just how deep rooted his family and pack prejudices went in his psyche. The other thing was that Dimitri had fucked before - heaps of women, none of whom had a place in this bed. What he hadn't done was given himself to another person and he wanted that person to be his mate.

"What you said last night," he said roughly, rocking again into Shane's touch. "I want you to give me what you promised me last night in the alley. What I told the Lieutenant you had done."

Shane groaned then, and let go of Dimitri's hands. Leaning over he murmured against Dimitri's lips, "Are you sure?"

"Yes," Dimitri breathed against Shane's lips before closing the distance between them. Their lips met and this time Dimitri let Shane take over. Shane played him, beautifully, expertly. Kissing him firmly, he gently encouraged Dimitri to open his mouth and slipped his tongue inside. He mapped out every part of Dimitri's mouth, spending a lot of time running his tongue over Dimitri's fangs which Dimitri found to be a huge turn on.

When Shane seemed satisfied that Dimitri had been kissed within an inch of climaxing, because damn the man was still sitting on him and the feel of Shane's cock against his abs and the man's balls teasing his own cock kept Dimitri on the fine edge of coming, Shane allowed his lips to move lower, kissing over his chin and jaw bone and then down his skin covered jugular vein. Dimitri lifted his chin to give the man more access - his submission not a gift given lightly and he knew that Shane was aware of that. The soft growl the man gave reinforced his belief that he was doing the right thing.

Shane kissed, licked and nibbled his way deliriously slowly over Dimitri's collar bone, his pectoral muscles, giving particular attention to Dimitri's stiff brown nipples. Dimitri growled as Shane bit him, nipping the nub sharply, but Dimitri grabbed hold of Shane's head and held him there. Dimitri had never thought his nipples would have a direct line to his dick, but having Shane nip and lave his way over his chest had Dimitri writhing hard against Shane, begging for more.

Finally Shane headed south again, down Dimitri's body. He mapped out the solid muscles that formed Dimitri's eight-pack, licking along each groove. Dimitri groaned and shifted beneath Shane's explorations causing his cock to bump Shane on the chin. Shane looked up at him then and grinned, his eyes almost black, before moving down, bypassing the needy cock in his face and nuzzling Dimitri's balls. Carefully he licked over each one before taking them gently in his mouth and tonguing them. Dimitri arched his back in pleasure. No one had ever done that to him before and fuck it felt so good.

"Shane, please," Dimitri begged, his low voice raspy with lust. If he didn't get some attention to his cock soon he was going to burst. Shane chuckled around Dimitri's balls and damn it all if the vibrations didn't make Dimitri want to come even more. But Shane must have taken pity on the man because finally his mouth encircled Dimitri's cock and Dimitri couldn't help himself. He thrust upward into that enticing wet warmth, shaking with pleasure as he felt Shane's tongue map out the sensitive skin under the head of his cock, before swirling down the vein that ran the length of Dimitri's shaft.

Dimitri felt the head of his cock hit the back of Shane's throat and Dimitri expected the man to stop there. But seconds later Shane relaxed and swallowed, taking the man deeper than he had ever been in a mouth before. He was going to come if Shane kept this up - he didn't know how he could stop himself.

"Fuck. Fuck. Fuck. Shane, you're killing me here," Dimitri cried out.

Shane nodded, which felt slightly strange because he still had Dimitri's cock deep in his mouth, but he eased back a bit. Dimitri panted hard, praying that Shane would understand how close he was. It seemed that Shane did, because moments later, after bobbing up and down Dimitri's cock for just a little bit more, he let the cock slide from his mouth. Dimitri groaned at the loss but then inhaled sharply as Shane's wicked mouth went below Dimitri's balls and started licking along his perineum.

Almost howling in delight, because damn it, that tongue on that sensitive piece of skin did feel that good,

Dimitri slid his feet up the mattress and opened his legs wide to give Shane more access. Using his devastating combination of sucks, licks, and nibbles, Shane moved closer to Dimitri's anus. Dimitri tensed for just one second when Shane's tongue flicked across it, but then he relaxed into the faint touch. It felt foreign, strange, but not unpleasant.

Encouraged, Shane pressed closer, using his broad tongue to soften the tight muscles protecting Dimitri's most private space. But Dimitri's butt was still too close to the bed for Shane to get decent access, and Shane raised his head long enough to ask for a pillow.

Arranging Dimitri with the pillow now firmly under his ass, tilting it to give Shane better access. Shane looked up at his mate who was flushed and sweaty, his cock hard and solid against his stomach.

"You okay up there," Shane asked softly.

"More than," Dimitri rasped out, "But please Shane, please can you speed things along just a little bit. I am hanging onto my control with a thread here - a very tiny thread."

"I could make you come right now if you like, lover. But then it would make it even harder for me to penetrate you because your delicious ass muscles would tighten up even more", Shane explained. "Can you hold on just a little while longer?"

Dimitri nodded, pleased that his mate was trying to be so careful.

"And," Shane said, as he bent his head again, "Don't be worried if your impressive erection here flags a bit as I prepare you, I'll get you back up again in no time."

Considering Dimitri didn't think anything would make his cock go down in the foreseeable future except a mind-blowing orgasm, Dimitri just nodded that he understood. His body tingled all over. His nose was filled with the scent of his mate. He knew he needed something, he just didn't know what. He just felt this need and it was driving him insane.

When Dimitri felt the tip of Shane's tongue actually enter him just a little bit, he damn near shot off the bed. Shane soothed and petted his thighs and belly before dipping his head down and repeating his actions. This time Dimitri was better prepared and he relaxed into the touch. The fingers Shane had lightly running up and down his cock certainly helped.

Soon Shane pushed his tongue deeper and before he knew what he was doing, Dimitri pushed back into the touch. There was no pain so far, just a wickedly sinful sensuality that appealed to Dimitri on a level he had never experienced before. Soon Dimitri was rocking into the touch, pushing his ass at Shane's face as Shane eagerly ate him out. If the man's moans and growls were any indication, Shane was really enjoying himself and Dimitri realized he was close to coming again.

Almost as though he was a mind reader, Shane slowed up his actions and then Dimitri felt the soft push of a harder digit - Shane's finger eased into Dimitri alongside his tongue. Dimitri groaned but he didn't stop rocking against Shane's face - it honestly felt so good. When Shane pulled his head back, Dimitri actually whimpered but he was soothed again as Shane petted him, stroked his cock and murmured softly, "Shush my lover, it's coming. I need to use the lube now, because the spit is just not enough. I don't want to hurt you and your virgin ass is so fucking tight."

Quickly Shane lubed up his fingers, three of them Dimitri noticed. Then he slid one of those fingers inside of Dimitri, taking the head of his cock in his mouth at the same time. Dimitri didn't know which way to move. The finger felt good, especially with the added glide of the lube, but the mouth on his cock was a known entity and Dimitri loved getting a blow job.

As Dimitri allowed himself to get lost in the sensation of Shane licking and sucking the head of his cock he felt Shane slip another finger inside his tight muscles. This time there was a slight bit of discomfort but it eased quickly as Shane kept sucking his cock and moving his fingers in and out of his ass. Suddenly Shane's fingers angled slightly and Dimitri groaned as a bolt of pleasure shot through his system.

"What the hell was that?" Dimitri asked his voice quivering even as his ass sought out that sensation again.

Shane dropped his cock long enough to answer with a grin, "the reason gay men have sex" before he went back to what he was doing.

"Do it again," Dimitri demanded. Shane obliged and Dimitri moved into the touch, forcing more. Fuck. That just felt so amazing Dimitri knew he could come from that stimulation without anything else. Who knew his ass could feel so fucking good?

Shane had widened the gap in his fingers now and Dimitri could feel the stretch, but it wasn't anything he couldn't handle. By the time Shane had added a third finger, Dimitri was fucking himself on Shane's hand in earnest, too lost in the pleasure to care that he actually had part of someone's hand up his ass. Dimitri just let himself feel. He could smell his mate and that comforted and aroused him all in one go. As the fingers moved in and out of him he quickly got to the point where it wasn't enough.

Letting Dimitri's cock fall out of his mouth, Shane said quietly, "Sorry, can't wait anymore. I'm going to fuck you now, lover. It would be easier for you if you were on your hands and knees for the first time, but I think your wolf will handle it better if you can see me when we do this. Is that okay?"

Dimitri took in the lines of tension on Shane's face and noticed for the first time how hard and leaking Shane's cock was. The man had been so very patient, but it was clear his control was damn near shattered. And so was Dimitri. He wanted this. He wanted Shane inside him so badly he ached.

"Please Shane, fill me. Fuck me, mate with me and claim me. I'm yours," Dimitri said, the truth of his words shining in his eyes.

Growling possessively, Shane removed his fingers and inching forward on his knees, he raised Dimitri's legs, putting them on his shoulders. Dimitri could feel the blunt head of Shane's cock push up against his anus and for a moment Dimitri tensed, worried that it wouldn't fit. But Shane had done a good job of stretching him as much as he could, and with a sharp little thrust the head of Shane's cock pushed past Dimitri's muscles and into the heat inside.

Okay, damn. Dimitri could feel that. He tightened up as felt the burn race through his nerve endings. Shit. Shit. Shit. Above him Shane had stilled completely simply letting Dimitri adjust to his size. Shane's cock wasn't huge by wolf standards, but all shifters were well endowed and Shane was bigger than most humans.

"Relax hon," Shane soothed, "breathe out and try and relax."

Dimitri didn't even realize he had been holding his breath. He let out a long exhale and consciously tried to relax his anal passage. As he pushed out, he could feel his body accepting more of Shane's length and Shane pushed in a bit more. Trying hard not to tense up, Dimitri breathed and pushed out again, and Shane gained even more ground.

Together the two men worked until Shane was balls deep inside of his mate. He stilled completely again - a sexy as shifter statue with a body so perfect Dimitri knew he was going to spend a lot of hours exploring his mate. But for now he had a more pressing need - he needed Shane to fuck him and fuck him deep.

Reaching his hands out, Dimitri grabbed Shane's hips and pulled him as close as he could with his legs still on the man's shoulders. The action caused Shane's cock to sink even deeper into Dimitri and they both moaned. Looking deep into his mate's eyes, Dimitri growled, "Move mate. Make me yours."

His wicked grin lighting up his face, Shawn rocked against Dimitri, setting a shallow rhythm to get Dimitri used to the sensation. As his strokes became longer, Dimitri could feel the need escalate between them. Within minutes Shane was pounding in and out of his mate's ass with Dimitri begging him to go harder and faster.

Yes, Dimitri knew he was acting like a prize slut but he really didn't care. Shane felt so good inside of him, so very right and when the man tilted his angle slightly so that his cock was brushing across Dimitri's prostate Dimitri knew he wasn't going to last much longer. Releasing one hand from Shane's hip, Dimitri fisted his own cock, desperate to come.

Still keeping up his punishing rhythm, Shane let Dimitri's legs drop as he moved his chest up over Dimitri's.

"Ready to be mine," Shane growled at him.

"Fuck yes," Dimitri yelled as he felt the beginning of his orgasm hit him. Shane bit down hard on the juncture between Dimitri's shoulder and neck muscles and Dimitri howled as his orgasm overtook him. And he was lost to it. Dimly Dimitri realized that his own wolf had come out to play and as he sunk his teeth into Shane's neck his cock burst again, his orgasm stretching on and on, bathing Dimitri in unimagined pleasure. Seconds later Dimitri heard Shane howl as his orgasm overtook him and Dimitri moaned long and low as he felt Shane's hot spunk bathe his inner channel.

Around them the mating bond swirled - two wolf souls joining just as the human bodies had - merging and then coming together. Two wolves forever entwined; their mating bond permanently in place. A bond that could only be broken in death.

Shane went to move off of Dimitri, but Dimitri held him close, pulling him against his chest. He felt satiated, complete in every way. He didn't care what anyone else thought. This was too perfect to be wrong, no matter what society, his family or his pack thought. The ache that had manifested in Dimitri's chest the day he pushed Shane away eight years ago was finally filled.

## Chapter Ten

As Shane lay with his head on Dimitri's chest, his mind was a whorl of emotions. There was the peace that had been absent for the week he had known Dimitri was his mate. That was an awesome feeling. Shane couldn't ignore the intense satisfaction settled deep in his gut, that he had pleased his partner sexually as well. Given that Dimitri was his mate, the desire to give the man exactly what he had promised did cause just the slightest touch of performance anxiety. Not that he would ever tell Dimitri that.

The fact that Dimitri had bitten him, both surprised and pleased him. Shane honestly thought that Dimitri would have to be buried deep in his ass before that would ever happen. Another huge shock had been that not only had Dimitri allowed him to top, but the straight man actually seemed to enjoy it.

All of this clashed awkwardly with the underlying thud in his head that *Dimitri was not gay*. He didn't like men. He didn't lust after men, like Shane had done since he had first shifted. Nope. Dimitri lusted after Shane, that much was obvious, but without the underlying security in his gayness, how was Dimitri going to handle the discrimination that came from their sexuality – the gay bashing in other words – especially within the police department. Shane knew that his personal reputation as a good detective had gone a long way towards any acceptance he had at the precinct, but Dimitri didn't have that history with the men they worked with.

"You are thinking too much," Dimitri said softly.

"I'm worried about you." Shane could admit that much at least. He hadn't even begun to think what this afternoon's activities meant in terms of his heart, or anything like that, and quite honestly, right in that moment, he didn't want to think about it. But a mate would be worried about their partner – that was almost expected. Having a straight mate, who would be considered gay as soon as their relationship was known to the humans around them, was justifiable cause for worry. And Shane would keep telling himself that, even if it was so he didn't think about hearts...or any of that other mush.

Unfortunately it seemed he and Dimitri had their wires crossed. "I'm not going to miss being with women, you know," Dimitri said, but Shane wasn't sure who he was trying to convince. "I spent a long time thinking this situation through. I know, with you never going back home, that the chances of you ever knowing we were true mates was virtually non-existent. I could have stayed in Jacobs Lake, married Angela and have kids on the way by now. But I wanted you. I came after you."

Leaning back a bit so that he could see his mate's face, Shane really studied his new mate. He could tell from the earnest expression on the man's face, that Dimitri was sincere. But the man had picked up on the wrong worry.

"You can't have sex with anyone else but me, from now on anyway," Shane said. "We both knew that, going into this mating. You're just lucky I'm versatile, or you could have real problems." The frown on Dimitri's face alerted him to the fact that his mate didn't understand what he meant, but Shane could fill him in on that later. He decided to try a different tact.

"Do you have any idea how hard it is to be a publicly gay man in the police department? In Stockton? In society in general?"

"I'm not gay," Dimitri said stubbornly and for a moment Shane felt a flash of anger. There were shades of pack teachings in Dimitri's conviction that were going to make their situation all the more difficult if Dimitri kept ignoring what other people would say about their relationship. Taking a deep breath, he said instead, "you have just lost your anal cherry sweetheart, and you loved it. For all intents and purposes, you are gay."

"I have never lusted after another man in my life." Fuck, Dimitri was stubborn. "Only you. I'm not gay, I'm..." Ha, see, now Dimitri couldn't come up with another word, because there was none. "Shane-obsessed," he finished lamely. Shane couldn't help but laugh.

"Hon, if, or should I say when, thanks to what happened today, our fellow officers find out you and I have slept together, the last thing they are going to be worried about is semantics."

"We can keep things seemly at work," Dimitri persisted. "It shouldn't ever be an issue."

Shane shook his head, and looked down his mate's beautiful body. It was just as well the man was a looker, because he was definitely lacking in some aspects of the brain department. Shane had never had anything but one night stands and club pickups since he joined the Stockton PD. He had never taken a date to any of the department's social functions and no one that he worked with had ever seen him with another man. But it didn't stop the few haters in the department making endless speculations about who he did, when he did it and what he did in bed. Straight men's fascination with the gay lifestyle, tempered with ignorance often made for dangerous people, and Shane had learned a long time ago to ignore a lot of what was said, both behind his back and to his face.

Deciding he needed to try and get Dimitri to understand, Shane sat up, not caring that he was still naked. Okay, that might have been on purpose, because the flash of interest in Dimitri's eyes was hard to ignore and Shane definitely liked seeing it there.

"You told the Lieutenant that we slept together. You described in detail something you had only known in thought at the time. By Monday morning, it will be all over the office that you are gay. Fuck," Shane had another horrible thought. "I'm going to have to beat men off you with a stick at the clubs."

"Why? I'm not interested in any other man but you." Dimitri seemed genuinely puzzled and Shane tried to think of a way to explain.

"Okay, let's say for now, that you are not gay and you wouldn't be interested in anyone at any club we went to. It's not going to stop those men being interested in you. They will want to touch you, feel you up, and they will probably proposition you. You'll be with me, so they will assume you are gay, even though you claim you aren't. So you will attract attention."

"Like you do." Now a jealous Dimitri with a surly tone was really cute, but Shane decided to keep his thoughts to himself. Instead he said, "Yes, like I do. You see, if they think we are a couple, then there are going to be some men that want a threesome, or who are jealous of the fact we are in a relationship and want to come between us. If they think we are both single, then, well, we're both fair game."

"But what if they think I'm straight. That should stop them, right?"

Shane laughed then. He couldn't help himself. "Oh sweetheart, there are some gay men who would see you as one big challenge. Converting a straight guy to the dark side is their biggest fantasy."

Dimitri seemed deep in thought for the moment, and Shane didn't want to say anything further. He was quite happy to let the man think things through if it helped him cope with how life would be for them as a couple. Stockton wasn't a bad place and had an active gay community. Gay marriage was allowed and recognized. But the police department was one of many government organizations where the old school network still operated. When Shane had first come to the department he had taken a lot of verbal abuse and some nasty pranks before he had been respected for the work that he did.

So Shane let his mate think, while he took the time to let his eyes wander over Dimitri's body, looking at the tattoos, muscle definition and Dimitri's handsome face. As he looked up, Dimitri caught his eye and Shane grinned. Yes he had been caught scoping out his mate's body – there was no way that could be a bad thing. It was a mate thing, if nothing else.

But Dimitri surprised him again. "I don't like the idea of other people touching you, especially other men."

"Is that a gay thing?" Shane couldn't resist the tease and he was pleased when Dimitri smiled at him, rather than taking offence.

"No," Dimitri said slowly, his gaze heated as his eyes took their turn running over Shane's body. "It's a mate thing. I already know you have been with a number of men here in town, thanks to you leaving me with Ruby for the last week. I don't want to see those men thinking they can come back for round two."

Leaning back against the headboard, letting Dimitri take as much of a look at his body as he wanted, Shane leisurely ran his hand down his torso to his cock, which was starting to harden under Dimitri's visual inspection. Lazily running his hand up and then down his shaft, he flicked a look at his mate and was thrilled to see blatant lust in Dimitri's eyes. He wondered what it would take for his mate to actually make a move on him – given that the guy still thought he was straight.

"Well, I guess you'll have to stick close to me then," he said out loud, as the hand on his cock moved a little faster. "Keep away the competition. You might have a rep with the ladies in Jacobs Lake. But I'm the one who has a rep here in town and I have made it a goal since I first moved here, to ensure my reputation never got tarnished with a poor performance."

Yes! Jealousy was a huge motivator for his new mate, Shane thought with a grin as Dimitri launched himself at Shane, claiming his mouth with a vicious kiss, his hand knocking Shane's away from his cock. Dimitri took him in hand, coming up from the kiss just long enough to snarl, "This. Is. Mine." Before he got back to the serious business of tormenting Shane's tonsils with his tongue, and his cock with that calloused hand.

Within minutes Shane was close to coming again. The way Dimitri kissed him with such confidence, his free hand exploring his body, was such a turn on. So caught up in lust he almost missed Dimitri's question. Shaking his head, he said, "what?"

"Does being versatile," Dimitri asked, harking back to their earlier conversation, "mean that you'll let me fuck you?"

Stunned speechless, all Shane could do was nod his head. He had worried that Dimitri wouldn't be keen on instigating anything sexual himself, given that he hadn't been with a man before. Now he couldn't wait to see what his new mate would do next.

*/~/~/~/~/*

In all of his years of having sex with women, Dimitri had never felt the way he did looking at Shane's naked body. Instead of perky tits, he was running his hand over solid pecs and tight hard little nipples that begged to be bitten. There was no plump hips to stop his hand – just lean muscle and buttocks that were so tight they could bruise a man as he pounded in between them. And damn if Dimitri didn't want to pound between his man's legs.

There was something about the hardness of Shane's body that called to him, like nothing else. After only knowing the softness of a woman's body, it was if Shane was giving him permission to be the man he always knew he wanted to be – rough, hard and so freaking horny he had better do something before he had nothing left to work with.

Remembering his porn notes, Dimitri left a trail of biting kisses down Shane's torso, delighting in his mate's moans for more. As he got closer to Shane's cock he hesitated just for a moment, 26 years of pack teaching running through his head. Then

Shane moaned again, the man's hands clasped tightly in the coverlet as though he didn't dare touch his mate, and Dimitri knew he had to get over himself.

Swallowing his nervousness, Dimitri buried his nose in Shane's balls breathing in the concentrated scent that lurked there. Shane smelled of vanilla and coconut, a soft scent that ran through Dimitri and warmed his heart, and hardened his cock even further. Determined to be bold, because Shane being his mate meant he needed to do this, Dimitri ran a tentative lick up Shane's cock, releasing his own moan as a drop of pre-come coated his lips. Fuck, how could he not have known that his mate would taste as delicious as he smelled?

Lapping eagerly now, Dimitri tongued over the tiny slit that graced the head of Shane's cock, eager to get more of that enticing taste. Shane's body writhed, as though in agony, but the man didn't touch him, didn't try and force his cock into Dimitri's mouth. It was though Shane was letting him do whatever he wanted, as he wanted, and that realization tore through Dimitri like wildfire. He could do whatever he wanted to this wonderful man, and Shane would let him.

Emboldened by that idea, Dimitri carefully nudged the head of Shane's cock into his mouth, his hands holding Shane's hips firmly to prevent any thrusting. He really didn't want to gag. Shielding his teeth with his lips, Dimitri closed his mouth over just the head of Shane's cock and suckled gently.

"Damn it, Dimitri," Shane said with a rasp, trying to fight Dimitri's hold on his hips and drive his cock further into the man's mouth. "You don't have to treat me like spun glass. I'm dying here."

Dimitri grinned to himself, and slowly let his breath out, moving down the shaft of Shane's cock as he went. Hmmm, the books were right, it was easier to get more length in this way. Taking another breath he carefully worked his way back up, using his tongue this time. He figured if this was something he liked having done to him, Shane would probably like it also and if the moans and cursing were any indication, he was right.

Now that he had got some sort of technique going, a technique that seemed to be working, Dimitri was able to actually revel in the sensations that sucking his man's cock was causing deep inside of him. There was something primal about having Shane's pleasure under his control. The way Shane's hips flexed as much as possible beneath Dimitri's death grip. The gasps and the moans, grunts and curses as Shane tried to speed him up.

But it was more than that. Shane's length felt right on his tongue. The man's taste titillated his own desire. He felt powerful and yet there was also that deep pleasure that came from Shane's obvious desire. Remembering what Shane had said, Dimitri raised his head long enough to ask, "If I make you come like this, can I still fuck you?"

His head propped up on pillows so he could watch the show, Shane seemed stunned for a moment, like the question didn't make sense. Dimitri liked doing that to his mate. He waited, knowing that Shane's brain was sex fogged, and damn it all, if that didn't make him feel good as well. This whole having sex with your mate thing was so much better than anything else he had ever done.

Finally Shane said, "Yeah, should be fine. But er...go slow, okay. I haven't bottomed for a long while." Giving a satisfied nod, because who wouldn't be pleased with a statement like that, Dimitri got back to giving his first blow job ever.

## Chapter Eleven

It was official. Shane was going insane. He tried to remember that this was Dimitri's first time. He was over the moon that his mate even went near his cock, let alone had it in his mouth. The suction was awesome, the heat of Dimitri's mouth wickedly sinful, but the damn man was going too slow and being too fucking nice about it. Shane went with men, because he wanted to be treated like a man, not a female who needed a gentle touch. The urge to grab the hair on Dimitri's head and shove his cock straight down his throat, was overwhelming.

"Fingers," he said out loud, thinking quickly, "You can use your fingers to prep me while you're sucking." Hopefully the added stimulation would bring him off, because Shane wanted to come so bad his balls were hurting. Dimitri lifted his head, and Shane was so entranced with the picture of Dimitri's lips swollen from sucking, he almost missed what the man said.

"I would far rather do this," Dimitri said with a grin that should be banned in all 52 States, and without any warning, he flipped Shane onto his stomach and then pulled at him by the hips, bringing Shane's ass into the air. Then again, no warning, no may I or please, the man ran his tongue straight over Shane's hole.

"Holy shit and fucking hell," Shane cursed as he dropped his head and shoulders into the pillows and gave himself over to the sensation. "You *are* trying to kill me."

Dimitri didn't say anything, but Shane could feel his grin against his skin. Then Dimitri's dexterous tongue went to work, and Shane lost the ability to speak. How could he, when all that was coming out of his mouth was one long moan after another. There was no way this could have been Dimitri's first attempt at this particular rodeo. Shane could feel himself coming apart just from the man's tongue. And that was without the confident way Dimitri's strong hands held his butt cheeks apart.

And then Dimitri did the unthinkable. Shane literally held his breath as he felt the tip of Dimitri's tongue penetrate his ass. Holy hell. There were no words, and for a guy that kept professing he was straight, Dimitri's tongue was working him like a porn star and Shane reached beneath him to palm his own cock. His cock was going to fucking burst if he didn't come soon.

"Don't touch," Dimitri growled and Shane pulled his hand away with a whimper. He desperately wanted to scream at Dimitri to fucking get a wiggle on, but he didn't want to shatter any of the man's confidence. It's his first time, it's his first time, he chanted in his head, willing Dimitri to get to the good stuff.

"Fingers," Dimitri said, "How many?"

Looking at Dimitri's cock, hard and ready for action Shane figured he would probably need the man's whole hand for prepping – it had been a really long time for him. But not wanting to slow Dimitri down any,

Shane said instead, "A couple, and lots of lube."

Dimitri gave him a narrowed look, but picked up the lube where it had fallen on the bed after Shane's earlier efforts. Coating his fingers, Dimitri put one hand on Shane's back and with the other, gently ran his finger around his asshole.

"Shove it in already," Shane begged. He felt hot and sweaty, like he'd been kept on the edge for days. Dimitri's scent kept washing over his nostrils, making his cock and ass throb with anticipation. He still hadn't come despite Dimitri's promise of a blow job, and he didn't dare say anything that might dissuade Dimitri from his purpose. Shane hadn't forgotten it was his fucking finger comment that pulled his mate's mouth from his cock.

Fortunately, for Shane at least, this time Dimitri complied. Shane felt his mate's thick finger push through his muscles and breathed a sigh of relief. Surely it wouldn't be long now, especially after only a couple of pumps with the one finger, Dimitri followed up with a second, scissoring as he went, opening Shane up further.

Relaxing his head back into the pillows, Shane moaned his encouragement, moving his hips back towards his mate to show he was good with what was happening. By the time Dimitri had added a third finger, and damn it all, Shane had only told him he wanted two, Shane could feel the burn rushing through his insides. Breathing deep he rode it out, knowing it would only get better.

"Can't wait any more," Dimitri said, his voice so full of gravel that Shane looked back over his shoulder. What an amazing sight. Dimitri's heated gaze was fixed on his ass hole, his chest was heaving and there was the hint of fangs showing below the man's lips. Fuck, Dimitri's wolf had come out to play. This would be interesting.

"More lube on your dick, then go for it," Shane panted out, bracing himself on his elbows. If Dimitri's wolf was in charge, then Shane was in for the pounding of his life. As he felt Dimitri's cock nudge and then push past the muscles around his asshole, Shane took in a deep breath in, and then out, trying to relax as much as possible. It didn't look like Dimitri was going to stop for anything.

Dimitri made it in to "balls deep" status through sheer persistence and brute strength. As soon as he was seated Shane could feel the man's muscles tense behind him, and knew he was going to move. Shane wasn't anywhere near ready. The burn was exquisite and Shane had never felt so full, but damn his body needed to relax more otherwise Dimitri was going to tear a hole in his bloody colon.

"Stop," he said quickly. Dimitri looked at him, the concern on his face. Fortunately Dimitri did as he was asked. "I need a minute to adjust," Shane explained as he kept his breathing slow and steady, relaxing and pushing out with his muscles, Dimitri remaining a motionless sex statue behind him.

After a long minute, Shane knew he could cope with whatever Dimitri could dish out. Throwing a cheeky grin over his shoulder, he said, "Okay lover, show me what you've got." The pleasure at seeing Dimitri smile was quickly overshadowed by the immense delight when his mate took him at his word, and started pounding into him. Dimitri's hands had turned to claws and were biting into Shane's hips. The man's breathing was hot and ragged, grunts pushed out of his body with every thrust, and that cock kept pounding into him with relentless precision.

Tilting his hips slightly, and dipping his back, Shane felt Dimitri's cock hit his prostate and his body sang. Holding that position, as best he could, given the strength of the man behind him, Shane knew his orgasm was literally seconds away. And it seemed Dimitri was close as well if the erratic nature of the man's thrusts, and the way the man leaned over his back was any indication.

"You're mine," was the only warning Shane got before sharp teeth bit into his neck and Dimitri's come started coating his insides. With a howl of approval Shane let himself go, his own climax going on for what seemed like forever. It had definitely been worth the wait.

Thank fucking God, Shane thought as he drifted in the afterglow. Behind him he felt Dimitri carefully pull out, his slow movements so at odds with the pounding moments before. Then Shane felt two strong arms come around his middle and he was pulled into a warm embrace, Dimitri's breath in his hair.

"Not bad for a first time," he managed to say softly, before he snuggled in for a nap. It might be dinner time for the rest of the town, but Shane was worn out. A short nap before meal time was definitely in order. From Dimitri's snores beside him it would seem that his mate was on the same page.

## Chapter Twelve

It wasn't until they were sitting on the couch enjoying the pizza that Shane had ordered in, that the little niggle that had been bothering Dimitri since they had been at the crime scene resurfaced in his head. "How did the Lieutenant know you had been with CJ last night?"

A frown gracing his gorgeous face, Shane thought about it for a moment. "Green said that he had an informant that saw the two of us at the club." Clearly thinking about what had gone on in the interview before Dimitri had got there, Shane went on. "The guy must have been close enough because Green knew I'd been groped, and that we had gone out of the back of the club together."

"But whoever it was, didn't click that I was at the club too, or that I went out of the back door as well. Nor did he report that CJ was back in the club approximately ten minutes later."

Shane got up and started pacing the floor, something Dimitri knew he did when he was thinking things out.

Dimitri was much the same. Watching Shane move though, was proving distracting and Dimitri felt there was something about Shane's questioning that might be a clue in the case.

"There's so many unanswered questions," Shane finally said, pulling his hair in frustration. "Why was someone watching me? I'm in that club three or four times a week. How did an informant know that CJ was dead so soon? It had only been a matter of hours after he was murdered. If I didn't know better I would say that Green is using these bloody murders to get me off the force."

"Is that a possibility?" Dimitri knew that Green hated Shane and guessed it was because he was an openly gay man. Even if that wasn't the case, it seemed damned suspect that someone was quick to go to Green with a tip, so soon after CJ's body had been discovered. Something that wasn't public knowledge at the time.

"We need to find out who Green's informant is," he said looking up at

Shane. To his surprise Shane sat down with a thump – his face pale and his eyes wild, something clearly on his mind. Shaking his head, Shane said, "It might be worse than we think. Green doesn't work weekends. He shouldn't have known about the murder until the Monday morning briefing. How the hell did he find out about CJ soon enough to turn up with the IA, at the crime scene, with knowledge about my seeing CJ the night before."

Dimitri thought about the implications behind what Shane was saying. "Maybe someone phoned Green because it is a serial murder investigation?" He suggested.

"But it isn't," Shane said. "Not yet. I spoke to Green about it before you even started here and he brushed me off. Said that gay bashing was common enough and these guys were just unlucky. He refused to believe it was the work of one man, or that the murders were connected."

"He'd spoken to the Captain about it though, so maybe Green is thinking along those lines even if he didn't say so to you." Dimitri thought that sounded plausible, but from the way Shane was shaking his head, his partner didn't think so.

"I don't think so. You heard what the Captain said. Green had mentioned my ideas and basically slapped them down."

"That could be because he doesn't like you. He still might think it's a credible idea in his own head."

Shane looked at Dimitri and with the worried look on the man's face, Dimitri had this overwhelming urge to put his arm around him. Shane knew a lot more about the workings in the department than Dimitri did and something about Green was upsetting Shane now and it was more than the fact Green had tried to finger him as a suspect in a murder. Deciding to ignore what he didn't know for now, he followed through on the hugging idea and when Shane melted in his arms, he knew he had done the right thing.

"I can't help thinking that CJ's death had something to do with his contact with me," Shane said and the break in his voice did something weird to Dimitri's heart muscle. Kissing the top of Shane's head, which had gravitated to his chest, Dimitri tried to think about the situation logically. Which was more difficult than usual, because Shane's scent drove him completely crazy with lust and he hadn't had anywhere near enough time to learn all the secrets of Shane's body. But he could sense that Shane needed more than a hot body right now. Shane needed his skills as a detective.

"You did say that CJ had been hurt before because people thought he was an informant," he said, hoping he wasn't making the situation more emotive. He didn't know how well Shane actually knew CJ and for all he knew, Shane could be totally gutted about his death.

"Yes, but that was when he was living on the streets," Shane said. "He was seen talking to uniformed cops and someone did him over for that. He's been my informant since he came out of hospital, and we've never had any trouble before last night."

"But the guys in the club, they know you're on the force, don't they?"

Shane nodded. "Yes. I've never hidden it and some of my tricks, hell, I'm sure they got off on it. And although CJ and I never did anything sexually, people always assumed we did and it was safer for CJ to let them think that. It's never done him any harm before."

"So you're thinking what exactly?"

Letting out a huff of breath, that heated Dimitri's chest and sent a zing straight down his pants, Shane said, "I'm not sure exactly. With the other three murders it was just frustrating – no leads, no clues. But I didn't know the murdered men. I had never even seen them in the clubs, or on the streets before. Hell, they could have been closeted for all I knew."

"But you do think the gay angle is the reason they were killed," Dimitri said, wanting to make sure.

"There wasn't anything else, and I looked, I can tell you. They all spent time in one of the three clubs the night they died. None of them were seen leaving with anybody. They turned up dead in an alley, tossed in a dumpster, found days later. At least one person, in all three cases, said that the boys were gay. And every straight murder we have had, we have been able to solve and none of them had the same MO as these cases."

"But CJ is a definite deviation from the norm," Dimitri pointed out. "He wasn't found in a dumpster, he was out in the open. He was found within hours of his death. The markings and the cause of death did look similar, but is it possible this is a copycat, rather than part of the serial?"

"We'll know for sure when we get the autopsy report. But I doubt it's a copycat. Some of the injuries inflicted were never released to the public, so if they are confirmed on CJ's autopsy then it would be safe to assume that it is the same person," Shane said with a sigh, curling around Dimitri as though seeking comfort. Dimitri tightened his grip and took a moment to just enjoy having his mate in his arms. But that nagging worry in the back of his head just would not go away.

"I'm more worried about you," he said, turning Shane's face up so that Shane could see he was serious. "No matter who killed CJ, and believe me, we will find the asshole, someone used it as an opportunity to try and trash your career. And the only person who seems hell bent on doing that, from what I can see, is Green. Or is there someone else we should be worried about?"

"No, Green's the only real problem. I get hassled a bit by a couple of the uniforms, but nothing bad enough to suggest they want me gone from the department. I don't know what am I missing here, but I feel there is something really important that is just on the edge of my brain." Shane said. His green eyes were sad, and Dimitri guessed that was because of CJ's death, but the man was focused on his work. Something Dimitri was struggling with, big time. After waiting for Shane for eight years, his cock felt it had a lot of catching up to do and having Shane in his arms was playing havoc with his senses.

Forcing his brain to think only on the problem at hand, and not how wonderful it felt to hold his mate, Dimitri said slowly, "I'm not questioning your methods, but I have looked over your case notes, in all three current cases. From what I could see, you spent a lot of time looking into the victim's lifestyles, their friends, family, workplace, and people that saw them in the club the night they were killed."

"Yes, so. That's standard operating procedure." Shane sounded a little bit peeved, like maybe Dimitri was questioning his methods, but Dimitri ignored it, a germ of an idea floating in his head.

"It's what you said about Green and how he might have found out about CJ and your involvement with him. When we were at the scene today, no one said anything about the person who found the body, and in all three previous cases, the bodies were found through anonymous tips. Have you ever thought about looking into who found these bodies?"

"There wasn't anyone at the scene today? I was too bugged out to notice to be honest."

"No," said Dimitri. "And if you factor in Green knowing about the murder, when he wasn't at work today, and the informant who told him about you and CJ last night..."

"Then you've just come up with an angle I hadn't even considered." The smile on Shane's face was beautiful and Dimitri was even happier when his mate flung his arms around Dimitri's neck and kissed him soundly on the lips. "You, my mate," said Shane, "are absolutely brilliant. So you fancy going clubbing tonight and see if we can find out who this informant of Green's is?"

"Kiss me again and I'll think about it," Dimitri said, even though he knew he would agree. He had a horrible feeling that this attack on Shane and his credibility wasn't finished, and he wanted to get to the bottom of it as soon as possible. Hunting for Green's informant was a good place to start. Then he stopped thinking, because Shane did kiss him again, and keeping in mind that they wouldn't be going to the clubs until much later that night, Dimitri kissed him right back.

## Chapter Thirteen

It was close to eleven that night before the two men decided to head out. Dimitri had wanted to get dressed in his suit again, but Shane convinced him that they should head back to his motel and get some casual clothes. When Dimitri protested that they were actually going to do some work, Shane reminded him that technically they were not supposed to be working on CJ's case, and the more casual approach would work a lot better. Grumbling, Dimitri had poured himself into black jeans that tight they should have been illegal, and teamed it up with a tight black button down shirt.

"I am definitely going to get you some leather pants. You have got the perfect ass for them," Shane said with a purr as he prowled around his now dressed mate. Dimitri looked positively edible and Shane felt his cock give a twitch in his own leather pants. Running his hand down Dimitri's back while the man fussed with his hair in the mirror, he said casually, "you want to get a bag of your stuff, and maybe stay over at my place a bit more after the club?"

"You're not sleeping anywhere from now on unless it's with me," Dimitri growled, his dark eyes catching Shane's in the mirror. "I am happy to pay for this poxy room for as long as you want me to give you some space, but we are sleeping together every night and we will be living together as soon as you give the okay for that. So the short answer to your question is yes."

Shane hid his smile, although he said nothing further as Dimitri grabbed a duffle bag from his closet and threw some clothes in it. He chuckled quietly to himself when he noticed that like him, Dimitri didn't wear underwear. Shifters like to strip quickly in the case of an emergency and underpants were a damn nuisance to get off. The thought of his mate wandering around all day commando was a delicious idea.

Although it might play havoc with his working day.

As for them living together, well, Shane knew he didn't want to be separate from Dimitri for longer than minutes in a day. The mating bond between wolves was strong, and the desire to be with each other a constant throughout their long lives. But Shane couldn't help but keep that little titbit to himself. It wouldn't hurt to make Dimitri wait a few days before he allowed the man to move into his space permanently. Shane wanted to see how Dimitri coped with being gay on a day to day basis in the real world, before he committed himself fully. If his heart gave a sharp twinge at the thought of Dimitri laying in his hotel bed by himself at night, Shane kept that to himself as well.

*/~/~/~/~/*

Saturday night at Club Truckers was always busy, and the club was packed when Shane and Dimitri arrived. Recognizing that this was Shane's home turf, Dimitri relegated himself to the role of body guard as Shane pushed his way through to the bar to get them both a drink. Dimitri felt his head throb as the sound of excited humans, loud music and the smells of sex and testosterone filled his senses. After his relatively quiet life at Jacob's Lake, he wondered how the hell Shane coped with this type of thing nearly every night of the week.

Grabbing a couple of bottles of beer, Black Cat Stout Dimitri noticed, Shane pointed to a booth that had just become vacant and headed over to claim it. "Is it a good idea to kinda cut ourselves off from people by sitting over here," Dimitri asked as he slid in beside Shane.

"People will come to us, you'll see. You're a new face and you're with me. You look hot and by sitting down tonight instead of prancing about on the dance floor, I'm letting people know I'm not available tonight. I thought it might also help you protect your virtue," Shane teased with his trademark grin.

Dimitri shrugged and sat back in the booth, his thigh against Shane's, his arm loosely resting on Shane's shoulder, watching the action around them. This was only his second time at the club, at any gay club, and the last time he had been here he had only been focused on Shane, and had paid next to no attention to the club, or what went on there.

Now every sense was assailed with what it was like to be gay. There seemed to be so many different types of men around – from painted up pretty boys, to big hairy looking men that looked like they needed a bath. A lot of the men were fit and good looking, as if they spent half their lives at a gym, but Dimitri couldn't raise a flicker of interest in any of them. Surely that meant he wasn't gay, right?

What struck Dimitri the most, and it was something that he would probably never tell Shane, was how confident and happy all of the men looked. There was a lot of physical interaction, men quite happily kissing, and more, with other men and nobody in the club seemed to worry about it. After the narrow minded upbringing Dimitri had, this open sexuality was going to take some getting used to.

"See anything you like?" Shane teased, leaning into his space, and for a split second Dimitri caught a hint of his scent. Looking into Shane's brilliant green eyes, Dimitri said with all seriousness, "only you," and was pleased with the huge smile that blossomed over the smaller man's face.

"Wow D-man haven't seen your friend before. Gonna introduce me?" Dimitri looked over to see a pretty little man sliding into the booth beside Shane. Similar to CJ the man had shoulder length hair and fine facial features. If he had to guess, Dimitri thought the man's lips, that were full, red and covered in gloss like women wore, were probably his best feature. Although the tiny t-shirt and the tight leather pants suggested that maybe other attributes were being marketed as well.

"Hands off, Gremlin," Shane said with a grin. "This one's not on the market and definitely not for you. He's my new partner on the force, Dimitri Polst. I'm just showing him around."

"Oh man, so you're working tonight? That just sucks." Gremlin pouted, or at least that is what Dimitri thought he was doing although he had only seen that look on a woman's face before.

"Nope, not working," Shane said cheerfully, as he put his hand on Dimitri's chest. "Out having some fun with my new partner. Catching up on what's going on around town. You know me."

The way Gremlin ran his eyes over Shane's body, like he would cheerfully drop his pants and bend over the table, suggested that the little man did know Shane, intimately. Dimitri growled under his breath. Gremlin might not hear it, thanks to the noise in the club, but Shane did and his hand pushed a little harder on Dimitri's chest.

"So you wanna..." Gremlin trailed off and let his face do the rest of the talking. A wink, a nudge, a flick of his head indicating the passageway out to the alley. Shane shook his head, and Gremlin nodded and slipped out of his seat. "Later D-man," he said over his shoulder as he went looking for his next target.

"You can't growl at every man that comes over here, lover," Shane whispered in his ear. "We won't find out anything if you're uptight and unapproachable."

"It's a little hard not to, when you've clearly fucked the man," Dimitri whispered back, flicking out his tongue and running it around Shane's ear. A shudder ran through Shane's body and he dropped his hand from Dimitri's chest to the top of Dimitri's thigh, and Dimitri felt himself harden from the contact. He slid down in his seat a bit causing Shane's hand to rest lightly against his cock. Fuck, that felt nice and Dimitri had never had a problem with PDA or even a spot of exhibitionism. The fact that he was in a gay club didn't even factor into it. In fact, it made the whole thing seem a bit more risqué.

"Feeling frisky, lover?" Shane teased blowing lightly into Dimitri's ear and running his hand lightly over Dimitri's pant-covered dick.

"Hmm, keep that up and you'll see more than you bargained for," Dimitri said even as he registered another man slipping into the booth, this time beside him. He bristled as the man moved closer than he would have liked, but couldn't move away because Shane was hemming him in on the other side.

"See you have a new toy, D-man. Can I play too?" The man said, reaching out towards Dimitri's chest. Quick as a flash, Shane slapped the man's hand away and glared at him.

"Hand's off, Tucker. This one doesn't play your sort of games," Shane snarled. "Either say something useful, or fuck off."

Tucker sat back against the booth, thankfully moving away from Dimitri, who didn't like the vibe coming off the arrogant man one little bit. Tucker was clearly an executive type, with short brown hair and mean eyes. His face could be considered textbook handsome, but Dimitri didn't like him on sight.

"Heard you got pulled in by the police this morning, D-man," Tucker said casually, examining the finger nails on one well-manicured hand. Dimitri could feel Shane stiffen beside him, but his face was an unreadable mask.

Shane shrugged and said, "You know how it is, Tucker. I'm gay. Vic's gay. Figure there's got to be a connection. All got sorted."

"Heard that there's some in your fine department that aren't too happy about that. One guy in particular."

Shane moved forward so that he was leaning on the table, fixing Tucker with a thoughtful grin. "Seems to me that you heard an awful lot for someone who doesn't get out of bed before mid-afternoon. Who have you been chatting to?"

Tucker grinned, and the look did nothing for the man's face. If anything Dimitri thought it made him look like a sick little weasel. Tucker hooked his hands in the waistband of his pants and framed his package, which looked pretty pathetic from Dimitri's viewpoint.

Pointing at Dimitri, Tucker said slyly, "let pretty boy here take me out the back and give me a blow job and I'll tell you."

Leaning back against the booth again, Shane mirrored Tucker's stance, framing his own package. Now that was something Dimitri could appreciate, and he couldn't stop the small smile on his face. If this was a pissing contest, Shane won, hands down. Unfortunately the look on Dimitri's face gave Tucker the wrong idea.

"Your boy seems keen," Tucker said. "So is it a deal?"

Shane thought for a moment, and then to Dimitri's surprise, he nodded. "Yep, come on out back Tucker. Dimitri will give you what you are looking for, won't you honey?"

How Dimitri managed to nod his head, he wasn't sure. But Shane was clearly counting on him to agree, even though the thought of having any man's dick near his mouth made him feel ill. Then he remembered he had tasted cock three times already today, and that hadn't made him feel sick at all. For some reason, in Dimitri's mind, sucking Shane didn't feel like a gay thing to do. But heading out to the back alley with Shane and Tucker made him feel so angry he was struggling to control himself.

## Chapter Fourteen

Out in the alley there was barely any light, but more than enough for Shane to see. The darkness would give him and Dimitri the edge over Tucker, and an edge was all that Shane needed. Leading them over to an ever darker spot, Shane nodded to the wall and said, "Get yourself propped up and ready, Tucker. Me and my man here don't have all night."

Sporting his sickly grin, Tucker leaned up against the wall and dropped his trousers and briefs, exposing a small, skinny hard cock. "Do me, big boy," Tucker demanded as he put his head back and prepared for his blow job. Good god, and this man thought he was being seductive.

Shane looked over to Dimitri who was clearly angry, but trusting him enough to go along with whatever Shane wanted. Blown away that his mate could feel that way after such a short time, Shane gestured to Dimitri to move forward. Dimitri frowned but pointed to the ground. Very slightly

Shane shook his head and ran a finger across his neck. Dimitri's raised eyebrows and small grin showed that his mate had got the message.

Stepping up to Tucker, and totally invading his personal space, Dimitri put one hand on Tucker's neck and his foot on the man's pants. Leaning down so he was right in Tucker's face, Dimitri growled, "now who have you been talking to, little man?"

Tucker squeaked and looked across at Shane. "Your man's not giving me a blow job. What the fuck?"

"My man's straight," Shane said with a grin. "But he knows a lot about breath play, don't you honey?"

Dimitri grinned again and leaned a bit harder on Tucker, his hand on the man's neck turning Tucker's face into a delightful shade of puce. Then he let up enough for Tucker to talk.

"This is police abuse, D-man, I'll have your badge for this," Tucker managed to get out, although talking was getting a little bit difficult.

"Could be a little hard to prove, given you came out here willingly when you thought you were going to get your cock sucked. Who do you think the department is going to believe? More to the point," Shane said leaning in and doing a spot of intimidation of his own. "How long do you think you will last on the streets when it's known you're a police informant? How long will you last in that cushy job of yours when I let them know what you do on your night off?"

Tucker struggled then, thumping Dimitri on his chest with his hands, and trying to kick his legs out, which was impossible given that he was tied with his own pants around his ankles. When he realized he couldn't get out, he slumped against the wall, his legs barely holding him upright.

"Now you've got that out of your system," Shane said pleasantly, "I want to know who you've been talking to and what you know. If you don't tell me, then my partner here will book you for solicitation."

"I'm not a prostitute!" Tucker glared at Dimitri as though daring him to make such a claim.

"Under Penal Code 647(b) PC, you did offer your cock, sexual services, in exchange for information, which as an informant you would be paid for. Close enough," Dimitri said.

"You might get off," Shane said, perfectly happy to be agreeable because he knew he had the little weasel right where he wanted him to be. "But think of what the publicity of being charged will do to you."

"I'll see to it you never get another fuck in this town again, D-man," Tucker said with a surprising amount of force given that Dimitri still had his neck in his capable hand.

"Oh yes I will," Shane assured him. "My work and my fucking have nothing to do with each other and if you had paid a bit more attention to me and what I do, then you would know that. Everyone else does. Now talk Tucker, or we will take this down to the station."

"Can I at least pull my pants up?" Tucker tried one more time.

"Nope," said Dimitri. "Talk fast and we'll be gone. Simple really."

"I bumped into Gav, you know him right? Tall guy, shaggy brown hair and beard? Always looks like he needs a bath and a feed?"

Shane nodded.

"Yes, well I bumped into him at Rizzo's, the little Italian place down town. He had a fistful of dollars and was spending it like there was no tomorrow."

"That's unusual enough," Shane said thinking hard. Gav was a typical bum, although Shane had seen him around a lot just lately. That couldn't be a coincidence.

"I asked him about it, you know, like you do. Anyway he told me that he had been given big bucks for finding the guy who has been killing all those gay guys on the news lately. Those cases you're working on."

"No one's been arrested for that yet," Shane said, now thinking fast. This smacked of a set up and there was only one person who could have done that.

"But you were, this morning," Tucker said. "That's how come Gav got paid. He's been following you for weeks, waiting to see you make your move. He saw you with CJ. CJ's dead. You got pulled in. Gav got paid."

"How do you know CJ's dead? The news hasn't been released yet. The police are still looking for next of kin," Dimitri said and Shane couldn't get over how comfortable his mate was, juggling his police mode with the hand that was still holding Tucker's throat captive.

Tucker looked surprised. "Gav told me. He phoned the guy who's paying him last night and told him you were getting cozy with CJ. Then this morning this same guy rings him and tells him to come around and get his money because the job was finished. This same guy told Gav that CJ was dead, and that you were his killer and the killer of the other three men as well. Gav has been spreading it around all day. Course, no one believes him but he's definitely flashing money around."

Dimitri dropped his hand and stepped back, the anger clear as day on his face. "You should count your lucky stars that Gav's still not on the job," he snarled, "Or you'd be the next one found in the alley dead. Now fuck off and keep your trap shut."

"But what am I going to do about this?" Tucker whined, pointing to his cock, that miracles of miracles was still hard.

Shane cocked his eyebrow and then grinned. "You like the rough stuff, aye Tucker? Like a bit of force in your man?" Tucker looked at Shane like all his Christmases had come at once. "Hop down to Leathers, tell the doorman that Shane sent you and told you to ask for Sin. He'll take care of you."

"Sin, right," Tucker said in all seriousness, buttoning his pants. "You...er...won't say anything about this to anyone else, will you?"

"Fuck off," Dimitri snarled and Tucker ran down the alley.

/~/~/~/~/

As soon as Tucker had disappeared, Shane let the smile drop from his face and Dimitri could tell he was angry and worried all at the same time. Pulling Shane close, he kissed him softly on the lips. Then deciding to avoid the obvious for now, he said with a grin of his own, "So Sin? Is he a threat or a promise for young Tucker?"

"Oh definitely a promise," Shane said. "Sin is the best sadist I know. A true master of humiliation, domination and pain. Tucker will love him, or hate him. But either way he'll get off."

Heaving a sigh, Shane sagged against Dimitri. "Someone's out to get me, and CJ's dead because of me. We've got to find Gav and god knows where he would be now he has money to burn. Things are not looking good, D. Can we go home?"

"Nope," Dimitri said firmly. "We are going back into the club and you are going to dance with me. I've never danced with a man before."

"But you heard what Tucker said. Everyone thinks I'm murdering gay men?"

"Did you notice anything different when you came here tonight? Did anyone get weird on you, or did you pick up any strange vibes?"

"No, I thought it was just like any other night, except I was with you instead of Ruby."

"Exactly. Tucker already said that no one believes this Gav anyway, and if you are out on the town, having fun, then maybe we'll pick up a bit more gossip. If nothing else word will get back to Gav that you aren't in the lockup, and who knows, maybe his curiosity will get the better of him and he'll come looking for us."

Shane ran his hands around Dimitri's waist and pulled him close. "A straight man wants to dance with little old gay me?" He teased.

"I want to dance with my mate. Those other men I was watching seemed to be having a lot of fun with it, so I thought I'd give it a try, with you."

"Do you even know how to dance?" Shane asked him as he led his mate back into the club.

"Well enough," Dimitri said confidently. He and Angela used to go dancing all the time, and while the club at Jacobs Lake might not be as big, or as sophisticated as Club Truckers, he was fairly sure he wouldn't look like an idiot. But then, when Shane pulled him close as they stood on the edge of the dance floor, and wrapped his arms around Dimitri's neck, Dimitri figured he didn't care if he looked like a first class fool. The feel of Shane in his arms, their hot bodies pressed together from thigh to chest, was more than enough to make up for it.

When they collapsed in a booth about an hour later, bottled water in their hands, Shane showed he had still been thinking despite his sensual dance moves, because he said, "What I don't understand is that if we make the assumption that the man who hired Gav is the same man who killed CJ, then why was Gav paid out and allowed to spread so much gossip about me? If the guy's a killer, wouldn't he have killed Gav rather than pay him? That would be the more logical thing to do."

"Trying to discredit you in the gay community; trying to discredit you in your job; not wanting to draw attention to the fact that he had a paid informant, although that didn't work; too cocky for his own good; or because he's an idiot who thought that you would be locked up. Or maybe it's because he's not the killer, but knows who the killer is." Dimitri ticked the items off his fingers.

"And what do you think?" Shane asked, taking a long swig of water from the bottle.

Watching Shane's throat work, Dimitri said huskily, "I think you've shown enough people you're not in lock up for now and no one seems to have a pressing need to talk to us. So I think that we should go home."

Shane looked over at him and smiled. That was all the invitation Dimitri needed.

## Chapter Fifteen

There should be a law against mobile phones working on a Sunday, Shane thought as he reached for the offending gadget in the half light of the early morning. He and Dimitri hadn't gotten back to his place until well after three in the morning and they hadn't fallen asleep until after 5am. Rubbing the grit from his eyes, Shane peered blearily at the tiny screen in front of him – Mace – what the hell would he want at this time of the morning.

"If you answer the fucking thing, then you'll know," Dimitri's gruff voice came from somewhere under the pillows. Flicking a quick glare at the man in question, Shane hit the relevant buttons on his phone.

"Yeah, Mace, what's up?" He said, trying to sound more awake than he felt.

"A body has been found down by the Marina. Thought you might want it," Mace said.

"Is it one of mine," Shane asked sitting up and fumbling for his pants. Shit, he wore his leathers last night and that wouldn't do for an early morning body view. Standing up, he walked over and flicked through his closet for some jeans. Stuff wearing a suit on a Sunday.

"No," Mace said, "not like the other ones, but the Captain said you might want this one too. It's Gav, you know? The bum from downtown? Always hanging around the gay spots."

Shit. Fuck. Double Damn. "Yes," Shane replied. "I know. Give me twenty minutes." He clicked off his phone and turned to find Dimitri already pulling on some blue jeans and a plain black muscle shirt.

"Gav," he said shortly. Dimitri nodded and waited for Shane to finish dressing. Without a word the two men left the house, and piled into Shane's car. Ten minutes down the road, and Shane pulled into a drive thru for coffee – if anything warranted a jumbo cup of java, another dead body did. Especially a dead body that might have held all of the answers Shane was looking for.

When they pulled up at the marina, the normal activity around a dead body was evident. Yellow police tape, three police cars parked at angles to try and contain what appeared to be a fairly open crime scene, and people milling about looking officious. Shane spotted Mace and headed over to find out what had been gleaned so far.

/~/~/~/~/

Dimitri followed a little more slowly. This was only his second crime scene at Stockton and he didn't want to make assumptions about what went on. He presumed Shane and Ruby had their own routine, and as Shane was currently talking to Mace, he decided to take a look at the body and try and do a bit of a sniff around without anybody noticing. It was all very well and good having enhanced senses, but a person could get looked at funny if he was caught sniffing a dead body – a smell most people tried to ignore or get away from.

The first thing that struck Dimitri was that Gav didn't look like any of the other gay men that had been killed. In comparison to the relative cleanness of the previous scenes, this was a gruesome crime scene, the amount of blood on the concrete shocking in itself. But the sight of flesh coming from the victim's mouth, where it had been cruelly shoved, was a message Dimitri couldn't ignore. He didn't need to turn the body onto his back to know that someone had relocated Gav's penis. Either someone thought that the dead man had talked too much, or this was yet another stab at the gay community.

Ignoring the obvious stench, Dimitri walked slowly around the body, with his head down. To any casual observer he was studying the body from all angles, but what he was trying to sniff out was the scent of the killer. Unfortunately Gav was someone who didn't appreciate the virtue of soap and hot water, and Dimitri couldn't get anything definitive. It wasn't until he knelt down by Gav's head that he caught the faintest hint of a smell that shouldn't be there.

"Find anything?" Shane asked as he knelt down beside Dimitri.

"Sniff," Dimitri said so quietly only Shane would hear him.

"Clive Christian," Shane muttered under his breath. "Fuck it all, well that clarifies one point. Gav knew the serial killer."

"But what we still don't know is whether the man who was paying Gav, and the killer, are one and the same person," Dimitri insisted.

"And we're not likely to get a lot of clues out of Gav anytime soon."

Dimitri pointed to Gav's face, with its grotesque gag. "This is new. Escalation or making a point?" he asked softly.

"The whole crime scene's wrong," Shane said huffing in frustration. "Left out in the open, far too much blood at the scene. I imagine the autopsy will show numerous wounds and yet nothing on the face except the gag. You could almost assume it was a completely different killer, except..."

"Except for Christian," Dimitri finished for him, nodding as a non-descript man in a suit came over.

"What have we got?" The man asked as Shane stood up and shook his hand.

"More of the same," Shane said. "Oh Brian, this is Dimitri Polst, my new partner. He took over from Ruby last Friday. Dimitri, this is Brian Anderson from the ME's office."

Dimitri took the limp sweaty hand offered him and nodded, but couldn't be bothered to smile. It wouldn't be appropriate while they were standing over a dead body anyway, at least in Dimitri's opinion. Brian was about five foot eight inches, with a soft body and the beginnings of a paunch around his gut. Dimitri guessed the man to be about thirty five, but it was difficult to tell.

"This doesn't look like one of yours," Brian said to Shane as he did his own quick examination of Gav's body.

Shane shrugged but offered nothing in reply. Dimitri could understand why. All Shane and Dimitri had to go on at this stage was some gossip from a masochist at a gay club, and a hint of a scent that no-one else was likely to pick up, unless they were shifters. And Brian was human. A competent ME, if the examination Brian was making of the body was any indication, but he didn't have shifter senses.

Brian stood up and waved to a couple of men who were standing by with a body bag. "I'll take him in but it will be Tuesday or Wednesday before I have anything for you. TOD based on rigor and temperature I would estimate at about 4am, but I will know more when I get him on the table."

Shane clapped him on the shoulder. "Thanks Brian. Let me know when you can. Come on Dimitri – I need some breakfast."

On the drive back into the city center, Shane filled Dimitri in on the information he had got from Mace.

The body had been found by a street cleaner, just after 7am but the man hadn't seen anyone else in the area. Uniforms were looking into the possibility of surveillance cameras in the area, but given that it was Sunday, finding anything concrete before Monday was unlikely. There were some cameras in the area, but how effective they were, or whether or not they caught anything useful was anyone's guess.

It wasn't until they had ordered breakfast at a cheap little café that sat off the main road, that Dimitri said, "Do you think we need to talk to Tucker again? He's the only link to Gav we have at the moment."

Shane grinned at him over his plate and said, "I'm not sure Tucker will talk to us anymore. He's likely to run the other way if he sees us coming."

"You mentioned last night that he doesn't get out of bed until after lunch, so we could probably catch him at home. I presume you know where he lives..." Dimitri trailed off. He didn't want to think about the possibility that Shane had fucked Tucker. The man was too much of a weasel and although Dimitri knew he would probably come across a number of Shane's previous connections as the two men worked together, he hated the thought that Tucker might have been one of them. There was something slimy and not that trustworthy about Tucker, and Dimitri would have hated him, even if the cocky little shit hadn't been looking to him for a blow job.

"I haven't been with him," Shane explained quietly. "I actually do have standards. But I'm at the clubs a lot, and you get to know familiar faces after a while. I dropped Tucker off home one night after he was too wasted to get a taxi and he told me he doesn't get up before lunch over the weekend, when I offered to take him back to get his car the following day."

Dimitri dropped his head and picked up his coffee. In that moment it seemed so much easier to focus on his cup rather than his mate. "This isn't going to be easy," he said quietly.

Shane frowned. "What the murders, or us?"

Something in Shane's tone made Dimitri look up, and he was surprised to see the hurt in Shane's eyes. "Both. Neither. I don't know. I just know it's a wolf thing – to be all territorial and not want anyone to touch their mate. I hate the thought that you've been with men like that Gremlin character last night."

"And I hate the thought that you had a solid relationship with someone – a female, who I could never compete with because I don't have the bits," Shane snapped back.

Dimitri watched as Shane took a deep breath to calm himself before the man said, "You knew who I was. All these years you knew about me. You knew I was your mate and yet you still tried to make a go of it with a woman. Now I don't know what changed your mind. I don't know why things went wrong with Angela. But things for me were very different. I knew I was gay from the moment I shifted, but I didn't think I had a mate. I've never met another gay wolf shifter. But I did know I couldn't ever, tie myself down to a human male, no matter how attractive they might be. But wolf shifters like their sex, so I had sex. But that's all I had Dimitri and I'm not going to let you make me feel guilty for that."

Now Dimitri felt like shit because Shane was right. He was the one who had run from their mating, well before Shane even had a chance to know about it. And he had genuinely thought he could have a permanent relationship with Angela – he even thought he loved her for a while – despite knowing that Shane was his real mate. Not for the first time he cursed their home pack, knowing that it was the narrow-minded attitudes that he was raised with that had caused both men, and to a lesser degree Angela, a whole lot of grief that could have been avoided.

Looking up at Shane Dimitri said, "I'm sorry and you're right. You have nothing to feel guilty about. But I'm not going to be sorry for being possessive. There are some things that are just in our nature and that is going to make some aspects of our job difficult for me."

Shane smiled, and Dimitri hoped that meant he was forgiven for being an idiot. "You have to remember that I'm possessive too, so we will both have to work on our people skills. You know it comes down to trust, right? Trusting each other not to do anything that will emotionally hurt the other."

"I'm not quite sure what you mean. I know we can't get a hard-on for anybody else again, but what if you fancy giving someone a blowjob? Is that covered by the mating bond or do I have to trust that you just wouldn't do that."

"I'm pretty sure that's covered," Shane said, laughing now. "Just the thought of you touching Tucker last night was enough to make me feel sick, and there was no way I could ever look at someone and think, oh man I have to suck that dick. I never did before so I'm not likely to change now."

"Yes, well the thought of sucking Tucker made me fucking angry," Dimitri said. "The thought of going near any male in a sexual way makes me feel...oh hell, I don't know. It would just be wrong and I don't know if that's because I am mated to you, or if it's because of the way I was bought up, so don't ask. I just know I would never do it."

"What about women?"

Looking down into his coffee cup, which was of course empty, Dimitri thought longingly of a double scotch. Or Bourbon. Or anything that would help him get through this conversation. Then he looked around the small café. There weren't many people sitting around, but there was enough to make Dimitri feel uncomfortable.

"Can we go somewhere else and finish this conversation?" He asked. When he saw the frown on Shane's face, he added quickly, "I need to share some things about me and Angela, and I need to try and explain what has happened to me, and I would just feel better about that if we could do it in a more private setting."

Still frowning, Shane nodded and drank down the last of his coffee. "We'll head home," he said shortly and Dimitri wondered if Shane had realized that he had used the word home in the same sentence as 'we'. That had to be a positive if Shane already thought of them as living together.

## Chapter Sixteen

As he drove Dimitri back to his place, Shane was seething inside. He was so sure that Dimitri was going to explain to him about how he still loved women, how he would miss being with a woman, but how he knew that he couldn't anymore because they were mated. Then the angel on his shoulder would remind him that Dimitri had already said that he wasn't interested in women anymore. Yes, said the devil on Shane's other shoulder, but the man's not gay either and he said that after Shane had shafted his ass for the first time. Not the best time to be making sweeping statements. The warring factions, that Shane could clearly imagine sitting on either side of his head, were giving him a headache. He was looking forward to his run later that night. Whether he intended to invite Dimitri or not would depend on what the man had to say.

Stalking into his house, knowing that Dimitri was hot on his tail, Shane headed straight for the kitchen and put on the coffee machine. He would have dearly loved a beer, even though it hadn't hit lunchtime yet, but he didn't like to drink on Sundays because that was when his wolf was allowed to come out and play. So the coffee would have to do.

Once made, Shane took Dimitri's coffee into the living room where the man had made himself at home on the couch. Despite his anger, Shane was stunned to notice how right it felt, having Dimitri in his personal space. He had lived alone since he had left home, seven years before, and he had never noticed how having another person around could make him feel so...complete.

Forcing those thoughts aside, Shane handed Dimitri his coffee and went and sat on a single arm chair to the side of the couch. Yes, he was putting up walls, and maybe that was a childish thing to do given that he and Dimitri could never be apart from each other now. But being mated didn't mean he couldn't get angry with, or hurt by his mate, and he wanted to minimize that as much as possible. He sat in silence, waiting for Dimitri to speak.

"I know I told you that I had been with Angela for three years. When we first got together, things were really good. I'd enjoyed a lot of sex with a lot of women before her, but there was something about Angela that clicked with me. She was funny. She liked the same things I did and she accepted my wolf. At first, I honestly did think I could marry her, have kids and stay in Jacobs Lake, even though I knew about you."

Dimitri looked over at Shane and it took all of Shane's will power not to go over to the couch and hug the man. Dimitri looked so conflicted. But right in that moment, Shane knew he had to protect his own heart, which was seriously hurting with the things Dimitri was saying. So he settled for a nod and a wave of his hand, indicating he wanted Dimitri to continue.

"Yeah, right, so in the first year, things were good between us. But as we got halfway into the second year together I noticed that my wolf was getting antsy when Angela was around. She didn't notice, but it was getting harder for me to ignore. That impacted our sex life because my wolf didn't want me near her, let alone be intimate with her, so I found myself making excuses to her. I had exams to sit so that I could be a detective, and I was still playing sport, so I had the perfect excuse if I came home tired at night. Angela seemed to accept it, and so I pushed on."

"You were living together?"

"No," Dimitri said, looking down at his hands. "But she wanted to move in with me and I had given her a key to my place. She used to stay over a fair bit. Cook me dinner. That sort of thing. On our second anniversary..."

Dimitri trailed off because Shane had physically winced at the word anniversary, he couldn't help it. Somehow that one simple word clarified all that Dimitri had shared with another person, which Shane had missed out on. He couldn't hide the hurt no matter how much he tried. His eyes were filled with tears he refused to shed, and he had to close his eyes to stop them from falling. He had to get over it and let Dimitri finish what he had to say, or he was going to be plagued with doubts about them forever – but it was so fucking hard to hear. He had to know where he stood with his mate.

When Shane opened his eyes, he could see that Dimitri was watching him intently, and Shane forced himself to stay calm and say nothing. "Go on," he said, when Dimitri didn't seem inclined to say anything further.

"I'm sorry I'm hurting you," Dimitri said. "But you need to know this. So yeah, second anniversary, Angela started talking about us getting engaged. I went along with it for a while because it made her happy, and my mom happy..."

"You told your mom?" Shane yelled, and then slapped his head because that was such a stupid thing to say. Of course the man had told his mother. She was probably over the moon expecting a quick wedding and pups in the near future.

"Yes, Mom and Angela had a good relationship," Dimitri said. "Mom was gutted when I broke things off with Angela, but I'm getting ahead of myself." He took a deep breath and carried on.

"The sex had gotten really infrequent and a lot of times I had to be rip roaring drunk for it to happen at all. By this stage I wasn't initiating any of it, and would only give in when I was too wasted to come up with an excuse. My wolf hated it, constantly reminding me that the smell wasn't right, and that she wasn't right for me. That she wasn't my mate. In the meantime I was dreaming about you all of the time. Remembering your smell, the way you felt for that brief moment in my arms..."

"You were going to beat me up," Shane interjected. He didn't see how Dimitri could feel there was anything romantic or even sexual about how they left things between them in the alley behind the school.

"Yes, I was," Dimitri said. "But a lot of the reason that I picked on you so much was because you irritated me for some reason, and I couldn't stop thinking about you, even before my first shift. It was easier to beat you up than it was to work out why you were in my head so much. When I smelled you that day, and felt your body against mine, I was hit with a tidal wave of emotions – want, protectiveness, need – fuck I just wanted to devour you whole, rub all over you, bite you and keep you forever."

"And yet you threw me on the ground and walked away."

"I walked away," Dimitri agreed. "Angela, by this stage was noticing that things weren't right with me. She...she suggested that maybe we needed to spice up our sex life and even talked a girlfriend of hers into coming over one night. That was a huge disaster. I felt like I was being cornered, my wolf wanted you and I freaked out big time. Went out, got shitfaced drunk and staggered home and proceeded to tell Angela the whole story."

Looking over at Shane, Dimitri said, "She didn't have a problem with you being a man. I told her all about true mates and she tore strips off me for what I had done to you, and to her. And she was right. But in the meantime I had made detective, my mom was pressuring me about when Angela and I were getting married, even the Alpha said it was about time I had a few pups. And I was falling apart."

Dimitri sat quietly for a moment, probably thinking back to that time. While Shane could see it probably was a difficult time for his mate, the man had brought it on himself. He refused to feel sorry for Dimitri, no matter how broken the man looked, and how urgently his own wolf wanted him to comfort their mate.

"Angela, by this stage, was pushing me to find you. We had already agreed that we were better off apart, because she did deserve to get married and have kids. We stayed good friends, much to everyone's surprise, and the rumors that we broke up because I was a sex hound didn't surprise anyone, so we left it at that. I wanted you, but I didn't, if you can understand. So I tried meeting other women – maybe another human woman my wolf would accept for a while, but I couldn't do it and it got to the stage that the only time I had stiff cock was when I was thinking about you."

Getting up from his chair, Dimitri crossed over to where Shane was sitting, and sank down to his knees on the floor. Shane clenched his fists so he wouldn't reach out and touch him. The temptation was too great, but he could see Dimitri hadn't finished what he had to say and he had to hear it all. He didn't think he could handle it, if Dimitri stopped now.

"The reason I told you all this," Dimitri said, gazing at Shane with those wicked brown eyes of his. "Was because I need you to know that I won't want anybody in my whole life again, except you. I have looked at women – gorgeously sexy women, who three years ago would have made my dick hard in an instant. Even before I met up with you here, I couldn't feel anything for them. I didn't get hard – it was like, you know how you can look at a car, or a person for that matter and you might think, 'shit, that's nice,' but it's just an appreciation of beauty. You don't want to drive or own the car, you don't want to go to bed with the person."

"I think a Ferrari F12 Berlinetta looks really sexy, and I would want to own and drive one. And I would totally want to have sex with Adam Levine, if he was that way inclined," Shane said, but he made sure that Dimitri could see the small smile on his lips, because yes, he was only teasing his man. His man. His mate.

No matter how hard it was to hear the story behind it, Shane did understand what Dimitri was saying.

Dimitri might look at women, but he would never have one in his bed again. He might struggle with being labelled gay, but Shane was starting to realize that might not be a bad thing, in terms of their working together. The two men were going to be around sexy men most nights of the week, especially while working their current cases. Was the fact that Dimitri only wanted him such a bad thing? Definitely not, considering he felt the same way about his mate.

But he didn't say that, because it wasn't the right time. What he said instead was, "So you fancy going on a run tonight? I've never seen your wolf form, and I can show you where I go every Sunday night."

☐

## Chapter Seventeen

Dimitri knew that his story about Angela, and how he came to the realization that he would never want another woman again, was hard for Shane to hear. He was learning that his mate had little 'tells' when he was trying to hide his emotions. A tightening of the jaw, closed eyes, and perhaps something even Shane wasn't aware of – rubbing his hand over his chest as though his heart was aching. Given that wolf shifters did not have heart attacks, Dimitri knew it was because he had emotionally hurt Shane with the things he had said.

It wasn't until he saw how Shane tried to hide his tears, when Dimitri mentioned his and Angela's anniversary, that Dimitri started to realize how much Shane had missed out on by just having casual sex all those years. That situation would be hard enough for a human, but Shane was a wolf shifter and wolves thrived on being around others. Shane had no family, no pack, no relationships, no one except the people he worked with. So what the hell did Shane do on Christmas, birthdays and vacations?

Dimitri wanted to know all those things, but first he had some more pressing matters to take care of. Because they had been woken with a phone call, Dimitri hadn't had the chance to even kiss his mate all day, and he ached to feel Shane's touch. Leaning in to kiss his mate for the first time since they woke up, Dimitri's senses came alive as first lips, then tongue, and finally roving hands started to torment his senses. He pushed forward with his body, still on his knees on the floor, and pulled Shane down a bit, so that his ass was on the edge of the chair. Then holding the man in place with his hips, Dimitri surged over Shane, fisting that length of longer hair on his head, and ploughing the man's mouth with his tongue.

Shane met him with equal passion. Dimitri had a feeling he would be bottoming at some stage in the afternoon. But for now his feelings of wanting to hold, fuck and claim his man were riding him hard, and after a few minutes of intense struggle, Dimitri felt Shane submit. And with that submission Dimitri's wolf surged. Sitting up, he attacked Shane's pants as though affronted by their mere existence. Tugging them down his mate's legs, Dimitri was momentarily flummoxed by the boots that Shane was wearing, but he soon took care of them as well. Naked from the waist down, Dimitri thought he had never seen anyone so beautiful. Shane's hair was mussed, his lips were wet and swollen and his eyes – fuck, Dimitri could get lost forever in the heat in his mate's eyes.

Focusing on Shane's hardened length, Dimitri didn't hesitate as he sucked the man into his mouth, his groan of appreciation of Shane's unique taste reverberating around the cock in his mouth, causing Shane to groan as well. Pleased he had learned something new in how to give pleasure to the man underneath him, Dimitri sucked hard, while his fingers eagerly sought his main objective. Guessing his intentions, Shane lifted his legs over the arms of his chair, effectively holding himself open for all that Dimitri wanted to do.

Groaning again, his mouth still full, Dimitri ran his fingers in a direct line from the base of Shane's cock, down between his balls and then across the perineum until he found the hole he wanted to sink into. Running his fingers lightly over the tight space, Dimitri quickly came to the realization that they needed lube, and lots of it.

"Lube," he growled, pulling his mouth away from that delicious cock. Shane closed his eyes for a moment as though he was trying to think and then he waved vaguely at the couch. "Try under the couch cushions," he said, as though it was perfectly normal to have lube stashed all over the house. Dimitri wasn't going to complain though, especially if it saved him from having to make a sprint to the bedroom.

Finding the squished tube exactly where Shane had indicated it would be, Dimitri decided to keep any teasing about his mate jacking off for another time. It wasn't as though the last week had been much better for him. Returning to his goal, Dimitri quickly lubed up his fingers and then Shane's ass, eager to feel the promised heat encompass his cock. Hoping like fuck the man was ready after a couple of scissors from his fingers, his ears lapping up the sound of Shane's pleas for now, Dimitri lined himself up and plunged in.

No matter how often he did this, and damn he hoped it was often, Dimitri was struck again at the rightness of being buried deep in his lover. The tight heat encasing his cock, the moans of the man beneath him, all felt more of everything than anything he had experienced before. He'd had anal sex with Angela, in the hopes that it might help his flagging sex life with her, but it didn't come close the sensation he was feeling now. With a tiny mental note that he really should call his friend and soon, Dimitri lost himself to the sensations of being one with his mate.

It was truly glorious and because it felt so awesome it was destined to be over far too soon. Shane was grunting with every one of Dimitri's thrusts, his body sprawled across the chair, his hands holding his legs in an effort to keep them open in such an awkward position. But Dimitri was beyond caring about his mate's comfort. With one hand on Shane's cock and the other gripping the man's shoulder to hold him in place, Dimitri pounded hard, his wolf rising in him – wanting to bite and possess. As Dimitri felt his balls tighten and his orgasm start to tingle in his spine, he sped up, dropping over Shane's chest and snarling "mine," before he dropped his teeth into Shane's mating mark on his neck.

"YES!" Shane yelled and then Dimitri felt Shane's cock throb in his hand, as Shane spilled all over their abs. As Shane's ass tightened even more around his cock, Dimitri was lost then. With one last thrust he felt his seed spill into his mate's willing body, draining his fear and worry in a series of pulsating throbs that tingled his balls, he had come so hard.

Holding himself up on his elbows on the sides of the chair, so that he didn't crush his mate, Dimitri gently licked the blood from Shane's neck, his pride at the sign of possession pleasing both man and wolf. Shane was marked clearly, and no other shifter would dare to touch what was his. Now if only he could find a way to brand his man so those damn humans that lusted after his mate would get the same idea.

Shane's arms moving around his neck forced Dimitri's thoughts of total domination from his head. Shane's eyes were clearer now but the smile on the man's face suggested to Dimitri that lust would hit them both hard again, very soon.

"You've had your go lover," Shane said softly. "Now get your ass into the bedroom because now it's my turn."

If Dimitri's ass fluttered a bit at Shane's dominant tone then no one but him was going to know about it. But Dimitri couldn't help but move quickly as he did what his mate had suggested. He clearly had more lessons to learn and he was a more than a willing student for anything Shane had to teach him.

☐

## Chapter Eighteen

Monday morning saw both Shane and Dimitri sitting in the bull pen waiting for the inevitable Monday briefing. Both men were quiet and holding jumbo coffee cups from the local takeout place. After a marathon sex session that spanned the rest of the afternoon, Shane took Dimitri out for a proper sit down dinner before driving them to Mt Diablo State park. Apparently Shane had an agreement with the rangers, or maybe because he was a detective, but he had a key to the gates that gave the two men access to the roads the rangers used. The run, the first one Dimitri's wolf had enjoyed since he had left Jacobs Lake had left both men tired but happy. A couple of mutual blow jobs when they got home and all in all it had been a good weekend, barring the two murders.

Dimitri was still trying to work out a way of staking a claim to Shane that would mean something to the humans they worked and interacted with. The most obvious idea was to marry him, and Dimitri did plan to ask once they had been together a while. Although it had always been in his plans to marry his mate, the thought of having to phone his mother and tell her he was marrying a man, was enough to make him think that putting off the inevitable for a while was a good idea. His mother had phoned while he and Shane had been at dinner the previous evening, and he had purposefully ignored the call as well as Shane's knowing look when he told him who it was on the phone. But fortunately Shane didn't say anything.

Maybe he could get the man a promise ring or something similar? But would Shane wear it without an actual proposal? Lost in his thoughts about what his mate would do, Dimitri almost missed the Lieutenant's entrance until Shane jabbed his elbow. It was clear from the scowling look directed his way that the Lieutenant hadn't forgotten about what Dimitri had told him on Saturday. If looks could kill both he and Shane would be dead. Willing his wolf to settle down, Dimitri sat silent and impassive while the Lieutenant droned on about the problems with the image the police had, budget concerns, and the problems within the gay community, including the recent murders.

"As you all know," the Lieutenant said loudly, "West is our key liaison with the gay community and now that he had been joined by his partner, Polst, perhaps the two men can get their heads out of each other's asses long enough to solve these cases. Unsolved murders make our department look bad, so if anyone here can help these two lovebirds out, then perhaps we can all get on with some real police work."

Dimitri sat stunned. He had just been exposed as a gay man to the whole department. By a fucking homophobe who hated him. And he wasn't gay. He felt Shane put his hand on his leg and he was terrified that everyone would see, and all he wanted to do was run. But the pressure on his leg increased, and Shane whispered

"Hold it together just a little while more, then you can run."

Not knowing how the hell Shane even knew what was in his mind, Dimitri sat and seethed until the Lieutenant finally finished up. As soon as the man left the room, Shane lifted his hand and said, "Now you can go. But hurry back." Dimitri didn't think. He just got up and left the room and his mate, and then finally the building. But even as he drove towards the park they had been to the night before, Dimitri didn't think he could ever run far enough to escape the taint of being gay. And now he was actually faced with it, he didn't know how the fuck to deal with it.

/~/~/~/~/

Shane was furious at Lieutenant Green for outing Dimitri the way he did, but he was equally hurt by the fact that Dimitri's only thought had been to protect himself and run, leaving him to deal with the fallout with their work colleagues. Checking his watch and seeing he still had twenty minutes before he was expected in the Captains' office, Shane sat at his desk, going over the reports from CJ's and Gav's murder scenes over the weekend. If he looked busy maybe his workmates would leave him alone.

"So you and Dimitri, hunh?" Shane looked up to see Trent and Mace standing over his desk. Shane just shrugged, not sure what to say. He had tried to explain to Dimitri that once their relationship was common knowledge, and that was inevitable in a gossip hub like the police department, then most people would accept it, while a select few would make a few digs. Shane had already gone through the worst of what the department had to offer – the insults, attacks on his locker, men failing to support him when he was chasing suspects. He had just put his head down and kept on doing his job and over time, things had eased off. It seemed that Green's comments at the meeting this morning had just bought Shane's sexual orientation back into the headlines again.

"He's a good looking man," Trent said. "Not sure I can blame you. But damn, that was fast work, even for you."

Looking up in shock at Trent's comments, Shane kept a wary look on his face. "Dimitri and I have history," he said cautiously. "We went to school together."

"So he came here to be with you?" Mace said. "That's almost...fuck, that's almost romantic or something."

Or something, Shane thought to himself. "Yes, well Green's scared him off, so don't get used to seeing the man around. I figure he'll have his resignation into the Captain before the day is over."

"Why would he do that?" Trent seemed genuinely puzzled and Shane sat back in his chair looking at his two straight colleagues. "Dimitri's not gay," he said bluntly. "He and I are in a relationship, but my partner doesn't consider himself a gay man."

"Like you do," Trent clarified.

"Like I am, yes. Being labelled as a gay man, in front of a department full of people who don't know him, and who he has to work with on a daily basis has probably sent him running for the hills."

If Shane felt an overwhelming sadness at the thought, he wasn't going to share his emotions with his work colleagues. He was gay, not weak. But he knew that if Dimitri did do a runner then he and his wolf were going to suffer – badly. Mate's usually died if they couldn't be with the one that claimed them. Fuck, and they had claimed each other. Why did the thought that Dimitri would rather be dead than be with him hurt so fucking much?

"So why did Green do it?" Mace said. "That's just fucking mean. Almost an invasion of privacy, or something."

Glancing at his watch again, Shane quickly explained what had happened on Saturday – his arrest and how Dimitri had been his unwitting alibi. Both men laughed when he told them how Green had gone running out of the interview room, but they agreed that the damage had been done.

Standing up, Shane said, "I hate to break this up but me and Dimitri had an appointment with the Captain about these murders. I guess I'd better front up."

Trent and Mace stood aside to let him go, but just as he went to leave the room, Mace yelled out, "You know that most of us don't give a shit about you and Polst, right? Hell, anyone who does is probably just jealous."

Smirking to himself, Shane gave a wave and headed to the Captain's office. Support from two of the men he worked most closely with was certainly helpful, although the support wasn't going to help if Dimitri didn't come back.

Knocking at the Captain's door, Shane went in when requested, closing the door behind him.

"Where's your partner?" Of course that would be the first question his Captain would ask. He looked at Captain Reynolds. The man was in his fifties, distinguished short grey hair cut short and kept off a rugged face. Shane had heard stories about the Captain's days on the beat. He was apparently a hand's on type of officer who had instilled fear in many members of the criminal underworld. Now Shane was faced with an uncompromising stare and he knew just how those criminals felt.

"Permission to speak freely, Sir." The Captain nodded. "Green made a point of embarrassing both of us at the meeting this morning, basically telling everyone that Dimitri was gay and that he and I were in a relationship. Dimitri didn't handle it very well and has left the building."

The Captain looked thoughtful. "Did either of you say anything when the Lieutenant had his say."

"No Sir. That would have been disrespectful and inappropriate."

"Hmm, a bit like Green was with you," the Captain observed, as though he expected Shane to say something. But Shane hadn't got to where he was in the department by complaining about his colleagues, or his superiors and he kept quiet.

"Am I likely to lose Polst over this?"

"It's possible, Sir. Dimitri doesn't consider himself a gay man. He has only had relationships with women before me, and this is a departure from his normal way of looking at things. That, combined with the fact that he hasn't been with our colleagues very long, and probably would have preferred to let the knowledge about our relationship go around the department naturally, could cause him to go back to Jacobs Lake, yes."

"Take a seat, Shane, we need to talk." The Captain looked really serious and had used his first name, and Shane wondered what the Lieutenant had been saying about him now. He sat down and tried not to look like his life was over. Because of course if Dimitri left him, it probably was.

"I can't think of an easy way to say this, so I'll come right out and ask. Is Dimitri your mate?"

"Sir?"

"It's not a hard question, Shane. I know you're a shifter and I am guessing the only reason why Dimitri would move from a really good position in Jacobs Lake, to take a low paying position here, is to be with you. Given that he asked about you two being in a relationship after you telling me that the man doesn't think he is gay, I guess the question is a formality. Is Dimitri your mate?"

Not knowing what to think, Shane had no choice but to tell the truth. "Yes, Sir."

"So if he leaves and goes back to Jacobs Lake, then you'll go with him?"

Shane shook his head. "Definitely not, Sir, and Dimitri wouldn't want me to. We couldn't be together there and I am no longer welcome at home. If he leaves, and that is a strong possibility, then I will stay here."

"The stupid actions by Green this morning could possibly be a death sentence to both of you then, if what little I know about mates and mating is right. It's a shame I can't get the man for inciting a hate crime."

Thinking about it, Shane rather thought it was a good idea. Green was trying to instill hatred within the department for gays, from his comments that morning, and according to the new politically correct policies all police departments had to adhere to, that was a crime. But as much as he would like to see the Lieutenant removed from his position, the resulting publicity would make the situation worse, not better.

"I appreciate the sentiment, Sir, but the damage has already been done. I do believe that if confronted about this, Green would find a way to make the situation worse and ultimately I still have to work here."

The Captain fixed him with that uncompromising stare as he thought the situation over. Then to Shane's surprise, the Captain laughed. "You are a better man than I am, Shane. If it had been me, in your position, I would want to see Green fired. But I respect your judgment and will let it go for now, but I want you to promise that you will come and see me if Green gives you any more trouble, or anyone else in the department for that matter."

"If I can ask, Sir, I still don't understand how come you knew I was a shifter. I've been very careful about concealing that part of my life since I have been working here and I didn't think anybody knew. Shoots, most humans don't know shifters even exist."

"The Captain over at Jacobs Lake is a good friend of mine. I know that all of the officers there are shifters, and when you came here I noticed from your application that you were from the same place. I had my suspicions then, but when Dimitri spoke to me about you two being in a serious relationship when you had technically only known each other for a week, I put two and two together."

"I hope this isn't going to cause any problems, Sir. I won't let it interfere with my work."

"You don't have anything to worry about from me," the Captain assured him. "But I am worried about Polst. I suggest you take the rest of the day off and find him. Try and convince him to stay. I don't want to lose either one of you."

"But what about the murders, Sir. I thought we were going to talk about classifying them as the work of a serial killer?"

"We can do that tomorrow," the Captain said firmly. "I told Dimitri that I accepted you two in a relationship provided it didn't cause any problems. If Dimitri leaves then you are going to have a lot more to worry about than the latest murders. Now go and find him and bring him back."

Nodding his head, Shane left the office and headed out to find a department vehicle. As he suspected, Dimitri had taken his car. But as he drove around, checking first his home, then the motel Dimitri was staying in, and finally even the park where he and Dimitri had gone for a run the night before, by nightfall, Shane had to admit defeat. His mate had done a runner and probably wasn't coming back. Dimitri had just signed a death sentence for both of them unless the stubborn man could get his head together. Not for the first time, Shane wished they could share the mind link that many mated pairs from other packs had. Unfortunately that trait had been bred out of the Jacobs Lake pack quite a few generations before. But Shane could certainly use it now.

☐

## Chapter Nineteen

By the time he had come to his senses, Dimitri had been driving for hours and the sky had been dark for some time. Looking around, he realized he was in St. George, about 50 miles from his home pack. Screeching the car to a stop, Dimitri pulled over to the side of the road and sat there shaking. His first coherent thought in hours was Shane. How the hell could he leave his mate like that? Why the hell had he automatically headed for his home pack? Anyone who knew him would know he had been claimed as soon as they saw him - he had the mating scar and his scent had changed the moment Shane had bitten him. Leaving a mate was inexcusable in any pack and his mother would kill him for that, if his Dad didn't do it first for claiming a man as a mate. God, how could he have fucked up so badly?

Pulling out his phone, Dimitri looked at it, wondering who to call. The only person he wanted to talk to was

Shane, but he guessed the man had every reason to be pretty pissed off at him right now. Looking at the time, he saw it was almost eleven at night. His mate would be at a club right now. Doing his job, and looking so fucking fine that every male with a pulse would have their hands all over him. Out on the town with no mate to shield him from unwanted advances, out doing his job with no backup to protect him – and all of it was Dimitri's fault.

With a groan Dimitri pressed the one contact he knew would give him some sound advice. After six long rings, Angela answered the phone and she didn't sound very happy either. "Damn it, Dimitri, do you know what freaking time it is?"

"Yeah, sorry Ang, I just needed someone to talk to. Can you spare a minute?"

Angela's tone softened in an instant. "Well, considering I'm in bed on my own, I guess I can spare you a bit of time. What have you done now my friend?"

"Fucked up more than you can believe," Dimitri said honestly. He quickly updated Angela with the fact that he and Shane were now true mates and the great weekend they had shared. He explained what had happened in the meeting, God was that only this morning, and how he had just hit the road running.

"And the killer of it all is that I'm driving Shane's car. I'm surprised the man hasn't reported it stolen," Dimitri said with a broken laugh.

Angela let him have his laugh and then, when he had got himself sorted out, she said, "Why do you keep persisting that you're not gay. You are hurting the man you are supposed to cherish above all others. You ran out on him today and left him there to fend for himself, and yet you have the cheek to be worried about what he's doing while you are having a mental crisis. For fucks sake, Dimitri. You said you had sorted this stuff in your head. You had months, no, make that years to understand what would happen if you did this claiming thingy with Shane. Then, when you should have been standing by your mate's side and coping with whatever fallout might have happened at work, you take off. Now you are on the side of the road, having a pity party and getting all bent out of shape because some homophobe said you were gay. So fucking what? Why does his opinion matter if you get to be with your mate?"

"Being gay goes against everything I've ever been taught, Ang. You know that."

"I know that the one person you should be thinking about right now is Shane. Not yourself. Not your prissy reputation. Your mate. I might not be a shifter, but you were the one who told me how amazing being with a mate can be. Are you denying that the sex is excellent, or that you feel like a whole person for the first time in your life? That Shane is someone you want to spend the rest of your life with?"

"No, of course not," Dimitri whispered.

"Then you are beyond idiotic and Shane deserves a damn sight better than you as a mate. One tiny little homophobic slur and you run for home. What are you going to do when the next person calls you a faggot, or heaven forbid, attacks you or Shane because you're holding hands. Run and leave him to fend for himself, just so you won't be considered gay? You've got a murderer in Stockton, for fucks sake, who is targeting gay men. You've got someone out to discredit your man in his job, and trying to pin the murders on him. What if he's the next one on the killer's hit list?"

"I've got to get back," Dimitri said, panic hitting his system hard. Angela was right – in his pity party and confusion he had totally forgotten about the murderer and the fact that someone was trying to at least discredit Shane. If the two things were related somehow then his mate could be in real trouble.

"You've got to find a motel and get some sleep," Angela said in that firm voice of hers that let Dimitri know she wouldn't accept any argument. "You're tired, you have been driving all day and have an equally long trip back. Get some rest and head back in the morning, or you'll wrap your mate's car around a telephone pole with you in it. And I might not know the man, but I can guess he wouldn't be happy about that."

"How am I going to make things up to him?"

"I don't have a clue," his infuriating friend said happily. "But I think you are well beyond the flowers and chocolate stage."

"That's not helpful," Dimitri muttered as he clicked off. But his friend was right. He did need some sleep. That is if his wolf would let him. The unsettling idea that Shane could be in danger, wouldn't let him go and he knew he had to get back as quick as he could. His place was with his mate, and to hell with homophobes like Lieutenant fucking Green.

But Dimitri hadn't been an officer for as long as he had, to ignore Angela's advice. Tired drivers caused accidents and with a sigh, Dimitri pulled up Google and tried to find the closest place to get a bed for the night. First thing in the morning he was heading back to Stockton, and he would do everything in his power to make Shane forgive him so he could stay close and keep the man safe. And if anyone else had a problem with that, then Dimitri would deal with that as well.

/~/~/~/~/

The following morning saw Shane back at his desk, going through the same routine that had kept him sane for years. Work, eat, sleep, with the occasional fuck thrown in for light relief – that had been his life since he left Jacobs Lake. It was how he had managed to curb his wolf's urge for pack and family. Some days it was all he could do not to scream from the loneliness he felt. He thought things would change when Dimitri had bitten him, but no. That was a fool's thought and Shane resolutely put the man out of his head. He had never been a fool over any man and he wasn't going to start with his mate. Sure his wolf was going to get harder to control, and yes he was probably going to pine away and die, but if he was strong, he could get these murders solved first. If he knew Dimitri, then the man was probably back in the bosom of his home pack, lying his head off about the whereabouts of his claimed mate. If he could come up with a plausible enough tale, then Dimitri's family and pack might be able to stop his pining away, but Shane didn't have the luxury of a pack or family. What he did have was a job to do and a killer to find.

The phone on his desk rang, and when he answered it he found it was Brian, the ME, requesting his presence in the lab. Praying that maybe the man might have finally found something useful, Shane swallowed his reluctance to go to the ME's office. The smell of chemicals and bleach always upset his wolf's nose and usually made him feel queasy.

Pushing through the office doors, mentally blocking his nose, Shane smiled at the mousy ME. "What have you got for me, Brian?"

Brian looked over his shoulder, as though expecting to see someone else, and Shane realized that the man was looking for Dimitri. "My partner's running some other leads," he said. "He can't make it." Now if only his wolf would stop whining in his head, then maybe even Shane could believe his own lie.

Apparently satisfied, Brian went over to a covered trolley, clearly carrying remains of someone. "I did the autopsy on the victim you knew, CJ, and there wasn't anything there to report, beyond what we already knew about the other victims. CJ was killed by strangulation, his face cut with what looked like the same knife or scalpel that was used on the previous victims, and although there was evidence he had been anally penetrated hours before his death, the presence of spermicide from a lubed condom, and additional lubricant, plus a lack of tearing or damage suggested he wasn't raped."

Shane breathed a sigh of relief. CJ had gotten lucky before he had met his killer, but he hadn't been raped before he was killed. Shane wasn't sure he would have been able to handle it, if he had known that CJ had been raped before he was murdered. The death was hard enough to deal with. The cuts on the face on all of the previous three victims had been done post-mortem. Shane presumed that the same could be said for CJ, because otherwise Brian would have said something.

"I did find some interesting stuff on this second victim though, Gav, I think you called him, also known as Gavin Wolshowski." Brian pulled back the cover on the tray to reveal a cleaner, but still very dead, Gav. Brian rolled the cover down so that the man's torso was uncovered and Shane moved forward. Gav's torso was covered in what looked like a hundred gash marks. Fuck, they looked like claws, or teeth – but too meticulous to be the work of a wild animal. Was it possible a shifter had killed Gav?

"Whoever did this was really angry at the victim," Brian said in the same dispassionate tone he always seemed to use when giving a report. "There are 103 different wounds and I'm having a hell of a job working out what caused them. If I didn't know better I would say he had been mauled by an animal, but in the case of an animal attack there would have been more carnage, not less."

"Cause of death was from this mark here," Brian pointed to a particularly deep wound just over the heart. "However, without medical help the victim would have bled out within minutes anyway, or drowned thanks to a punctured lung. His penis was removed after death. What I did find, was a number of different fibers caught in the victim's beard. I don't know how many, if any were from the killer, but they have been sent off for processing. I also got a saliva sample." Brian looked up at Shane. "It seemed the killer spat on the victim, after death."

"So are you thinking this is a different killer, to the others, or the same person in a weird frame of mind?"

Brian shook his head. "There's no real way of knowing. If I was looking at this case as an isolated incident I would have guessed there were two individuals involved in killing Gav – or one man and some type of wild animal. There is definitely a human involved because the penis was removed with a knife. The knife that was used to remove the penis could be the same one as was used on the faces of the other victims, but those marks were more to deface the victim, rather than cause any deep damage. The fact that we found fibers on Gav is a first, but then all of the other victims were clean shaven so maybe the killer does clean off the victims, which would explain why we haven't found any physical evidence. Maybe he overlooked Gav's facial hair. The amount of anger and the wounds on the torso, in this last case, and the fact that a knife was used, could suggest that if this was the same killer, then Gav had made him very angry. What is distinctly different in this case is that the killer or killers would have been covered in blood."

"Surely, you would have to be angry to kill anyone anyway. Are you saying that there's no evidence of any type of emotion in the killing of the other victims? That they were like a paid hit or something?" Shane was curious. This might not be hard evidence, but Brian had been known to have some useful insights before.

Brian sighed, and started covering up Gav's body. Idly Shane wondered if the dead man had family. If he didn't, then Shane would pay for his funeral. The man had been through enough indignity to end up with a stark cremation and no service. Especially if a shifter was responsible for his death.

"The first three victims," Brian said carefully, "reminded me of a form of ethnic cleansing. The kills were precise and professional. The killer came up behind the victim, grabbed them by the throat and squeezed the life out of them. Once dead, the killer probably laid the victims down on the ground, slashed their faces as if their looks offended him, and then thrown them in a dumpster. CJ and Gav were different."

"It's not easy to simply strangle someone with your bare hands, especially if you are coming up on that person from behind," Shane said, thinking hard.

"No, you're right," Brian agreed. "It would suggest that the killer is someone who is much taller than the victims, and lot stronger, if the bruise evidence is anything to go by. From the bruises on the first three victims I would say that the killer used gloves as the finger marks are more impressions, rather than distinct finger outlines. In CJ's case, it is possible that the killer was bare handed and I am keeping the body for a while longer to see if any additional bruising comes to hand. We may even get a print, although that is unlikely," he added with a rare smile.

"So," Shane said slowly, "if, hypothetically, we are dealing with the same killer, then he starts off just killing pretty gay men. Then something about CJ sets him off, and he uses more force with him than with the others..."

"CJ also had bruises to his knuckles and feet – the victim tried to fight. But someone had cleaned under his fingernails, so we got no evidence there."

"But CJ defending himself could account for the additional force," Shane said, just thinking out loud now. "By the time the killer gets to Gav, who isn't pretty and who wasn't known to bathe, the killer changes his MO because he doesn't want to physically touch him – going totally psycho on him with something and finishing off with the knife in a different way."

"If you are dealing with the one killer, and if all of the cases are related, then the killer's reason for killing Gav had to have been different than the reason he was killing the others. But it's a big if. I'm more inclined to think that if the same killer is responsible for all of the deaths, then given the state of Gav's torso, he has an accomplice who has some weird toys. I'll be doing impressions on some of the marks to see if I can get an idea on what caused them, but I've never seen anything like it before. I'll let you know what I find."

Sighing, Shane nodded. "Yes, thanks Brian. Look the Captain has officially taken me and Polst..." God, he could barely say his mate's name without wincing inside. "...off of CJ's case because I knew the victim. He's given it to Trent and Mace, but they have been told to keep me in the loop, so you might want to update them. I'm going to see the Captain now, to see if we can get these deaths reclassified as a serial killing. That will hopefully bring a few more resources in, so we can stop this madman."

"Good hunting, detective," Brian said as he turned back to his work. Shane headed to the Captain's office with renewed purpose. Death by manual strangulation was a slow way to die and he had been pleased that CJ had at least tried to fight his attacker. But the bottom line was that CJ was dead, along with three other men whose only worry should be what they could do with their hair when they were going out.

Gav was a wild card with what looked like animal wounds on his body, that may or may not have been caused by a shifter. If it wasn't for the fact that Gav had been Shane's only lead at finding out who was trying to pin the other murders on him, Shane would have treated the case separately. But he had a hunch that there was one man responsible for all of the killings, even if he wasn't the killer per se. Shane just had to prove it, and find out who the hell was responsible. Given the dearth of clues in each case, Shane wasn't too proud to ask for help. He just hoped he could keep his conversation with the Captain on a professional level, because he didn't think that he could cope if he had to tell his boss that Dimitri was MIA, or that it was unlikely the man was coming back.

☐

## Chapter Twenty

By the time Shane crawled home for the night, it was almost two in the morning. Being a Tuesday, Shane knew that the street workers would have more time to talk, and he would get more info from them, than if he went to the clubs. In one respect he had been glad that Dimitri hadn't been with him, because the man's imposing presence would make it harder to get people to talk to him. But damn, the ache he felt at Dimitri's absence was like a physical presence that invaded every cell in his body. Dimitri hadn't been gone for even 48 hours yet, but Shane felt physically ill from missing him. Given that wolf shifters didn't get sick, that was hard enough to accept by itself.

Shane's purpose for going out had been to find out if the street workers had been hassled by particularly large men. Not clients because the killer almost certainly hated gays. Most of the obvious suspects were law enforcement officers, but he had a couple of car tags he needed to check first thing in the morning. The boys who worked the streets were good at keeping an eye on each other, and it was common practice for the ones that Shane knew, to take the car tags of any vehicle that another boy got into.

Foot trade was a little harder to trace and Shane figured some time spent on stakeouts might be the only way to get a definitive handle on who was walking the streets at night. Shane knew that the killer wasn't targeting the rent boys. He was going after club twinks. But unless the killer was a demon, or something similar, then he had to have been seen somewhere – walking to a club, following a potential victim, getting away from the crime scene. Could the marks on Gav's body have been caused by a demon, or should Shane be looking for another shifter in town?

Mulling the problem over in his mind, Shane let himself into his little house and threw his jacket on the nearest arm chair. He was sweaty, tired and...what the fuck. Why was his wolf doing a happy dance now? Then the delicious scent of jasmine and citrus hit his nose and he groaned under his breath. It would seem his mate was back. Flicking on the light, Shane looked over to see Dimitri sprawled on his couch, apparently fast asleep.

He stood for a long minute, looking down at the man who had claimed his heart. Shane wasn't stupid enough to deny that little fact to himself, although he would be damned if he told Dimitri, especially now. His mate looked really tired, the lines of stress evident around his eyes, despite the man being asleep. Sighing, Shane grabbed a throw rug from the back of the couch, and laid it out over his mate's hunky body. Turning to leave the room, he had almost made it when he heard a growled, "Shane?"

"Go to sleep Dimitri," Shane said softly, refusing to turn around. "We can talk tomorrow." Hurrying up the stairs, before his body betrayed him, Shane went through into the bathroom, wanting nothing more than to shower and sleep. His mate was safe, and back, although who knew for how long. But Shane knew that nothing good would come out of their talking when they were both tired and stressed.

Unfortunately, even though the hot shower had relaxed him, it was some time before Shane finally dropped off to sleep.

/~/~/~/~/

Dimitri woke with a groan, and not in a good way. His back had seized up from trying to get comfortable on the couch all night long, and he felt grungy from spending almost two full days in the car. Listening for sounds in Shane's apartment, he heard the sound of running water and guessed that his mate was in the shower. Thumping his cock, which had risen rapidly at the thought of a wet and sudsy mate, Dimitri carefully eased himself into a sitting position. He knew he wouldn't be welcome in the bathroom.

Ten minutes later, Dimitri was still sitting on the couch when Shane came downstairs looking really sharp in a dark grey fitted suit. Seeing Dimitri awake, Shane got a funny look on his face for a moment, but it just as quickly disappeared. Instead, Shane said, "I have to get the department's car back to the garage. Can you bring my car in today?"

"Yeah, yes. I can do that," Dimitri said. "Erm...but I..."

"Good," said Shane firmly, as he headed towards the front door. "Then I'll see you at the office."

"Shane we need to talk," Dimitri said hurriedly, as Shane went to leave.

Shane turned back and glared at him, this time there was no mistaking the anger on his face. "I know we do, but I'm due at work in twenty minutes and I haven't had my coffee yet. We will talk back here, if you're still around, this afternoon when it's not interfering with our work. If you're not coming in today then let me know so I can get a taxi home." And with that, Shane slammed out the front door, leaving Dimitri to wonder how the hell he was going to calm the anger he saw on his mate's face.

"Well, sitting around on the couch isn't going to do it," he muttered to himself, getting up to have a shower. Maybe he could make a better impression if he went to work.

Forty minutes later, feeling a lot more like his old self, Dimitri walked into the homicide division like he owned the place. He would have made it in thirty minutes, if he hadn't spent ten minutes sitting down in the garage, trying to remind himself that it didn't matter if his workmates thought that he was gay. They all had jobs to do and Dimitri knew that if he could just ride out any gossip over a couple of days, then the situation would down as everyone found other things to speculate about.

The smile on Shane's face at the sight of him, was worth any discomfort. Shane was sitting at his desk with Trent and Mace and they were going over some papers.

"Ah, here's the sleepyhead now," Trent said, greeting Dimitri with a smile of his own. "Family shit sorted out all okay?"

"Er…yeah, thanks. All sorted," Dimitri said, quickly realizing that Shane must have covered for him. "What have you got?"

"DNA and fibers on Gav. Come on, don't get comfy. We've got some leads to follow." Shane's smile was still on his face as they said their goodbyes and headed out of the office.

"Thanks for covering me," Dimitri said quietly, as they walked to Shane's car. Shane held his hand up for the keys, that Dimitri threw over and they got in.

"It was the Captain's idea," Shane said as he started the car, and pulled out of the garage. "Did you know that he knows we're shifters?"

"How the hell would he know that?"

Shane smirked. "Apparently he's friends with your ex-boss. Seems they talk on the phone quite often, and Reynolds even goes to Jacobs Lake for his vacation. He asked me point blank if we were mates."

"And you told him yes, of course." Inside Dimitri groaned. If the Captain knew, then eventually he would tell his ex-boss that they were both in Stockton, and oh, hell, he would have to tell his mother. The only thing that would make her more upset at his being mated to a man, was being told about it from somebody else. Then he had another thought.

"Aren't you worried about your family finding out you're in Stockton?"

Shane shrugged, maneuvering through the traffic with practiced ease. "My parents won't even allow my name to be mentioned in their presence apparently – but then they know that I'm gay already, so it won't bother them if I have a mate or not. They just won't care. I have to admit that I was worried that some of the pack would come after me once it got around the pack about my sexuality, but when they didn't, I came to realization that I just wasn't important enough to anyone, for them to care about what I did, or who."

Ouch, Dimitri felt that one strike his heart big time. If Dimitri hadn't spent the weekend learning more about his mate, he would have thought that Shane's casual tone, with minimal infliction, was an indication that he didn't care. But his mate was hurting and it showed in the tightening of his jaw, and the sadness in his eyes. Dimitri waited for Shane to say something about his own behavior – how Dimitri had acted exactly the same way by taking off the way he did. But Shane kept driving, finally pulling into a parking space by a row of shops.

Shane pointed to a menswear shop that sat on the corner of the others in the row. "We're going there to try and get a customer list. It seems the fibers on Gav's beard came from a high end suit – probably Armani or Hugo Boss, although we should know more within the next week. This is the only shop in town that would stock anything like that, so if they are cooperative, we might have a bit of luck in tracking down who killed Gav at least."

Shane looked across at Dimitri, with a thoughtful look on his lovely face. At least Dimitri thought it was lovely, and looking at Shane full on for the first time in two days, made Dimitri realize just how fucking much he had missed his mate while he was having his meltdown. Just as he thought about what Shane might do if he kissed the man, yes, even though they were in the main street of Stockton, Shane said quietly, "we might have a shifter problem" and damn if that didn't put all thoughts of kissing right out of Dimitri's head.

"What do you mean, a shifter problem?"

"The body – Gav's. He wasn't killed like the others. The cologne and the fibers suggests that the same guy who killed the others, was at least on the scene when Gav was killed. But the marks on Gav's body look like teeth or claws, or a combination of both. I would swear he was killed by a shifter."

"Do you know any…?"

"Not in Stockton, no. I've never come across one."

"Fuck!" Dimitri swore as he tipped his head back on the car seat. Shifters killing others happened no more or less than it did in the human world. There were good and bad shifters, the same as in any other species. But if a shifter did kill a human it was normally by human methods. All paranormals had kept themselves hidden in plain sight in the human world for centuries, and every shifter knew the importance of keeping their secret.

It was partly because of the logistics of trying to impose human justice on a shifter, which made the secret so necessary. Shifters needed to let their animal form roam free once in a while or they would go insane. Vampires needed blood. The Fae needed access to nature. Demons and Angels needed access to their higher power. None of those things were ever considered when human jails were constructed.

What that meant, for Shane and Dimitri, is that even if they found the shifter responsible for Gav's death, then he could never go through the human justice system. If the person was a wolf shifter, then pack justice usually prevailed, or as in the case with other shifters, a herd or similar system was in place. The only difference was in big cat shifters, who were usually dealt with by the Shifter Council.

All of this flashed through Dimitri's head as he tried to get a handle on what that little tidbit of information meant for him and Shane. If there was a rogue wolf shifter in the area, then it would be up to Shane or Dimitri to take him out, or at least get the rogue out of town. Then Dimitri had a thought.

"I didn't smell anything at the crime scene – did you?"

After thinking for a moment, Shane shook his head. "No, I picked up the whiff of the cologne when you mentioned it, but with all of the other smells around, and the fact that I never thought to scent for a shifter, I didn't get anything. By the time Brian showed me the marks, any smell was gone."

"I didn't notice anything at CJ's crime scene either, and that body was fresh and CJ was clean. I might be able to tell what type of shifter was involved if I saw Gav's body," Dimitri said. "We had a few shifter murders in Jacobs Lake. Not many, but if we could get a handle on what type of shifter we were looking for, then it might make the killer easier to find."

"That would be helpful," Shane said. "But what's pissing me off is that this information also skews the physical profile of who we are looking for. If a shifter is involved – one who can hide his scent, then we are looking for two possible killers in each case, instead of one. I had assumed, based on how CJ and the others were killed, that the individual had to be a big, strong person because it's so fucking hard to manually strangle someone. Now, if a shifter is involved as well, then my assumptions about size could be a moot point."

"How do we know that it wasn't a shifter in the first place?"

Shane grinned. "The cologne. I bought some, but can't wear it because my animal doesn't like it. I can't see any animal spirit liking the use of artificially created scents, no matter how lovely they smell in the bottle."

"Shit, that makes sense," Dimitri said, pleased that Shane was able to smile and talk to him like a normal work partner would. Now all he had to do was get their personal life back on track.

"Well, we'd better see if Mr. Jorgenson, the owner of this store, is going to be in a cooperative mood today. Then we'll run over to the morgue and get another look at Gav's body, hopefully without an audience."

"Then?" Dimitri couldn't help asking as they got out of the car and wandered into a nicely appointed store.

"Then we go home," Shane said, his tone giving nothing away.

## Chapter Twenty One

As Dimitri followed Shane's shapely ass up to the counter, he hoped like hell some sex was on the table during the afternoon. Shane's scent was driving him crazy, and the tight pants Shane wore, were leaving nothing to Dimitri's vivid imagination. Dimitri already knew that Shane didn't wear underwear and the thought of that luscious cock, free balling it in that expensive material...Dimitri discretely adjusted himself as Shane greeted, who was presumably the store owner.

"Mr. Jorgenson, how is business today?"

"Not so bad, Mr. West, Can't complain," Jorgenson wheezed. The store owner was short, at five foot four, but he was carrying a lot of weight, which probably accounted for the breathing problem Dimitri noticed. The man's lack of hair and florid face did nothing to enhance the man's look, but Jorgenson's smile was friendly, if a little wary.

"So what can I help you and your friend with, Mr. West. Is this an official visit?" At least the man got straight to the point.

"I'm afraid so, Sir," Shane said politely. "This is my new partner, Dimitri Polst. He took over from Ruby last week."

"Ah, Ruby, my little sweetheart," Jorgenson beamed. "She must be due to have the baby soon, ha?"

"A few weeks," Shane agreed. "So, I was wondering, I am trying to find some leads on an individual who favors high priced suits, and as you are the only shop in town that would carry such items, I was hoping we could get a copy of your customer list."

"Mr. West," Jorgenson spluttered. "Surely you are not suggesting that one of my customers is a bad man?"

"No Sir," Shane soothed. "Just a man who might be able to help us with our enquiries, nothing more."

"My customers expect me to respect their privacy, Mr. West. Surely you can respect them?"

Shane nodded. "I do Sir, and believe me, none of your customers will ever have to know that we have spoken to you. But..."

"But if we have to get a warrant," Dimitri broke in, quite happy to play bad cop to Shane's polite manner. "Then there are no guarantees."

"I don't like your new partner," Jorgenson said darkly. "I much preferred Ruby."

"There are times I feel the same way," Shane said smoothly. "But please, your cooperation would be appreciated."

Flashing another dark look at Dimitri, Jorgenson disappeared behind a curtain at the back of the shop and Dimitri assumed the man was going to his office. Shane had wandered over to where a selection of the same suits they were investigating, were hanging in exclusive splendor. Pulling out an almost black suit, from its rack, Shane looked at him critically.

"This would look good on you," he said, frowning as he looked up and down Dimitri's body. "You really should wear your suits with a bit more tailoring."

Dimitri glanced at himself in the mirror. The suit he had on, he thought, looked pretty good. Admittedly it didn't fit as well as Shane's did, but then he wasn't one for advertising his assets, like Shane apparently was.

"Do I want to ask what is wrong with the one I have on?" Dimitri couldn't miss Shane's glare, but his mate put the suit back on its peg. Shit. Maybe this was a gay thing? Or a mate thing? In either case, from the look on Shane's face Dimitri had just fucked up – again! Wanting to see Shane smile again, or at least stop glaring at him, Dimitri slipped off his jacket and handed it to Shane without a word. He plucked the jacket Shane had recommended, off its hanger and slipped it on.

The suit was made of a finer wool than Dimitri was used to, and looking at himself in the mirror, he did have to admit that it made the jacket hang off his broad shoulders in a flattering way. He did up the buttons, and looked again. The thinner lapels suited his shape and emphasized the width of his chest. Given that the color of the suit was so dark, it emphasized his hair and eye coloring. Overall, the jacket did look better than the one he was wearing.

Glancing down at the discrete price tag Dimitri gulped and then ignored the hit to his wallet. If Shane liked it, then he would buy it. The suit was a small price to pay if it put him in Shane's good book.

Turning to smile at Shane, Dimitri could see Jorgenson watching them from the counter. "You are quite right," he said to Shane. "If the pants look just as good, I'll buy it. Thank you."

"The pants will probably need some alterations," Shane said with a smirk. "You are taller than the average customer." Turning to Jorgenson, he said, "My partner here is interested in this suit. Is it possible for him to try the rest on – the pants will probably need some adjustments?"

"The jacket too, don't you think?" Jorgenson wheezed on over, and stood with Shane looking at the jacket, Dimitri was still wearing. "I was thinking of pulling it in slightly at the waist, and maybe half an inch longer in the torso," Jorgenson continued.

"We have to allow for shoulder holsters," Shane said apologetically. "Taking the jacket in would allow the holster to show, and that would ruin the line of suit, don't you agree? And I think its current length would work given the amount of exercise my partner here, might have to do in that suit."

"Of course," Jorgenson beamed and Dimitri had the uncharitable thought that the only thing it took to please this little shop owner was the promise of a decent sale. Thankfully Jorgenson didn't require him to try the pants on although he did insist on taking his measurements, which was an embarrassment in itself, given that he was another shifter who never wore underwear. He could have sworn that Jorgenson copped a feel while he was taking his inside leg measurement, and he complained as such to Shane, as they left the shop complete with a printed customer list and contact details.

"Of course he did," Shane said as they got back in the car, his smile back on his face. "It's one of the perks of his job."

"And I had to pay for the privilege," Dimitri muttered under his breath, thinking of the thump his credit card had taken buying just one suit. He could have clothed himself for a year in Jacobs Lake, with what he had just purchased.

/~/~/~/~/

Shane felt he had gotten his anger at Dimitri under control by the time they had left the clothes shop. He knew it was a mean thing to do, pretty much guilt-tripping Dimitri into buying an expensive suit. But the jacket did flatter his mate's awesome build, and Shane figured Dimitri had better get used to him giving advice on his wardrobe. Unfortunately the visit to the morgue didn't yield any further clues, although Dimitri said if he had to guess, he thought Gav's killer was a cat shifter because of the depth of some of the wounds.

After a quick lunch, where Shane deliberately kept the conversation case related, they headed back to Shane's house for their talk. Dimitri seemed nervous, which was helping Shane's mood, but he couldn't shake the feeling that he was going to get monumentally dumped by his mate.

As soon as they got into the house, Dimitri went to take Shane in his arms, but Shane quickly evaded his grasp. "No," he said firmly. "We have things to talk about and getting physical with you is not conducive to a serious discussion." He pointed to the couch. "Sit over there," he said, sitting down in the arm chair that Dimitri had fucked him on over the weekend.

Forcing those - decidedly hot - memories from his mind, Shane looked at Dimitri and said, "So tell me where your head is right now, because I have to tell you, after you taking off for two full days, simply saying sorry isn't going to cut it."

"I know it was a stupid and cruel thing to do, taking off like I did. I honestly don't know what came over me. I was just so horrified at the thought of everyone we work with thinking I was gay, and I panicked. I didn't realize what I was doing until I was fifty miles from home."

"Well, forgive me for thinking you're more than a little pathetic," Shane snapped. "We talked about this. You told me you had thought this through. I told you after what you said to Green on Saturday, that everyone would know by Monday. I thought he might have been a bit more subtle about spreading the news, but I wasn't surprised by what he said. And he didn't call you gay, he called us lovebirds, suggesting we were in a relationship. Which I thought we were. You claimed me for fucks sake. Bit me, fucked me, and then ran off at the first sign of trouble. You said you wanted to marry me – and in all of that, didn't it strike you that people might think that was a gay thing to do? Marrying another man?"

"I thought about it in theory, but when Green started spouting off about us, all I could think was what the fuck would I do if my Dad found out."

Shane sat back in his chair and seethed. He knew he should be understanding – fuck it was hard for any gay man to come out, and Green had no right to do what he did. But it seemed to Shane that Dimitri had bitten him purely and simply so he could fuck him, and damn it that didn't make him feel like a fool.

Trying for a totally casual tone, Shane said, "So I presume you are heading back to Jacobs Lake then? I'm sure you can come up with some story as to why you've been claimed but don't have a mate in your arms. Shouldn't be too difficult."

Dimitri looked up at Shane, shock plastered over his face. "I don't want to leave you. I never thought about leaving you. But I refuse to be considered a gay man."

Shane narrowed his eyes and glared at Dimitri. Sometimes his mate was so thick. Shane didn't have time for people who insisted on placing labels on others either, but the fact of the matter was that if Dimitri stayed with him, lived with him and had sex with him – another male – then the people they associated with would assume he was gay. Or at least bi-sexual.

Then, with a germ of an idea floating in his head, he stood up, removing his jacket. "Fine," he said. "You're not gay." He deliberately started unbuttoning his shirt buttons, revealing his chest. "You're not even bi. I'll accept that, seeing as you're so damn sure. You are a straight man with no thoughts, ever, of being with a male ever again. What a shame I'm a male."

Shane tugged his shirt from out of the waistband of his pants and let it slip from his shoulders. He didn't have to be a wolf shifter to see the lust in

Dimitri's eyes, but he totally ignored it.

"We'll call our claiming a necessity," he said lightly, undoing the button on his pants and kicking off his shoes. "Something you had to do to claim your fated mate and nothing more. Say you were driven by hormones and then you were horrified by what you had been forced to do, and that you will never do it again."

"A curiosity for you, now satisfied," Shane continued, as he lowered the zipper on his suit pants. Dimitri's eyes were fixed on the opening in his pants, glazed and dark with passion.

"Not something you will ever have to do again. Not something I will let you do again, because my kink has nothing to do with converting straight men," he said, letting his pants fall to the floor. Stepping out of them, he picked up his clothes and made to walk out of the room.

"Where the fuck are you going?" Dimitri growled, standing up in one fluid movement. Noting the significant bulge tenting Dimitri's pants, Shane smirked at him over his shoulder and flexed his ass.

"I'm going to have a nap. Seeing as you're not gay you will want to sleep on the couch. I have more than enough toys to satisfy me in bed – but as the thought of having a large dildo sticking out of my ass would probably offend your straight personality, I'll amuse myself, in private. There's no place in my bed for someone who doesn't accept who I am – gay!" Shane grabbed hold of his solid shaft and pumped himself once, then twice, because it felt so good, and sauntered from the room, as naked as the day he was born.

Five…four…three…Shane counted off in his head as he went up to his room and walked over to the bottom drawer of his dresser. Two…umpf. Two strong arms grabbed him and threw him on the bed. An angry, horny, naked Dimitri filled his eyes as the man leaned over him.

"I don't do labels, mate," Dimitri snarled. "But the only hand on your cock will be mine. The only one shoving a dildo up your ass will be me. And I don't give a fuck what anyone has to say about that."

Shane couldn't resist teasing – Dimitri was so damned gorgeous when he was angry – all flashing eyes, snarled lips and hot tense body. "And you don't think that makes you a little bit gay?"

"That doesn't make me gay," Dimitri growled. "I missed you. Want you. Get so fucking hard over you it hurts. It's you, who consumes my every thought. It's you that governs my cock, my brain and my fucking heart. Just you. And if you have to fucking label it, call me yours."

"Mine," Shane agreed a split second before Dimitri savagely took his mouth. Hmmm, thought Shane happily as he took in the passionate anger in the kiss – anger and all that possessive nature really did push Shane's buttons. It wasn't something he had ever been able to enjoy before, and guessed it came from being with his mate, but damn it was really something worth hanging onto.

Unable to be a passive bystander while Dimitri sucked his soul through his mouth, Shane's hands got busy, roaming over all of that luscious skin. Dimitri was muscled everywhere, and Shane could feel as each muscle rippled under his touch. Shane felt Dimitri run one deliberate hard hand down the side of his torso until he reached his buttocks, cupping and then shifting Shane's leg over his own body so that he could reach Shane's puckered hole.

The tension in Dimitri's body was tangible, the man was primed for action and not inclined to stop. Shane shuddered as he felt one dry finger breach his hole, his outcry swallowed by Dimitri's mouth. The pain was fleeting but Dimitri wasn't about to be put off. Shane gave up his own explorations for a minute and fumbled to find the lube he had stashed on his bedside table. He might be able to take a finger dry, but there was no way in hell Dimitri was getting that fat cock of his into his hole without some lube – a serious amount of lube.

Dimitri, in the meantime was plying some serious efforts into getting a second finger in to join the first. Shane managed to wrench his mouth free and after taking a couple of gasping breaths he yelled, "Dimitri! Lube you fucker," shoving the tube at his mate.

"I need in you," Dimitri growled, but he sat up, his proud cock jutting from his body, looking every inch the battering ram Shane figured he was going to feel in about two minutes flat if his mate had his way. Not that Shane was feeling any better, he wanted his mate with a fire that couldn't be quenched – he was just letting Dimitri go first.

With well lubed fingers probing at him now, Shane was able to relax enough for Dimitri to open him up a bit, although he knew it wouldn't be enough. Well before he was ready, he could feel the fat head of Dimitri's cock nudge his opening and then Dimitri put a bit of strength behind his push and Shane desperately tried to stop himself from tensing as his mate fair forced his way inside.

Shit. Fuck. Fucking hell. Every nerve ending in Shane's body came alive. Sure there was pain, but pain was fleeting. What caught Shane in a tailspin was the way his mate surrounded him, his scent, his long hard body, strong arms resting on either side of Shane's head as Dimitri plunged into him, time and time again. Shane tugged on Dimitri's neck, and the man came willingly, using his tongue to mimic the action of his cock that was trying to plumb new depths to Shane's insides.

Shane loved it all – the power, the strength and the sheer possessiveness of his mate, all flowing through his body via one heavily pounding cock. Finding his feet, he planted them flat on the mattress to give him more traction and arched his back to meet Dimitri's thrusts. When he felt Dimitri's rough hand grasp his cock, Shane couldn't hold on. Arching his back, screaming into his mate's mouth, pouring his spunk all over Dimitri's hand and his own chest. Seconds later, Dimitri raised his head and roared as Shane felt the man's release pulse deep inside him.

☐

## Chapter Twenty Two

Taking more care pulling out, than he did getting in there, Dimitri carefully eased himself from Shane's body and flopped over on his back, his hand still curled around Shane's cock. To his amazement Shane was still hard, even after coming like a rocket just moments before. Although, given that they had both been without each other for two, almost three full days, Dimitri couldn't blame him. He could go another round himself, he thought looking down at his own half hard cock, still slick with juices and lube, resting against his abdomen.

It seemed Shane had the same idea. His mate propped himself up on his elbow, looking down at Dimitri with a half-smile on his face. "You know," Shane said in a quiet voice as one of his hands made lazy circles on Dimitri's chest. "You have a lot to learn about the importance of preparation, if you keep wanting to top men."

"I don't want to top other men," Dimitri said lazily, relaxing under

Shane's fingers that were now circling his left nipple. "I do however, love topping you. And you, mate of mine, are a wolf shifter, so you should be able to handle a bit of rough."

"A bit of rough?" Shane asked, his eyebrow's raised. "Hmmm," Shane seemed to agree, but then Dimitri's butt clenched when Shane said, "okay, and now it's my turn. It so happens, I like a bit of rough myself."

Shane bent down and gave Dimitri a searing kiss, and Dimitri relaxed – his mate wouldn't hurt him. He kept thinking that right up until he felt a searing pain jolt his insides, as Shane shoved, what Dimitri was sure was his whole fucking hand inside of him – dry. Bolting upright, Dimitri pushed Shane off of him, and sat there, glaring at his mate.

"What the fuck?"

Shane held up his middle finger and grinned, but Dimitri wasn't happy. "What, you're giving me the bird now, after shoving your fucking hand up my ass with no lube."

Waving his finger, Shane said, "not my hand lover. Just this one finger. Exactly the same as what you did to me, but the difference between us, is that I wouldn't do more than that without lube, or some gentle persuasion around the anal muscles. You, mate of mine, were prepared to fuck me dry and your cock is a damn sight bigger than my finger. Now roll over and stick your ass in the air. I want to fuck you."

"I don't feel like it now," Dimitri sulked. He felt guilty for hurting his mate, and more than a bit shitty because he'd always been a good lover, with women at least. It seemed that Shane didn't feel the same way.

"You will," Shane said happily, "Now roll over."

Grumbling under his breath, Dimitri rolled over and dutifully slipped his knees underneath his hips, raising his ass. He felt ridiculous, his ass in the air when he didn't feel like sex at all. But he did relax when he felt Shane move behind him, caressing his back gently.

"Simply perfect," Shane murmured. "You are so beautiful like this, lover." Dimitri settled his face down on his arms, thinking that he didn't have to be horny to let his mate enjoy his ass. He would take all that Shane had to offer, because he really did owe the man for not kicking him out. Yep. He'd just let his lover get off, and who cared if he didn't get anything out of it. He could do this for Shane.

And he thought that for all of two minutes. Ten minutes later, Dimitri was begging to come. Literally verbally pleading with Shane to let him come. His balls were so tight they ached, his ass desperately needed to be filled, and his entire body felt like it was going to fly apart if his lover didn't get his cock in his ass, right now. But Shane would not be hurried as he kissed, caressed and then rimmed the hell out of Dimitri's ass. Dimitri didn't know if he was in heaven or in hell. It was all so good, and nowhere near enough. He was being wickedly tormented.

Every touch was like fire on his skin, every prod of Shane's tongue in his hole left him wanting more. He ached, he moaned and yet he couldn't come. Because Shane, his conniving sneaky mate, had a hand wrapped firmly around the base of Dimitri's shaft, preventing the orgasm Dimitri frantically needed to let go.

Dimitri barely felt it when Shane's cock finally got down to business. His asshole welcomed the invasion of something more solid that Shane's clever tongue. Raising his upper body onto his elbows, Dimitri pushed back, wanting that connection so badly.

"Shush, lover," Shane crooned, as he rocked gently into Dimitri's body. "My turn, remember? My way."

Mumbling under his breath about sexual sadists, fucking mates, and Shane's ability to keep him from reaching his orgasm when he wanted one enough to beg, Dimitri allowed Shane to set the pace. The hand on his hip was firm, the one on his cock, tight, and yet Shane pumped slowly – long, slow, strokes of his insides that had Dimitri's legs turning to jelly. It was intoxicating and Dimitri's body alternated between wanting to beg for something harder and faster, and enjoying the pure bliss of a mate who was making love to him.

Making love to him.

Not fucking him. Not pounding him into the mattress. Loving him and showing him, yet again, how good sex between them could be. Not that it hadn't been good before, but as Dimitri found himself pulled under Shane's erotic spell, he realized what he was going through was so much more. More than he'd ever had with Angela or any other girl. More than he'd gotten from Shane before, and much, much, more than Dimitri had given his mate in return.

As Dimitri allowed himself to soar, he could feel the love that Shane put into every caress, every thrust of his determined hips. When Shane's hand on his cock turned from clenching to gentle pumps, Dimitri gave himself up to his orgasm willingly. One that seemed to go on forever. Clenching his ass muscles tight around his mate, he felt Shane stutter, swell and finally release, Shane keeping up his gentle thrusts, prolonging things for both of them.

When Shane pulled out, Dimitri collapsed on the bed, half turning and pulling Shane into his arms. They were sticky, sweaty and both needing a shower, but Dimitri felt that if he didn't hold onto Shane tight his entire soul would fly apart. Shane loved him, and even if his mate never uttered those words to his face, Dimitri knew, and the feeling humbled him to his core.

"Learn anything," Shane said sleepily, his head on Dimitri's chest.

"Everything I needed to know," Dimitri agreed as he tightened his arms around his mate and slipped into sleep.

/~/~/~/~/

"I think we should be looking for the shifter," Dimitri said, watching Shane ease his ass into a hot looking pair of leather pants. They were heading out to the clubs again, but this time they were going to focus their enquiries on trying to find two men who worked as a pair, and who were hassling gay men.

"We are," Shane said absently, as he bent to put on his boots. He foraged around in his drawer, he knew that damn thing was in here somewhere. Yes. Smiling in triumph, Shane pulled out a light silver vest made of material so sheer it was indecent. A Christmas present from Ruby that Shane had never worn because it really wasn't his style. But it would work for tonight.

Slipping it on, he couldn't ignore the incredulity in Dimitri's tone when the man said, "You can't be serious? You're wearing that?"

"Yep," Shane said, foraging through his top drawer this time. Oh yes, fucking hair gel. He hated it. Couldn't understand why any man would wear the shit in his hair. But Shane was on a mission tonight, and it didn't have anything to do with proving that Dimitri was actually gay.

Shane was starting to think he really didn't care what Dimitri called himself. Wolves didn't do labels. They met their mates, fucked and claimed each other, and then lived together for the rest of their lives. Regardless of gender, sexual orientation, race or religion. The Fates were never wrong, and true mates needed to be with each other. Dimitri had tried to stay away. Had tried to forge a life without him. But in the end his wolf prevailed, and Shane knew that Dimitri had strong feelings for him.

All Shane had been trying to do, when he was goading Dimitri earlier – and hot damn if that didn't turn out so much better than he had expected – was to try and toughen his mate up a bit. Being called gay was the least of the men's problems. Gay bashing was rare now, although it had been quite a problem in the 1980s, but it did happen and Dimitri's sheer size might hold off an attack from one person. But a gang of drunken thugs, hell bent on beating the gay away could be a real problem. Shane had learned to deal with the slurs and the abuse, partially because he accepted his sexual orientation. If Dimitri didn't accept at least what other people would think, then that would make any abuse he went through that much harder for him to cope with. And Shane didn't want his mate running back to his ex-pack every time he thought someone was questioning his sexual orientation.

Fingering the gel through his short hair, Shane tilted his head from side to side looking at his reflection critically in the mirror. He looked good, but he needed something more. Another rummage through his drawers revealed a black leather cuff, some silver chains that he hung around his neck and arms, and a black kohl pencil. Perfect. Leaning in to the mirror, Shane carefully outlined the top of his eyelids, and after another critical look at the picture he was creating, underlined the bottom lids as well.

The man that looked back at him, was nothing like the detective persona that Shane usually presented – even when he went out in the evenings. Hating the thought, Shane had to admit he looked pretty. The kohl brought out the color in his eyes, and accentuated his high cheek bones and full lips. The chains, leather and silver top gave him a pretty party boy look. Exactly what he was going for.

Shane looked up in the mirror to see Dimitri glaring at him. He had insisted that Dimitri wear all black and the man had on a black fitted muscle shirt that accentuated every one of the muscles in his shoulders, chest and arms. Tight black jeans and boots made for a bad boy's wet dream and Shane grinned. Dimitri was now the perfect foil for his pretty boy looks.

"What the fuck are you up to, Mate?" Dimitri snarled. "How can you go out looking..." he waved his hands vaguely in Shane's direction.

"Like a pretty boy wanting a fuck?" Shane suggested. Turning from the mirror, Shane sauntered over to

Dimitri, flexing his hips, knowing that his ass looked nibble worthy in his favorite leather pants. He leaned up against Dimitri and batted his eyelids at the glaring man. "Would you fuck me?"

Growling, Dimitri crushed Shane to his chest, plastering them together so that Shane could feel the massive erection Dimitri was hiding behind his zipper. Not that he was much better, feeling his own cock harden deep in his pants.

"I don't want you going out like this at all," Dimitri snarled. "In fact I think I'll tie you to the bed and go out on my own. I get that this," his big hands cupped Shane's ass and pulled him closer, "is for work. Please tell me that normally you wouldn't be caught dead in a top like this." He plucked at the silver top dismissively.

"It was a present from Ruby," Shane said. "And no, I've never worn it before. But our murderer is targeting twinks, and if he doesn't know me, then there is a good chance he will target me, because I plan to be as visible as possible tonight."

"And if he does know you – knows you're a detective? After what happened to CJ, you know that is a real possibility." Dimitri couldn't keep the snarl out of his voice and Shane could understand. His plan had more than a few holes in it and he was counting on his mate to provide him with back up.

"Then this get up is going to infuriate him. A known police detective playing twink amongst Stockton's gays. Who better to be on his hit list?"

"I don't like it," Dimitri said, although Shane noticed he still held Shane close. "What am I meant to be doing while you are parading around like fuck fodder?"

"We'll head to Truckers," Shane said thinking fast. "As a couple initially. Then we'll have a public fight, and I will storm off as though I'm going home, leaving you at the club. Hopefully, if our killer, or shifter, or even a lookout is there, then someone will follow me, and we will hopefully have a bit more to go on."

"It's really hard to scent a shifter in a club. There are so many other smells around," Dimitri said, and Shane was pleased that his mate had gone into detective mode. It might take Dimitri's mind off the idea that Shane was literally putting himself up as bait.

"I know, which is why I have to get out of the club, without arousing suspicion. If I leave with you, then everyone will leave us alone, but if I go alone..."

"Upset because you've had a fight with your lover, then you look like a victim," Dimitri finished for him. Shane nodded, grateful that his mate understood, even if he didn't like it.

"Well, thinking of you as bait has taken care of any erection problems I might have had," Dimitri said, pushing himself off of the wall he had been leaning on and wrapping his arms firmly around Shane's back. "No matter what, I won't be far away."

"I know," Shane said, looking deep into those dark eyes that had floored him the first time he had seen Dimitri in the Captain's office. "I trust you to watch my back."

☐

## Chapter Twenty Three

Dimitri didn't think he would ever like Club Truckers. It wasn't that it was a gay club, or that it was full of humans. He could handle the loud thumping music, excited chatter and even the smell of sex and sweat, which would normally be an aphrodisiac for him. But what he couldn't stand, and he didn't think he ever would, was the fucking attention that his mate was getting.

It wasn't a jealousy thing – in 'Oh he's so much prettier than me.' Nope. That wasn't it. Dimitri knew his broody good looks were attracting more than enough attention. Attention he thought he could deflect with a menacing look and a growl. Unfortunately, he quickly found out that for a few of the pretty boys who were hanging around, that type of approach seemed to arouse them more. So instead he roped his arm around Shane's chest and pulled the man into his lap. That helped, but didn't dissuade the predatory type of human male.

It seems that Shane was known as a top. A good top if the crap he had to listen to was any indication. Now that that same man was dressed like a pretty bottom, sitting on Dimitri's lap, it seemed that there were a number of Dominant wannabe's who wanted their chance at the fickle Shane. Dimitri was getting heartily sick of it, and if it wasn't for Shane constantly reminding him that they were on a job, he would have dragged his mate off home ages ago. Dancing with Shane helped, but even then he had to keep Shane real close to stop the wandering hands, lusting over a man that was clearly his.

After a couple of hours, Shane wound his hand through the top of Dimitri's hair and leaned in close, whispering in his ear, "Show time."

"Thank fuck," Dimitri whispered back. "If I have to listen to one more fucking wannabe claiming they want to share your ass, I swear I will kill someone."

Shane pushed off his chest as though angry and stood up, stumbling a little as he did. Considering Dimitri knew that Shane was far from drunk, he figured it was part of the act.

"You want to share me?" Shane shrieked and Dimitri's winced – his wolf didn't like this drama queen persona one little bit. "I thought we had something, I thought we were in love – and you want to share me!"

"Get over yourself," Dimitri said dismissively, leaning back in his booth seat. He had more than enough experience with women getting clingy back in his days of casual fucking.

"Get over..." Shane spluttered. "Why you...I gave you...and you...UGH. You bastard. I never want to see your ugly face again." On that last missive, Shane threw the drink he had been holding all over Dimitri's trousers and stormed off, tears in his eyes.

"Fucking drama queen," Dimitri muttered for the benefit of the avid listeners around him. He knew he couldn't go running after Shane, although every inch of him wanted to. Even though he knew it was a fake fight, it still upset his wolf. Wolves never played emotional games, and his wolf just knew that their mate was upset. His wolf wanted to go and grovel, or get all dominant on their mate – basically his wolf didn't like an upset mate and would do anything it could to make Shane happy again.

"Soon," he whispered to himself. But for now he had to trust that Shane knew what he was doing. He headed off to the bathrooms to clean up the mess Shane had made of his pants, and then he would slip out the back of the club and track down his mate. The longer he was away from him, the more uneasy he felt.

/~/~/~/~/

Shane didn't have a problem faking tears as he ran from the club, in an apparently distressed state. All he had to think of was the possibility of his mate taking off back to Jacobs Lake and the tears came easily. He brushed off offers of support from those who knew him inside of the club, and weaved his way down the street, towards the darker alleys, in the hopes that if anyone was watching him, they would think he was drunk. Drunk, upset and vulnerable. If that didn't bring the killer out of the woodwork, then nothing would.

"Hey, are you okay?" Came a small voice from the shadows of the alley Shane was passing. Looking over, Shane wiped his face as though clearing his tears, and saw a small, really pretty man dressed in clothes far too big for him, watching him with concern. Most people wouldn't have seen the boy where he was standing, but Shane's wolf picked out every detail.

Remembering his role, Shane shrugged, "Yeah, boyfriend trouble. You know." He looked around as though he was lost. "I don't know what I'm going to do, where to go, you know."

The pretty boy twisted his hands, and looked as though he was warring with himself over something. Then he looked up, and even through the shadows, Shane saw the indecision on his face. "You could come with me," the boy offered. "I...er...I have a place. It's not far from here." He indicated further into the alley.

Now Shane's curiosity was piqued. He had never seen this little one before, on the streets, or in the clubs. The boy was clean, but the clothes were old and clearly not brought for him as they were way too big. Probably not homeless, but far too pretty to be out on the streets by himself in the dead of night.

"That's real kind of you," Shane staggered, as though he was going to fall, and the boy came forward to help. It was then that Shane caught a whiff of the forests – cedar and fuck, strawberries and the underlying scent of a shifter – cat, if he wasn't mistaken. He looked at the pretty boy in shock, only to see that his new friend was looking at him in the same way.

"You...you're..." the boy gasped and made as if to move away.

"Oh no you don't." Shane whipped out his arm and caught the boy as he tried to melt into the shadows. To his shame he saw the boy cringe and put his other arm over his head as though he was going to be hit. Shane loosened his grip, but didn't let go.

"I'm not going to hurt you," Shane whispered, trying to soothe the boy. "I just want to know who you are. I've never met another of our kind here before, apart from my mate. Do you live here in town?"

The boy slowly lowered his arm. "You have a mate?" He whispered back.

Shane nodded, and said, "So you see, I'm not going to hurt you and I don't want you for sex or anything. What's your name? Are you here with others of your kind?"

"Kalel," the boy said softly. "And no, I came to the city alone. My Mother..." Kalel broke off and looked like he was going to cry and Shane understood. Most cats were solitary animals and when they came of age, or their mother met another man, then the cubs were kicked out. This boy couldn't be far past his first shift, and had been left to fend alone.

"Then perhaps you'd better come with me," Shane suggested, loathe to let Kalel run off into the night and never be found again. Or worse, found like CJ was, in an alley, dead.

"I can't." Kalel looked terrified. "He said he'd kill me. I'm meant to bring you to him. He tracks me with this," Kalel pulled down the neck of his hoodie and Shane could see what looked like an electronic collar around his neck.

"Who did this?" He growled, trying to soften it when he saw the frightened look on Kalel's face again. "Is this another shifter?"

Kalel shook his head. "No, this big man. I don't know his name. But he makes me bring him...men like you."

"Shifters?"

"Gays," Kalel whispered. "I'm so sorry. I didn't want to do it. I didn't mean to, please, you have to let me go."

Understanding hit Shane like a force ten gale. His killer wasn't partnered with a second gay hating male. He was using a pretty boy shifter to lure other upset men to their death. A boy who had wandered into the city, lost and alone, and was now being used as bait and somehow, had been forced to kill Gav.

"What hold does this man have over you?" Shane said, trying to be compassionate, while his mind was racing.

"He knows what I am, and he said...he said that he'd kill me and expose me to human scientists if I didn't..." Kalel was crying and Shane's anger grew at this mystery man.

"You are coming home with me," he said firmly. "Me and my mate, we'll find a way to keep you safe."

"Won't your mate...I mean won't she be upset if you bring me home?"

"*He*, won't have a problem with it at all," Dimitri said quietly, stepping forward from the shadows. "Is this our shifter?" he said to Shane, looking him over intently as Shane nodded, his dark eyes almost glowing in the half light. Kalel squeaked in alarm as he took in Dimitri's size.

"You're mates?" Kalel gulped again as Dimitri came closer.

"Yes, true mates," Dimitri said firmly.

"I didn't think....I didn't know men could..." Kalel broke off, clearly embarrassed.

"We'll talk about it when we get you home," Shane said, gripping Kalel as if the boy would run off again.

"But my collar," Kalel said. "He'll find me and he'll kill you because you're gay. He hates gay men."

"Well, Dimitri here isn't gay, so that's not a problem," Shane said as Dimitri led them to his car. "And I can take care of myself."

"Not gay?" Kalel looked between Dimitri and Shane in confusion.

"It's a long story, boy," Shane said as helped Kalel get into the back of the car. "A long story."

☐

## Chapter Twenty Four

Dimitri's first instinct, when he saw how close Shane was to the pretty boy in the alley, was to kill the little man and worry about the consequences later. After spending hours in the club, watching his mate being pawed over and lusted after, he was the first to admit that his temper was on the fine edge of overkill. Now, as he drove Shane and Kalel back to Shane's house, he was glad that he took a moment to think before he acted.

The little cat shifter was the key they needed to find out who had murdered CJ and the other innocents. While it was highly likely that Kalel was responsible for killing Gav, Dimitri knew he couldn't let the shifter go through the human justice system. It just wouldn't be right and it risked exposing shifters to humans.

As he pulled into Shane's driveway, Dimitri looked in the rear vision mirror and saw that Kalel had fallen asleep. "Should we wake him?" He asked Shane who was also peering over the backseat.

Shane shook his head. "No, let's just get him into the house. I need something to eat and a fucking shower – this shit in my hair is driving me nuts."

Dimitri wasn't worried about the state of his mate's hair, but he was all for Shane showering off the smell of the other men who had groped him during the night. And he was throwing that obscene top in the rubbish, the first chance he got. If he ever saw Shane wearing crap like that again, it would be way too soon.

Opening the back door of the car, Dimitri surveyed their new stray. Kalel was very pretty – there was no other word to describe him. He had a mop of white blond curls, big blue eyes, when they were open, and a cute button of a nose. His full mouth probably gave most gay men in Stockton a hard on, and if his mouth didn't do it, his lithe body would. Even as a non-gay man, Dimitri could see Kalel's appeal. Combine killer looks with an innocence that couldn't be faked and it was no wonder that the dead men trusted the cat shifter.

Shaking his head at the unfairness of the situation poor Kalel had gotten himself into, Dimitri reached in and carefully scooped up the young man from the seat. Shane had already unlocked the door and had probably gone straight up for a shower, so Dimitri deposited the shifter onto the couch, and went through into the kitchen. He couldn't cook a lot, but he did do a mean bacon and eggs, and he knew Shane had both in his refrigerator.

Although he was strongly tempted to join Shane in the shower, he felt at least one of them would need to keep an eye on their visitor through the night. If what Dimitri had overheard was correct, then whoever was controlling Kalel would come looking for him the moment he realized that his little bait boy had slipped his noose. Kalel was the only one who could identify the man behind the killings, and so keeping him safe was paramount if Dimitri and Shane wanted to stop any further killings.

Dressed only in a pair of jeans, Shane came wandering through to the kitchen just as Dimitri was plating up. As the enticing mixture of vanilla and coconut hit his nose, Dimitri groaned. His anger at the night's work might have passed, but that had given way to a strong need for his mate. If the cocky smile Shane wore as he hopped up onto one of the kitchen stools was any indication, it seemed his mate knew exactly what was on his mind – and it wasn't eating the bacon, eggs and toast Dimitri had cooked up.

"Thanks for cooking," Shane said, popping a piece of bacon into his mouth and chewing appreciatively. "Hmmm," he groaned, "this is really good. Just how I like it."

"Only you could make eating a piece of bacon look sexy," Dimitri grumbled as he filled his own plate. If he wasn't going to get any sex then he might as well eat something.

"So what do you want to do with our new friend in there? Did you hear what happened to him?" Shane asked, tossing his head towards the living room.

Dimitri nodded as he thought about the situation Kalel was in, and what they might be able to do to help him. The problem was that Kalel had killed another man. Okay, it was clearly on somebody else's orders, but he would still be just as responsible under human law, unless Shane and Dimitri could prove that Kalel had been forced. And that would be just about impossible unless the killer actually confessed. No. Kalel would be better staying away from the human justice system all together. It would be best if they used Kalel to find the real killer, and then then they could try and locate somewhere shifter orientated where Kalel would be safe. He needed to be taught to control his shifts and learn to merge better as a human.

"We could keep him," Shane offered as he cleaned off his plate. Dimitri growled at that. He didn't know if he wanted the temptation of the blue eyed cat shifter hanging around his mate at home – even if the boy was so young, and he and Shane were mated, the boy would still be a temptation.

"You don't trust me," Shane said shortly, as though he could read Dimitri's mind. "If you could get your head out of your pants for a moment, you would realize it is the best idea. Kalel is too young, and too vulnerable to attack from humans and other shifters alike. He was turned out by his own mother as soon as he hit his first shift, and with looks like his, he would be in an abusive situation the first night he hit town. He has no job, no means of support, and no way to defend himself unless he shifts. That makes him prey."

"So what do you suggest we do for him?" Dimitri said. He knew Shane was right, and if this had been any other situation he would have been one of the first to offer Kalel help. Hell, if the man wasn't so obviously gay, Dimitri would have sent the boy to his home pack. His mother would adore Kalel, but given the packs' homophobic stance, someone would be out to kill the little cat shifter before he had been there a week.

"Give him a home with us. Get him some schooling, college maybe. Help him find some part time work so he can be a bit more self-sufficient. Basically help him until he has the confidence to stand on his own two feet." Shane slipped off his stool and came and stood between Dimitri's legs, wrapping his arms around his neck.

"Lover, I know what it is like to be alone. To have no money and no one to help you. It's a fucking jungle in the city when you don't know anyone, and it's worse for a shifter, you know that. Look at what has happened to Kalel already. I've got to help him, can't you understand that?"

Dimitri cupped his hands around Shane's hips and pulled his man closer to him. He reminded himself that Shane had done exactly that – left home after his first shift. Moved far away, where he had no family, friends or pack support. Shane had an education, but Dimitri had no idea how Shane had gone from being a homeless seventeen year old, to a respected Detective on a human based police force. One day soon he would sit his mate down and demand the whole story.

"I'll agree to whatever you want," Dimitri said softly. "You have far more compassion and understanding of Kalel's situation than I do. And if he needs to be with us, until he gets on his feet, then that is what we will do."

"By the way," he said as another thought hit him. "You never did say that I could move in here with you. Were you going to kick me back to my motel if I didn't agree with you?"

"I didn't know you were waiting for a formal invitation," Shane said, kissing across Dimitri's forehead and down his nose. "Given how dominant you are and everything, I figured you would just turn up here with your bags, and start unpacking." He brushed his lips across Dimitri's with such a seductive sigh, that Dimitri was almost too distracted to hear Shane continue. "I even emptied out half of my closet and one of my dressers, just for you, and I have never done that for anyone else."

Dimitri's heart leapt. Despite all of the shit, Dimitri had put his mate through, Shane still wanted him, in his life and in his bed, permanently. Groaning softly, he covered the few inches separating them, and gently licked across Shane's lips, seeking entrance. When Shane opened for him, as though it was the most natural thing in the world, Dimitri kissed Shane properly then. And for the first time since they met, it was as gentle and as loving as Dimitri could make it.

So caught up with exploring Shane's succulent mouth, which still held a hint of the bacon and eggs he had devoured, Dimitri completely missed Kalel coming into the kitchen, until the young shifter gave an embarrassed squeak.

"I'm sorry, I didn't mean to interrupt anything," Kalel said bashfully, looking down at the floor.

"You'd only be interrupting if we were both naked, and even then we probably wouldn't care," Shane said, turning in Dimitri's hands, but not moving away. "Come and help yourself to some food and don't mind us."

Looking like the eager boy his was, Kalel hurried to the kitchen counter and quickly plated himself up the rest of the food. Scoring the stool that Shane had been sitting on, he sat down and started eating immediately, as though he was worried someone was going to take his plate from him before he was finished.

"There's no rush," Shane said gently. "And there's plenty more if you want it. I know you're a growing boy."

Kalel flushed a deep red, but he did slow down his eating. After he had enjoyed about half a plateful, he looked up and looked at Shane and Dimitri as though they were some alien species.

"What is it?" Dimitri asked, not sure he liked being the object of such close scrutiny. "Go on," he said when Kalel blushed an even deeper red and looked down on his plate. "You might as well spit it out."

"Well, it's just, I'm a bit confused," Kalel said. "You said you two were mates. Shane said you were straight. But when I came into the kitchen there was nothing straight about the way you were kissing each other. I don't get it. I mean Shane is clearly gay. You are clearly not. But you two were kissing and it wasn't like the kiss you give your aunty or something."

Dimitri wasn't sure he liked the fact that Shane was doubled over with laughter, although he did appreciate the sound. His mate was truly gorgeous when he smiled, but when he laughed it was like the whole of Dimitri's world fell into place. Everything was right with the world, if Shane was laughing. But the cause of his mate's laughter was a different matter.

"Shane and I are as fully intimate as any other mates would be," he said stiffly, wondering why he was even trying to explain. "I just don't label myself as a gay man."

Kalel seemed to think about it for a moment, and then gave a shrug, that only the innocence of youth could pull off. "Okay," he said and he went back to his plate.

□

## Chapter Twenty Five

After Kalel had finished eating Dimitri questioned him a bit more about the man who was using him. All Kalel could tell them was that he was a big man, human, and that he had told Kalel to call him "Boss." This "Boss" had taken Kalel to a shelter on the edge of town, and got him a room there – something that was unusual enough for Shane to pay attention. Most shelters were crowded and they didn't have permanent rooms, but Kalel said this one was apparently run by this Boss and was where they kept gay boys, to teach them how wrong it was.

"It's a gay treatment place?" Shane was horrified at the thought of Kalel being in somewhere like that. He wasn't aware there was such a place in Stockton.

"Yes, real private. Run by a bunch of nutcases if you ask me," Kalel said, apparently unconcerned about the whole thing.

Shane narrowed his eyes as a thought struck him. "Are you gay?"

Kalel dropped his head and a worried look crossed his face. "Yes," he whispered, so softly it was hard for Shane to hear. "But I told Boss that I was a virgin, which is true, and he said it wasn't too late to change my perversions."

"How did he find out you were a shifter?" Dimitri cut into Shane's line of thinking. Shifters weren't aware of their true orientation until after they had gone through their first shift, so it made perfect sense that Kalel was a virgin. But he was also clearly gay, almost femme, and the thought of all that innocence being corrupted by anti-gay fanatics was enough to make Shane's blood boil.

"It was my own stupid fault," Kalel cried out. "I knew I should stay away from humans, but I was so hungry."

Moving over to pull Kalel into a hug, Shane felt his heart tug for a totally different reason. He knew all too well what it was like to be hungry and alone. "What happened?" He said as gently as he could, stroking Kalel's curls. He knew Dimitri wasn't happy with the contact, but the shifter had been through so much and Shane's touch seemed to settle Kalel a bit.

"I was trying to get some food out of a dumpster, in an alleyway in town. He came up behind me suddenly and yelled and I got scared. I shifted before I knew what had happened and fell into the dumpster and then I couldn't get out in my cat form. I'm not very big in my shifted form."

"So what happened next," Shane said ignoring Kalel's comment about his size. Cats came in all sizes and Kalel's form would likely grow as he got older.

"The Boss leaned into the dumpster and laughed at me. Said I was just as useless as a cat, as I was as a human. I had to shift to get out and my clothes were torn and...he was laughing at me...and I was naked..." Kalel broke off almost in tears and Shane hugged him close, pleased when Dimitri came to sit on the other side of them, gently stroking Kalel's back.

It was no wonder that Kalel had been taken in. Being in such a vulnerable position, with no support, he would have taken any help that this Boss-shit-person had given him. And given that the man knew about shifters and clearly hated them as much as he hated gays meant he was hardly going to be helping Kalel stand on his own two feet. No. Instead he had taken an innocent shifter and implicated him in the murders of five people, and Kalel was lucky if he was eighteen years old.

Shane met Dimitri's eyes, and he didn't need to be a mind reader to know that his mate was as angry at what had happened to Kalel as he was. Dimitri's eyes were blazing although the hand on Kalel's back was so gentle. Shane could feel the love he had for his mate increasing with every minute.

Fuck. Love? Not now, Shane told himself. Think about it later. Focus on Kalel and worry about...yeah, a lot later.

"Can I see your collar?" Shane said to Kalel, instead of a dozen other things he could have said to his mate.

"I can't get it off," Kalel said, sniffing as he raised his neck so Shane and Dimitri could see. The sturdy collar was made out of some sort of plastic-type materials, fixed with a buckle and a small padlock, and on the back it was wider and bulged, probably to harness the technology. Shane had never seen anything like it, although from the growl that Dimitri gave, he had.

"It's a fucking dog tracking collar," Dimitri snarled, as he took the small padlock between his fingers and twisted it, easily breaking the bolting mechanism. Once that was broken, Dimitri unbuckled the device and pulled it off of Kalel with another growl.

"Boss said I was an animal and needed to be treated as such," Kalel said quietly, shrinking into Shane's chest as though afraid of Dimitri's anger.

"I'm not angry at you, Kalel," Dimitri said in a gentler tone, although Shane knew his mate was still furious. "But no one, human, shifter, or otherwise, has the right to collar another unless it's the type of thing they are into. You are not an animal, and to think..." Dimitri broke off, clearly too angry to speak.

"He uses it to track me," Kalel whispered. "When I don't bring him someone, or one time, when I tried to run off."

"So how long will it be, before he comes looking for you?" Shane asked.

Kalel shrugged. "I'm not sure. Tomorrow I guess, when I don't turn up for my session at the shelter. He knows there are some nights I just don't find anyone and he only waits an hour or so before he disappears. If he's not in the alley where he's told me to go, then I am to take the boys to the shelter."

"What happens to the boys you do take to him in the alley?" Shane knew he was pushing but he had to get

Kalel to actually say what he had done.

Kalel looked like he was about to bolt, but with Shane's arm around him and Dimitri's hand on his back there was nowhere he could go. He twisted his small hands, his face a picture of anguish.

"It wasn't my fault," Kalel finally whispered. "The first time, I didn't know and then after, he told me they would blame me and put me in jail."

"What did he do, Kalel?" Dimitri's voice was low and firm, but Kalel would know he would have to answer.

Kalel looked at some point over Shane's shoulder and said, "Boss killed them. He came up behind me. He pushed me aside and just grabbed the boy around the neck. Boss is big, they were so little and he just kept squeezing."

"Why did he cut their faces, if they were already dead?" Dimitri wanted to know.

But Kalel was looking at Dimitri in shock. "How did you…how did you know what he did? Are you working with him? Are you going to kill me now? You are, aren't you? You're going to kill me."

Kalel struggled against Shane's arm, clearly prepared to run, and Shane couldn't let that happen. Kalel wouldn't be safe on the streets, and he certainly wasn't safe in Boss' clutches. Holding onto Kalel tightly, he pulled the man against his chest and waited until Kalel stopped struggling.

"Hush, Kalel," Dimitri said firmly. "We're not going to kill you and we're not going to put you in jail. I'm sorry. We should have said something sooner. We, Shane and I, are detectives on the Stockton police force. We're investigating five murders that we think have all been committed by the same person."

"But I did kill someone," Kalel said, horrified and apparently not at all appeased by what Dimitri had said. "You have to arrest me and I will go to jail. I killed some guy that Boss was paying to track..." he broke off and looked at Shane as though he was seeing him for the first time.

"You," he said. "You, it was your friend that Boss killed. He was trying to frame you for the murders. Said you were a faggot cop who shouldn't be on the force."

/~/~/~/~/

From the shattered look on Shane's face it was clear that he was still affected by CJ's death and Dimitri wasn't sure how to deal with that. Both men had suspected that whoever was behind the killings had a personal vendetta against Shane, but to hear it so blatantly stated, and to know it for a fact, would have been hard to for Shane to hear. Dimitri understood that Shane was the type of man who would always feel responsible for CJ's death, and he hated that.

Knowing his mate needed comfort, and unwilling to do that with Kalel in the room, Dimitri took Kalel's shoulders firmly and turned the cat shifter towards him.

"You are not going to jail. I can promise you that. No shifters can go to a human jail and we will find a way to work things out. We know you killed Gav, the informant, but it wasn't your fault. We will sort out how to track down this Boss person tomorrow, okay? But you are safe here. Do you understand that? You are safe and we won't let anyone hurt you. We just want to stop Boss from killing anymore innocent men. Do you understand what I'm saying?"

Kalel studied Dimitri's face intently as though looking for the truth. Whatever he saw there seemed to satisfy him because he nodded. "Just don't let me go back to him, please," he said. "I'll do anything you want, even go to jail if I have to, but please keep Boss away from me."

"We will, we promise." Shane's voice was strained but firm. "Now let me show you the spare room, and you get some sleep. If you wake up before us in the morning, please don't leave the house, okay? Can we trust you to stay here?"

Kalel nodded and although Dimitri wasn't sure that their little cat shifter was actually telling the truth, he didn't smell any deceit. For the moment at least, Kalel seemed to understand he was better off under their care, than he was on the streets, or with Boss.

Shane got Kalel settled – showing him the ensuite bathroom, and getting him clean towels and sheets for the bed, while Dimitri went around making sure the house was secure. Dimitri felt a bit better when he saw that Shane had locks on every window and the door was solid. Although Shane probably did that because he didn't want to be surprised by any ex-pack members, to be attacked because he lived alone did cause a pang of pain to go through Dimitri as he thought about all that Shane had endured – alone.

Dimitri couldn't comprehend what it must have been like to spend so much time alone, without a family or pack around him, and his heart ached at the thought of how lonely Shane would have been for all of the years they were apart. Knowing that loneliness was all of Dimitri's fault, was something he was going to have to accept and live with.

For now, however, Shane needed comfort and that wasn't something that Dimitri was used to giving. But he was going to give it a fucking good try.

□

## Chapter Twenty Six

Okay, he genuinely did want to offer Shane comfort. It had been an emotional night for his mate, and Dimitri wanted to do the right thing. But what exactly was the right thing when your mate throws you against the bedroom door and is plastered against you frantically sucking the life out of your lips? Dimitri's cock certainly had an idea, and Dimitri didn't think his brain was far behind his dick in the same idea, but...wasn't he supposed to be giving his mate some comfort – good old-fashioned TLC? It's certainly what the women in his life had always wanted – no sex. Cuddles, a shoulder to cry on and lame ass words about how everything will be all right.

"Fuck, I want you," Shane growled. "I want your ass – bent over the bed, waiting for my cock. I need it bad."

Well that was a good thing, right? Shane expressing his need – clear communication. Good relationship skills. Now if Dimitri could just get his legs to work. Oh yeah, there they were. With shaky hands Dimitri pulled the shirt over his head, and dropped his jeans to the floor. Fuck, forgot the boots. For a moment Dimitri was all tangled up in boots and jean legs, but he got it sorted and hurried to get into the position Shane had wanted.

"You are so fucking beautiful like this." Dimitri could feel Shane behind him, trailing his hands down his back, swiping his fingers down the crack of his ass, teasing his hole, dipping a finger in and then removing it. Dimitri sank his face into the coverlet. He didn't think he had ever felt so exposed, or so wanton in his life.

"You want this? You want my cock deep in that tight ass of yours?" Shane asked as Dimitri heard the click of the cap on the lube. Fuck yes, he realized, he did want it. This was so much easier than sitting and cuddling his man, stroking him and trying to use words to make his mate feel better. If a hard fuck would do it, then Dimitri was all for it.

"Yes," he groaned as he felt Shane breach him with two fingers. It hurt, but the pain went quickly as Shane found that pleasure spot inside of him, and bam, Dimitri was ready to blow.

Shane must have known, because he growled, "Don't come. I want you to come on my cock. I want your ass to grip me tight when I pound inside of you."

Fuck yes, Dimitri groaned, wanting that too. His need to climax backed off slightly as Shane thrust with a third finger, the burn giving just enough sting to settle Dimitri into a pleasurable haze. Pushing his hips back at Shane, in a silent demand for more, Dimitri groaned again when he felt the fingers withdraw. Seconds later he felt the unmistakable nudge of Shane's cock against his entrance, and then his mate shoved himself inside.

Fuck! "Breathe, babe," came Shane's sultry voice, and Dimitri took a shaky breath. And then another one, and by the third breath he found he could go back to breathing automatically, as the pain in his ass receded and he felt really full. Pleasurably full. Dimitri could also feel the ripple of tension in the man behind him – Shane was so on edge, but he still waited for Dimitri to be ready for him.

"Go. Move. Do it," Dimitri got out in gasps. Shane pulled back and slammed into him, knocking the breath from Dimitri's body again and pushing him up against the bed. Grabbing hold of the coverlets, as tightly as Shane was gripping his hips, Dimitri hung on for grim death as Shane pounded behind him – babbling all the while.

"Fuck yes, so tight, so hot, so good. My mate, my man, my love. Your ass around my cock, so fucking good," Shane mumbled as his hips kept up a punishing rhythm. Quickly Dimitri felt himself reach the point of no return, and damn it all, Shane hadn't even touched his cock. But with Shane's pounding accompanied by a constant stream of praise and dirty talk, Dimitri didn't even bother to try and reach his dick.

Letting the feelings rise inside of him, like a tidal wave on a path of destruction, Dimitri came, groaning loud, his muscles tightening around the cock that was still punishing his ass. Three thrusts later and Shane yelled, "Oh my God." One solid slam later and Dimitri felt the warmth of Shane's seed coat his insides. Shane draped himself over Dimitri's back, whispering nonsense and kissing every spot he could reach.

After about five minutes, Shane stood up, carefully pulling his still half hard cock from Dimitri's body. Dimitri shivered now the heat of Shane's body was gone, and he clambered up onto the bed, barely having the energy to pull back the coverlet and slip between the sheets, still on his front. Shane came back with a damp washcloth, wiping Dimitri clean with a gentleness that belied his previous pounding.

Feeling Shane cuddle up against his body, an arm and a leg draped over his back and thighs, Dimitri was at the point of falling into sleep when he heard Shane whisper, "love you."

/~/~/~/~/

Shane lay awake tormented by feelings and half-formed thoughts, Dimitri snoring softly beside him. He hadn't meant his admission of love to spill out, and he hoped like crazy that Dimitri had been too far gone in sleep to hear him. Shane had come close to spilling his heart more than once, but Dimitri's inherent "straight man" persona made it difficult for Shane to express how he felt.

Shifters fell in love quickly, with their true mates at least. With anyone else, not their mates, Shifters were the same as everyone else. They could feel love, but it wasn't anything like they would enjoy with the one the Fates had picked out for them. Shane guessed that was the type of love that Dimitri had felt for Angela – after all he was going to marry the girl.

And that was what was hurting his heart now. Shane didn't think that Dimitri would ever love him. Dimitri wanted him sexually. Was possessive over him. Didn't have a problem living with him, or sharing his bed. But those were all feelings caused by the mating bond. Love was something separate, but as Shane lay in the darkness he had to concede it was what he felt for his mate.

"Damn, why couldn't the Fates make him love me too?" Shane whispered into the night. No matter how he looked at this, loving Dimitri was going to hurt him, and yet the more he thought about it, the more Shane realized there was nothing he could do about it.

Then there was the whole "Who was trying to fuck with him" scenario. Someone, this Boss personage that Kalel had been taken in by, had used Kalel to bring him vulnerable gay men. Shane wondered how Kalel had snared CJ, who was more streetwise than any of the other victims. Of course, thinking about that, led to thinking about how Shane was responsible for CJ's death. It might not have been his fingers around his friend's throat, but CJ had been killed that night because he had been seen with Shane. It was that simple.

Trying to think of anyone that he had pissed off enough to have that person want to frame him for murder, Shane fell into an uneasy sleep.

/~/~/~/~/

Dimitri's body might have been dead tired, but his wolf was always alert and so, whether he wanted to be or not, he woke to the faint sound of breaking glass. Shaking Shane, who was still draped over him like a cuddle blanket, Dimitri put his fingers to his lips the moment Shane's eye's opened. Nodding his understanding, both men slipped off the bed and into pants, before heading to the door and listening intently.

Faint sounds of footsteps, in the house, and low voice tones. Whoever had broken in clearly didn't want to wake the house occupants up. Then Shane growled and Dimitri sniffed – wolf shifters. Their would-be burglars were wolf shifters. Frowning as he sniffed the air again, Dimitri groaned quietly. He knew those scents.

"Stay here," he whispered frantically to Shane.

"It's my fucking house," Shane whispered back.

"Just stay here, please?"

Feeling Shane's glare on his back, Dimitri slipped out of the bedroom door, padded down the stairs and came up behind two men he knew well. Grabbing his brother and his brother's best friend by the back of their necks, Dimitri couldn't stop his growl.

"What the fuck are you two doing here?"

"Hey man, is that any way to greet your brother and his best bud? What do you think we're doing here? Mum said you weren't talking to her, so she sent us down to see what you were up to," his brother, Peter smiled up at him, as though it was the most natural thing in the world.

"And you had to break in?" Dimitri growled again. "You couldn't use the door like normal people?" Striding over to the couch, dragging his two captives with him, Dimitri shoved them down and stood over them glaring.

Peter was smaller and younger than Dimitri, only twenty two years of age and about six foot in height, but he already had the muscled back and shoulders of a shifter. He shared Dimitri's dark looks, but his hair was long and his face had the clean shaven look of youth. Ben, Peter's best friend since Kindergarten was the same height and build but his long hair was blond, hanging in wavy curls around his face.

"Thought you might be busy, bro," Peter said with a smile and a wink. "Didn't want to disturb you, if you get my drift."

"How did you even know where I was staying?" Dimitri asked, ignoring the innuendo, all the while his mind turning. It would only be a matter of time before Peter saw the mating mark on his neck, and if Shane came down from the bedroom, there would be hell to pay. His parents would find out...oh fuck.

"Some guy down the police station said you were bunking in with your new work partner and gave us the address," Peter said, like it was the simplest thing in the world. "So what you got for breakfast? We're starved, long trip and all that."

Dimitri stood, torn. He could shuttle his brother and his friend out of the house and take them out for breakfast. Give them some story about being busy and pray they didn't notice the scar on his neck. But that wasn't fucking fair to Shane. Come hell or high water, Dimitri had claimed Shane as his mate and it wasn't right to leave the man hidden away in the bedroom because Dimitri was too chicken shit to admit he had a male mate.

Taking a deep breath to center himself, Dimitri nodded towards the kitchen. "Go see what you can find. Put on enough for five of us. I'll go get Shane up."

"Your partner?" Peter asked headed for the kitchen.

"My partner and my mate," Dimitri called back over his shoulder as he went up to the master bedroom.

□

## Chapter Twenty Seven

Shane didn't know what to think as he sat down to eat a meal prepared by his brother in law and his friend. Dimitri hadn't said anything to Shane when he came into the bedroom to retrieve a shirt. Shane had already put one on, figuring that Dimitri wouldn't want anyone to see his mating mark, and that was before he had worked out who the hell had broken into his house.

Having already taken a meal into Kalel, who had been sitting up wide eyed on his bed when Shane went in the room, Shane had explained quickly that they were visitors from Dimitri's pack and probably homophobic. Kalel had no problems hiding out in his room – he didn't want to face more wolves if he could help it and Shane couldn't blame him.

Now Shane was sitting, eating automatically, his brain going a mile a minute. He had distinctly heard Dimitri tell Peter that Shane was his mate, but so far Peter and Ben hadn't said anything about it. Peter was filling Dimitri in on the gossip of the pack – which seemed to consist mostly on who was shagging who. As Shane had given up his pack years before, he didn't see the need to include himself in the conversation. It wasn't as though anyone at Jacobs Lake had worried about him over the years he had been gone.

"You don't say much, do you?" Peter said, jolting Shane from his thoughts.

"Not a lot to say," Shane said shortly. "I left the pack a long time ago. Their gossip doesn't mean a lot to me now."

Peter looked puzzled. "You're from Jacobs Lake?"

"Originally. I left when I was seventeen."

"So you knew you and Dimitri were...?"

Shane shook his head. "No. If I had known Dimitri was my mate, I wouldn't have left him."

"Wow," Peter said, his awed expression hampered somewhat by the bacon and eggs he was stuffing in his mouth. "How romantic, I mean, the Fates sure are clever. Imagine both of you not knowing and then ending up in the same police department. Pretty cool, bro."

"I knew before I moved here," Dimitri said shortly. He looked over at Shane and then back at his brother. "I knew Shane was my mate just after my first shift. He didn't because he hadn't shifted yet, and I stayed away from him once I knew, so that he wouldn't find out."

"Bro!" Peter yelled. "That's harsh man. Really harsh. How could you do that to your own mate? Fuck it man, you were going to marry Angela, and yet you knew about Shane? That's just fucking mean."

"Yeah, well what was I going to do?" Dimitri yelled back. "You know how mom and dad are. You know what the pack is like. We'd have been fucking shot if we had claimed each other at home. That's why I moved here."

Peter looked at Dimitri for the longest time, not saying anything. Then he looked at Shane, and Shane was surprised to see pity in the boy's eyes. "You're okay with this? You knew about this and you're okay with it?"

"Dimitri told me. When I would finally talk to him, that is," Shane admitted. "It is what it is."

"Why wouldn't you talk to him? You had to know he was your mate when you met him here. You couldn't have known at the time what an ass he is."

Leaning back on his chair, Shane grinned. "Let's just say, not telling me we were mates while I was still part of the pack, was the least of Dimitri's crimes against me."

Peter looked between Dimitri and Shane, still confused.

"I bullied the shit out of him at school," Dimitri finally said.

"Fuck, this mating shit must be really strong," Peter said, clearing the last of his food from his plate. "You're lucky Shane didn't cut off your balls and serve them to you on a plate, bro."

"I like his balls where they are," Shane said with a wink as he got up to clear away the dishes.

"Did you leave the pack because you knew you were gay?" Ben spoke up for the first time, looking at Shane.

"Yep," Shane said cheerfully, stacking the plates in the sink. "I guessed before I shifted and I knew as soon as I did shift. So I headed home, told the folks and headed out of town before anyone could pull a gun on me. I have a good life here."

"I'm gay," Ben said quietly. Everyone was silent for a moment, then Peter hit him on the arm.

"Dude, it's not catching. You can't get gay just by being with my faggot brother and his mate."

Ben hit Peter back. "Don't use the word faggot, asshole, it's not nice. I didn't guess I was when I came in this house, you idiot. I mean I've been gay since my first shift. I've always known."

The look of utter confusion on Peter's face would have been cute, if the situation wasn't so serious. His eyes were bugging out of his head and his mouth had formed the perfect "O".

"But," Peter said, flustered to hell. "I've seen you with girls, man. You go out with heaps of girls." Then his eyes narrowed. "Just like my brother did. Fuck, you're really gay?"

Ben nodded, his classically handsome face a bright pink. "You've seen me with girls, but I've never done anything with them."

"Dimitri did – have sex with girls I mean," Shane said, suddenly finding the dishes in the sink a lot more interesting than the conversation at the kitchen counter. "But then Dimitri doesn't consider himself gay. He's just a guy who happens to have a guy as a mate."

When Peter and Ben burst out laughing, Shane smiled to himself. It seemed he wasn't the only one who thought Dimitri's stance on his sexuality was funny.

"Shut the fuck up, all of you," Dimitri snarled. "You don't have to be gay to take it up the ass."

Peter and Ben just looked at Dimitri and then burst out laughing again and this time Shane joined in. "Of course not sweetums," he said going over to Dimitri and popping a kiss on his head. "No one thinks taking a cock up the ass is gay. Unless the one taking the shafting is another guy." He danced away from Dimitri's slap with another laugh, and went back to the kitchen sink.

"Enough about me, anyway," Dimitri snarled. "What are you going to tell mom, Peter, now you've found me? And Ben what are you going to do?"

Peter agreed not to say anything to his mother until he got back, and he and Ben thought it was a good idea for the two of them to stay in Stockton for a few days. Dimitri agreed to put them up at the motel where he still had a room, and sent them off with the GPS instructions dialed into Peter's phone. The boys wouldn't leave the house until Dimitri and Shane promised to take them to Truckers that night – it seemed Ben hadn't had nearly enough experience in being gay and his only sexual experiences came from Grindr hookups.

"Makes you wonder, doesn't it?" Shane said as he and Dimitri flopped on the couch.

"Wonder what," Dimitri said, distractedly. Shane figured his mate was still freaked out at having to tell his mom he had taken a male mate.

"How many men in our old pack have male mates," Shane said with a grin. But then his face fell when he thought about Ben. Ben was gay enough that he couldn't stomach the thought of being with a woman and he could only get a hard-on around a like-minded male.

"You know we have to help Ben, don't you?" Shane said, thinking about how hard it must be for the young man.

Dimitri looked at him for a long moment, and then dropped his head back onto the couch with a groan.

"We're going to need a bigger house," he said. And Shane agreed. If they invited Ben to stay, and Kalel, then they were running out of room.

Kalel came out into the lounge, his big blue eyes wide. "Is it safe to come out now?"

"Yep," said Dimitri, "although that was my brother and his friend. Don't let them bother you, they won't cause you any harm."

"Okay," Kalel said easily, dropping down on the couch. Then he groaned and sniffed the cushion. Worried, Shane asked him what was wrong.

"The dark haired one, he was sitting here, wasn't he?"

Shane looked at Dimitri, who looked at Kalel. "What?" the young cat shifter said with an innocent look. "Okay, I might have snuck down to take a look while you were all in the kitchen talking. The scent in the hallway was delicious and made me so hard."

"The dark haired one," Shane said, making sure of his facts.

"Yes," Kalel said. "The blond is cute enough but the dark haired one makes my dick hard just looking at him – and I can't get enough of his scent."

Shane grinned at Dimitri. "Looks like your brother's not going to be running to your mother anytime soon. Not if Kalel's his mate too."

"Fucking hell, an even bigger house." Dimitri said. "And I thought things would be quiet here."

□

## Chapter Twenty Eight

Shane felt wired and tense as he, Dimitri and Kalel walked into Club Truckers that night. They had spent the day using the computer to find out who owned the private anti-gay place where Kalel had been kept, but all of the records kept coming back to a shell company and it was going to take time, and a lot more resources to dig deeper there. Shane had started going through the list of customers from the clothing shop. It wasn't long, only about twenty names, but everyone Shane ran a check on had come up with a clean record. Of course, the fibers could have come from a suit that had been brought on the internet, or while the guy was on vacation or anything. So it really wasn't much of a lead.

The collar wasn't much help either. Dimitri had tracked it to an online company that originated in China. Trying to get some guy on the chat service, who clearly had limited English skills to understand they were conducting a police investigation and wanted access to the customer details of the person who had purchased the collar was damn near impossible.

Dimitri rang into the office and asked Mace to try and find a Chinese interpreter who could ring the company and ask them for the information directly. He didn't hold out much hope, and neither Shane, nor Dimitri could come up with an idea on how they could trace the collar any further, if the company wasn't cooperative.

Shane sat down with Kalel and tried to find out more details about Boss, but unfortunately Kalel wasn't a lot of help. He didn't have police training – he could only tell Shane that the man was a bit shorter than Dimitri, was really big all over, wore expensive suits and seemed to favor a specific cologne. When Shane pulled out his bottle of Clive Christian's X Factor, Kalel confirmed it was the same scent. But all Shane had really got out of the conversation was that the man who had kept Kalel and used him so badly, was the killer. And Shane already knew that.

It didn't help that all Kalel wanted to talk about was Peter. Dimitri sat him down and explained that Peter was only into girls, and might not take kindly to having a male mate. He explained how homophobic the Alpha of the Jacobs Lake pack was, and how hard it would be for any wolf shifter who was caught with a male mate in that area. Kalel had been upset to think that his true mate might not want him, but he was even more upset at the thought that his mate would lose his pack if he claimed him. Shane assured him that he was really young, that provided Peter didn't claim him he could have sex with other men, and that maybe, like Dimitri, Peter might need a bit of time before he accepted a male mate.

They had agreed to meet Peter and Ben at the club, and when Shane walked inside he could see the two men sitting at a booth at the back of the club. Sending Dimitri off to get them drinks at the bar, Shane walked with Kalel over to the booth, introducing the young cat shifter to Peter and Ben. Kalel, true to his promise to Shane, didn't say or do anything to indicate that he knew Peter was his mate. He sat between Ben and Shane, looking around the club with interest.

There was certainly enough to look at. Although the place wasn't packed, it was still fairly busy and Kalel attracted a lot of interest with his pretty boy looks and body acutely outlined in the tight clothes Shane had got for him. When Dimitri brought over beers for himself and Shane and a soda for Kalel he purposefully sat on the edge of the seat like a hulking Dom, which kept a lot of the wannabes away from the booth. But it was hard to block the stares and Kalel, being young, clearly wanted to dance.

"Come on Kalel," Shane said. "Let's go and have a dance and let these straight men enjoy their drinks."

"Hey," Ben protested, waving at Peter and Dimitri. "I said I was gay. Don't lump me in with those two."

"I'll take you out there after," Shane promised. "For now, why don't you boys watch and see how it's done. Come on Kalel."

Kalel followed Shane eagerly, although Shane could tell he was really nervous. "I don't know how to dance," he whispered in Shane's ear.

"You're a cat shifter," Shane hissed back. "Let the music flow through you and your body will do the rest. But don't get separated from me, okay? We don't know if your Boss freak has anyone on lookout here tonight."

"I won't leave you," Kalel promised, his eyes wide with fear.

The first song was a slow one and Shane pulled Kalel into his arms, ignoring the glare from Dimitri and, surprisingly, Peter. Seems Peter had gotten a whiff of the little cat shifter and had come to the same conclusion Kalel had.

"Just relax and feel the music," Shane whispered encouragingly into Kalel's ear, noting the exact moment Kalel overcame his nerves and gave into the music. Shane had been right, Kalel was a natural and when the beat sped up and the two men danced alone it was like watching porn. Shane stayed close, enjoying the show and making sure that no one else got too close. If Peter didn't come through then Shane would find someone to help Kalel get over his virginity problem, but he refused to let Kalel's first time be a bathroom or alley hookup.

After about forty minutes, Shane was ready for a drink and he dragged an unwilling Kalel off the dance floor. The young man flopped into the booth and took a long suck of the straw in his soda.

"Phew, that was fun," he said innocently. "I could dance all night long. Do you want to have a go, Dimitri?"

Shane tried to hide his laughter when Peter growled. Dimitri's younger brother looked thoroughly pissed off, his dark eyes, so like his brothers' glinting in the dim light of the club. Dimitri heard it, and said, "Yep, come on pup, show me what you've got."

Dimitri let Kalel pull him out of the booth and sauntered with him over to the dance floor, and Shane sat back to watch. There was no denying Kalel's pretty looks, but Dimitri was so tall, dark and foreboding in comparison, it would prove to be a hot show. Shane settled back into the booth and relaxed.

"How can you let your mate dance like that with someone else?" Peter hissed, making his way to Shane's side. Shane flicked him a quick look. Peter didn't seem to be able to take his eyes off of Kalel and Shane looked back to see what had his young brother-in-law so worried. Dimitri had Kalel pressed up against his body, back to chest and the two men were dancing in perfect sync. If Shane wasn't already aware that Dimitri couldn't get a hard on for anyone else, he would have been worried, but as it was, he knew that his mate was teasing the crap out of his brother. To know that hot body would be ploughing his later, gave Shane a decided twinge in his pants.

"Kalel's a virgin," Shane explained quietly. "A cat shifter, who has had a really hard time since he came to the city. Dimitri and I just want to show him a good time without letting any of the other louts here get their hands on him. When he dances with us, he's safe. Besides, Dimitri and I have claimed each other, I don't have anything to worry about."

"But what if Kalel gets off on him?" Peter sounded positively angry at the idea.

"I'll make sure Dimitri showers when he gets home," Shane said flippantly, although inside he didn't like the idea any more than Peter did. Seems his cocky mate was doing a spot of payback for Shane's own dance exhibition and fuck it all, it was working. Shane adjusted himself and kept a bland look on his face.

When Dimitri's hands slid slowly down Kalel's hips, Shane thought he was going to combust. But before he could do anything Peter was up, out of the booth and striding over to the dance floor. Shane watched as Peter hit Dimitri's arm, and indicated roughly that he wanted to take over. Dimitri smirked at him and said something, but Shane couldn't hear what was said over the music. After a bit of back and forth, Dimitri came back to the table, the smirk still firmly on his face, and Shane watched as a look of wonder came over Peter's face as he took Kalel into his arms. It was as though time had stood still for the two young men, and when Shane saw Peter slowly reach down and gently stroke Kalel's face, Shane smiled. They would work things out.

"Pleased with yourself, lover," he said looking at Dimitri.

"It worked, didn't it?" Dimitri was positively smug as he leaned back in the booth and pulled Shane's back onto his chest.

"What the hell is going on?" Ben asked, looking between Shane and Dimitri, and Peter and Kalel who were still holding each other, barely moving to the music given how wrapped up in each other they were.

Dimitri quickly explained that Peter and Kalel were mates and Ben cracked up laughing. "Love 'em and leave 'em Pete has a gay mate? Oh, that's precious," he said, laughing hard. But Shane didn't miss the hint of wistfulness in Ben's eyes.

"Your chance will come," he said, patting Ben's hand soothingly.

A dark shadow blocked Shane's view of the dance floor and Shane looked up into stern black eyes set in the face of an angel – an avenging angel with full red lips, a straight nose set in a triangular face, a well-trimmed goatee hugging his chin. Dressed entirely in black leather, his long black hair hanging down his back, the man was the epitome of domination and intimidation. Shane felt Dimitri growl behind him, a low warning, but Shane grinned.

"Sin, my man. What brings you into the vanilla neck of the woods? This isn't your normal scene."

Sin let a half smile grace his lips, and shrugged. "Came to thank you for the little present you sent me the other night. Wasn't what I was looking for, but I passed him onto Master Bull, who was definitely suited to the little runt's needs. I hear Bull collared him and everything."

Shane thought back, and then remembered – Tucker. "Tucker and Master Bull, ha, I never would have guessed, but then you certainly know best on that side of things. So how's life treating you? Oh, by the way, this is my partner, Dimitri."

He felt Dimitri flick his fingers in greeting, but neither man moved to shake hands. Shane smirked – these two dominants weren't likely to get on that well with each other.

"Yep, life's good. Still looking for a permanent you know, scene's getting a bit stale." Sin looked over at Ben, who was gazing at the man like he was life's greatest treasure. Shane could practically see him drooling. "This boy available?" Sin asked Shane as though Ben wasn't even there.

Shane thought for a moment, he could feel that Dimitri had tensed beside him. Then, looking over at Ben again, he nodded. "Yes, but he's a noob Sin. A 'get to know you' type if you understand what I mean."

Sin smiled and really that shouldn't be allowed, because the very infrequent times the man did allow a smile to grace his beautiful face, it was so wickedly decadent, and full of a promise to deliver.

"Message received," Sin said, smile still in place. "Come on boy. Dance with me." He held out his hand. Ben looked at Shane once, got the nod and grabbed Sin's hand like a lifeline. Still grinning Sin followed Ben onto the dance floor, watching Ben's ass like it was a Christmas gift.

Shane relaxed back into Dimitri's chest and pulled the man's arm around him.

"Was that wise?" Dimitri breathed into Shane's ear, sending tingles down Shane's spine.

"Hmm, Ben and Sin? Hell yeah. Yes, Sin is big in the leather crowd and yes, he's a sadist, but he's got a cock that won't quit and Ben's not a twink. Sin will take it easy on him. Besides, did you see Ben's face? I could hardly say no." Shane laughed and he was pleased when he felt Dimitri chuckle under his back. He had been waiting for the inevitable have you fucked him which would have been a laugh. With both Shane and Sin as permanent tops, until Dimitri Shane reminded himself, it was never going to happen. But Sin was a useful contact to have in the leather community, and Shane considered the man a friend.

The two men watched Ben and Sin, and Peter and Kalel on the dance floor for a while, to the point where Shane started getting antsy. The blatant groping, the music and the faint smell of sex in the air, combined with Dimitri's hard body behind him, sent

Shane's motor revving. Remembering Dimitri's moves with Kalel, Shane turned and said quietly, "Think you can dance with me, the way you did with Kalel?"

"I thought you'd never ask." Dimitri's eyes heated as he looked into Shane's and Shane felt it all the way to his groin. Yes! Knowing he was another one who was going to get lucky later, Shane happily followed Dimitri's tight ass onto the dance floor and let himself be swallowed up in his mate's embrace. Who cared if it wasn't a slow song? With Dimitri's arms around him, their bodies plastered together, as they moved slowly to the music, Shane didn't want to think about anything except his mate. So he didn't.

☐

## Chapter Twenty Nine

Shane woke with a splitting headache – damned unusual for a shifter. Certain he hadn't drunk that much the night before, he went to feel his head, only to hear the clank of metal as his arm moved. Metal. Okay, either Dimitri had stepped up his game, or Shane was in trouble and as his other senses came online, option two seemed to be the verdict.

Without opening his eyes, he could tell he was lying down, on some sort of hard surface covered with some type of cloth. He couldn't feel any heat in the room, so guessed there was no windows, or it was still night time. Sniffing cautiously he could make out Dimitri's citrus and jasmine scent in the air, and he cautiously opened his eyes.

Yep, he was restrained on his back, to a table, in one of the dankest rooms Shane had ever seen. A distinctly musty smell, mold and damp assailed his nostrils. Turning his head, which was the only part of his body he could move, he saw Dimitri similarly laid out about three feet from him. It would seem his mate hadn't woken up yet, and as much as Shane would have appreciated the company, he let Dimitri sleep for a bit. Thumping his head back on the table, Shane tried to remember what the hell had happened. The sharp pain in his skull reminded him that thumping your head when you are already in pain was a really silly idea.

Shane thought back. They were at the club. Kalel had gone back to the hotel with Peter. Shane remembered pulling Peter aside and telling him that bad men were after his little cat shifter, and to keep Kalel close by at all times. Peter was happy to agree – it seemed the two men were heading off to find the internet, given that neither one of them had a clue about how gay sex worked. Popping a couple of links on Peter's phone, Shane waved them off. Ben had already disappeared with Sin, who promised to keep an eye on his young man also.

Their charges all safe and looking to get laid, Shane had focused on Dimitri. The 'testing Dimitri's skills as a driver when you are giving him a blowjob' type of focus. That must have been how they got jumped. A spectacular blow job in the car, Dimitri growling about how he was going to plant Shane's face into the mattress and give him the pounding of his life, and then a sharp prick (not the good kind) and lights out. Fuckers must have been waiting in the house.

Wrenching his neck around to a decidedly uncomfortable angle, Shane looked at his restraints. Police issue cuffs. Shane knew he could break them, or shift and get out easily enough, but he wasn't sure that was the best idea. If he shifted, he risked exposing shifters to any number of humans, not to mention the fact it would trash his clothes. Peering around the room, Shane tried to see if he could locate any cameras.

The room was constructed out of concrete blocks, with a couple of steel chairs against the wall. Apart from that, the tables were the only other objects in the room. As Shane had suspected, there were no windows and the only light in the room came from a small skylight set in the ceiling. There was only one door, and from what Shane could see, it was made of stainless steel, and appeared to open electronically as there was no door handle. Just a keypad set in the wall beside it.

Shane was working out their best possible escape plan, when he heard Dimitri groan and then a muffled, "what the fuck?" He decided to try a spot of levity – after all if you couldn't laugh at your situation you were pretty well screwed.

"So big man, if this was your idea of pounding me into the mattress, you need a few more lessons," he said, twisting his neck so he could see Dimitri's face.

"I still owe you," Dimitri growled, opening his eyes and taking in their situation. Craning his neck up to look at the cuffs, Dimitri spread his arms as wide as he could with the cuffs and then with an added burst with his arms, he broke the cuffs apart. Stretching his arms out and rolling his shoulders, Dimitri sat up and quickly pulled the cuffs holding his ankles to pieces, shaking his legs out when he did so.

He looked over when he must have felt Shane watching him. "What?" he said. "You know the adage. Better to die on your feet..."

"Than to die cuffed to a table," Shane finished for him, imitating Dimitri's moves, and getting free from his cuffs too. He sat up, and was immediately swallowed up in Dimitri's embrace. Hot hands ran over his body, and equally hot lips scorched his. Just as Shane thought his lungs would burst, Dimitri pulled back, his dark eyes searching his. "Are you okay?" The anger in Dimitri's voice was evident.

/~/~/~/~/

Dimitri was beyond pissed. Someone had been in their home, and yes he did count it as his home, even if he hadn't moved in yet. The bastards had been lying in wait for him and

Shane to get home, and the only reason why anybody would be holding them, that Dimitri could see, was because of Kalel's collar. Dimitri remembered they had left the collar on the kitchen counter when they went out. He should have been more focused on their surroundings, but the fun time at the club, and the promise of a fuck had addled his brain and now both he, and more importantly his mate were in danger.

Shane was over by the door, probably trying to work out how to open it. Dimitri went over also – it was either the door or the skylight and the skylight looked a little small, although Dimitri figured he could get Shane out of there, if he had to.

"Sniff the door," Shane said quietly. Dimitri dutifully sniffed and a familiar cologne hit his nostrils. God, he was really starting to hate that smell. "I couldn't smell it in the room," Shane said. "But with all of the mold and shit around that's not surprising."

"Yeah, well no surprises that we've been taken by the fucking killer,"

Dimitri said, pacing the floor. "What I don't understand is why he hasn't killed us too?"

"Because we know where Kalel is?" Shane suggested, walking back from the door and sitting back up on one of the tables. "It makes sense. He tracks us using the collar. Realizes Kalel isn't there. May have thought that we would have had Kalel with us when we got home. When Kalel wasn't with us, he brought us here to make us talk. If he kills us before he finds Kalel, then he runs the risk of Kalel getting to the police."

"But that suggests that whoever has done this, knows who we are, or at least you," Dimitri said, his mind racing.

"I think we already know that's a high probability. Who knows, maybe this killer thinks that Kalel has already talked and that we have the boy in protective custody or something?"

"I hate this not knowing," Dimitri growled, his pacing increasing in intensity. "I just want to..." he broke off frustrated. His wolf hated any form of confinement, and he was sorely tempted to shift, but he knew that wouldn't help the situation.

Shane stepped in front of him, placing calming hands on Dimitri's chest. "There's nothing we can do at the moment," he said softly, his face soft and in Dimitri's eyes so damn pretty. "Yes, we could probably get out," Shane continued. "But if we wait here, then with any luck we will get the answers we are looking for."

"I just hope the boys aren't looking for us – they're damn good trackers," Dimitri grumbled as he let Shane pull him to one of the tables. Sitting so they were facing the door, Dimitri put his arm around Shane's waist and pulled him close. No matter who came through that fucking door, he would protect his mate with every inch of his skin, and if that involved killing a gay-hating killer, then Dimitri's conscience could live with that.

/~/~/~/~/

Dimitri had no idea how much time had passed before he saw the door to their slide open cell silently. The man framed in the doorway was the last person Dimitri expected to see, but the waft of cologne hit Dimitri's nostrils at the same time as Dimitri's eyes registered the gun in Lieutenant Green's hands.

"Well, you two have caused me no end of trouble, especially you West," Green said stepping into the room and waving the gun at Shane. "Now where the fuck is my little cat shifter, I know you've got him."

"Somewhere safe and protected," Shane said calmly, and Dimitri was impressed with his mate's strength of character. Even a shifter could be killed with a well-placed bullet, but Shane acted as though facing a gun-wielding killer was something he did every day. Dimitri didn't take his eyes off of Green, looking for any opportunity to divest the man of his gun.

"That little shit is my pet, boy. He owes me and he belongs to me," Green said, coming closer. Come on, Dimitri thought, just a few more feet.

Calling his mate boy was the least of Green's crimes.

"Kalel is a person," Shane said and this time there was a tinge of anger in his voice. "He is nobody's pet, and no one's possession. You had no right to collar him, unless that is what you are into, you sick fuck. Is that what you like? Collaring pretty boys and getting them to suck your pathetic dick?"

Dimitri didn't see the shot coming, but he smelled Shane's blood a second later, and he didn't stop and think. He was off the table and in his wolf form in less than the time it took to blink, and on Green, mauling the hand that held the gun. Green yelled and screamed, but Dimitri wasn't stopping. He'd had killing on his mind since he had woken up in restraints, and Green was the perfect target.

"Dimitri, stop," Shane's voice broke through his angry haze. Looking up, Dimitri watched Shane ease himself off the table, and carefully hobble closer to where Green was still prone on the ground, Dimitri's wolf form on his chest.

"Dimitri, hon, you can't kill him. Those boys. The ones he killed. They deserve justice," Shane got out in gasps, and Dimitri could see his mate must be in a lot of pain. His sharp eyes caught the seeping of blood from Shane's thigh, and he knew he had to get his mate medical attention.

"You can't prosecute me," Green sneered, his arrogance apparent despite his mauled hand. Dimitri growled low, and put his head near Green's throat and snapped. Green lost a bit of his arrogance, but he was still far too smug for Dimitri's liking.

"You've got nothing on me but the word of a homeless faggot – a faggot who's as responsible for the killings as I am," Green continued, and Dimitri figured the man must be totally stupid because he could rip out Green's throat in a heartbeat.

"There's no forensics, no witnesses, except one who won't be believed. I've got good standing in this town and what have you got. Nothing," Green spat out. "Your fag mate CJ had more sense than you did. At least he knew he was going to die, and believe me West, you and your faggot partner are going down."

"You're responsible for five deaths, six if you count Gav," Shane gasped. "I will find a way to bring you trial. Those boys had families, lives to live and people that loved them."

"There were seven boys, two of them haven't been found yet," Green said with a grin. "Seven slutty faggots, strangled by my hands. Crying and pleading for their lives. Offering me money, sex, anything to save their pathetic skins. I tracked them down, strangled them and then I marked their faces with a knife when I was done, so even their corpses would look like the trash they were. And you've got nothing."

"Except a confession," Captain Reynolds said, walking in with Trent and Mace, his cell phone in his hand. "Caught on disc, bragging, in front of four law enforcement witnesses who will all testify to what they heard, as well as me. Your career is finished, Green, you are definitely not a person of good standing in this or any community. In a word, you are finished."

Green was silent for a moment, his face red, his eyes flicking back and forth, looking for an escape route. Now that the others had come into the room, Dimitri went to stand with Shane, who leaned on his shoulder, the pain from his leg wound clearly making it hard for Shane to stand.

"I can get you the murderer of Gav, the homeless guy," Green said. "West and Polst know who he is, and where he is. He deserves to be in jail as well."

Reynolds looked at Shane who said, "The boy was a minor, coerced and forced into his actions by Green who was present at the time. He has extreme extenuating circumstances," Shane looked down at Dimitri and then back up at the Captain, "and we feel there will be nothing gained by booking him for the murder, especially since the murder weapon was never found, and there was no other evidence. He is too young to be made to confess, which he did, and because of Green and what the man did to him, we stand by our decision."

"He's safe, this boy?" Reynolds asked.

Shane nodded. "Yes, Sir. No one will be able to coerce or abuse him again. We," he indicated Dimitri sitting by his side, "have made sure of that."

"Good enough for me. I expect a full report on my desk by tomorrow morning. Although, given the state of your leg West, you might want to get that checked out first. Trent, Mace, take this guy into custody. Don't worry about keeping him isolated because of his career as a police officer – he's slurred the good name of everyone in our department with his actions and maybe some time with some criminal buddies, might help him rethink his attitude," Reynolds said.

"You can't do that to me. This is all your fault," Green screamed, lunging for the gun with his uninjured hand. He raised it and pointed it at Shane, Dimitri jumping at him, just as he fired. Dimitri felt the impact as the bullet hit him, but it didn't stop him. Teeth bared, Dimitri crunched down on Green's neck, severing the man's artery. Only when he was satisfied the odious man was dead, did Dimitri release him, staggering back to his mate.

"Fucking hell," Reynold's said as Dimitri collapsed to the floor. He felt Shane's hand on his fur, searching for the bullet, but then the room got dark, and all of a sudden Dimitri had this overwhelming urge to sleep.

"Dimitri shift," he heard Shane calling him, but he didn't know if he had the strength to respond. "Shift damn it! If you fucking die on me, I'll go and get Sin to fuck me – hard."

He wouldn't would he? Dimitri felt confused, but with the last of his energy, Dimitri shifted, and lost consciousness.

☐

## Chapter Thirty

Dimitri's first sight, when he finally opened his eyes, was Shane curled up in a chair by the bed, fast asleep. His mate looked pale, thin and there were dark circles under his eyes. Dimitri sniffed but couldn't smell any blood, so hopefully that meant that Shane had gotten some medical attention. The next thing he registered was that he was unbelievably thirsty – like a complete desert in your mouth type of dry. Spying a jug of water on the bedside cabinet, Dimitri reached for it, stopping when a shaft of pain ran down his arm.

"Fuck," he swore loudly, prodding his gauze covered shoulder with the other hand.

"Leave it alone," Shane said sleepily, getting up from his chair and pouring the water Dimitri was craving. "You've been shot through the shoulder. The bullet came out when you shifted, but you still needed a dozen stitches or more. Captain didn't think either one of us should go to the hospital, being shifters and all, so he got Brian to come out here and stitch us both up."

"Brian?" Dimitri tried to pick through his scattered thoughts, grateful for the water which he sipped cautiously. Fuck, the feel of cool wetness sliding down his throat was so good. Then he remembered the name. "ME Brian? The guy who cuts up dead people for a living? He stitched us up?"

"Yeah," Shane grinned as he hobbled back to his chair. "Captain made him promise to make it look pretty. Look for yourself." Shane rolled down the waist band of the sweats he was wearing down past his thigh and Dimitri saw a row of eight stitches, all neatly holding together a healing wound.

Raising his eyes from Shane's tempting thigh, Dimitri said softly, "Come and lie down with me."

Shane shook his head. "I don't want to joggle your shoulder. You got more stitches than me, and you lost a lot of blood. That's why you passed out."

"Please." Dimitri had the sad little puppy dog look down pat, and he knew how to use it. Shane sighed, but hobbled around the other side of the bed, and climbed in beside Dimitri, carefully arranging his leg, so that it didn't come anywhere near his mate.

Dimitri rolled onto his side, and put his good arm out, resting on Shane's waist. "You sure you're okay?" he asked gently, worried at how tired his mate looked.

Shane nodded and gave a half smile. "Yeah, it's just, it was chaos after you passed out. Reynolds trying to work out how to turn Green's death into a viable shooting. Trent and Mace coming to terms with the fact that you and I are shifters. The boys...ha...it was the boys who called for backup. Seems all four of them came back here after they couldn't get us on our phones, we need new ones by the way, and when Kalel told them what we were investigating and the implication of the collar, Sin took them all down to speak to Trent and Mace. Trent went and spoke to the

Captain and Ben and Peter tracked us to here. The rest they say, is history."

Dimitri stroked Shane's skin carefully, processing what Shane had said. "How the hell was Green's death going to be described as a shooting – I munched the guy's neck."

"Don't remind me, okay. You kiss me with that mouth. Actually, if you hadn't have been out of it, you would have found it funny," Shane said. "The Captain called in Brian, all on the hush, hush, and he and Trent were wandering around Green's body, trying to work out how to get a shot in that would cover the bite wounds. Mace, pulls out this massive gun, takes two shots and Green had no neck at all – problem solved."

Dimitri did chuckle. He could just imagine the big guy doing something like that. Trent was the finesse, Mace was an all action sort of guy. "So how did they take the whole shifter angle?"

"Surprisingly well. Ben had already explained it all to Sin – apparently Sin was worried about hurting him in the dungeon and Ben explained why that wasn't a problem. Ben's in love I think," Shane added with a grin. "Trent and Mace had a few jokes at my expense about my cleared cases record, claiming they could do as well if they had a dog's nose, but they seemed fine with it. I guess we'll find out when we get back to our desks, and that won't be for a while."

"How come?" Dimitri said, worried that his killing of Green might cause them both problems. Or perhaps their handling of Kalel.

"We both got shot," Shane said. "Reynolds sorted out the shooting. Green will go down as the killer of all of the six men, including Gav, so Kalel's cleared. Trent and Mace are trying to track down who the other two victims might be and where their bodies are, so that their families will have closure. But the Captain said there is no way he could explain to the whole department how two men, shot in the line of duty, could return to work in a matter of days. We've got paid sick leave for two weeks."

"I'm sure we'll find something to do for two weeks," Dimitri grinned, the pain in his shoulder forgotten, as he carefully tugged Shane closer.

"Hmm," Shane said with a tired smile. "Well there won't be any of that until after we have both shifted and gotten rid of these stitches. And another thing we do have to do is find a bigger house."

"I guessed Ben would want to stay, and Kalel of course, but how did he and Peter make out?"

"Oh they did more than make out," Shane gave a genuine smile this time. "You have a new brother-in-law. Peter claimed him and reckons he is not going back to Jacobs Lake. He's going to transfer to the college here, to take up criminal justice can you believe?"

"Oh wow, Mom will be furious. Two sons with male mates, in law enforcement. Not sure that was on her plan for our future lives."

"You are going to have to talk to her at some stage," Shane said, slowly stroking Dimitri's face, and suddenly Dimitri didn't want to talk about his mother anymore. He knew he would have to have that conversation, but not when his mate looked like he needed some sleep."

"Have you had any sleep in a bed at all, since all this happened?" He said, stopping Shane's hand, by picking it up and kissing along his knuckles. Although he desperately wanted to kiss those gorgeous lips, Dimitri figured he had better at least clean his teeth first.

"Nope," said Shane, looking over at the clock. "And I'm only going to get about an hour if I sleep now. The boys promised to be back by six with food."

"What are they doing?" Dimitri asked as he helped Shane settle into the crook of his neck, wrapping his arm around Shane's shoulder.

"Looking at houses," Shane said and Dimitri felt Shane's smile on his chest. "Turns out Sin is a real estate agent."

Chuckling at the thought of the leather clad Dom showing houses for a living, Dimitri settled in for another nap. After some food, he and Shane could shift and then shower, and then...well they had two weeks to get everything else sorted.

☐

## Chapter Thirty One

*Five days later*

"That will be the pizza. I'll get it," Dimitri yelled, hurrying from the bedroom, wallet in hand. He and Shane were busy trying to get Shane's things packed up ready for their move, on the Saturday, actually make that less than twelve hours away. Peter and Kalel were working on the kitchen, and Sin and Ben were tackling the lounge.

"I've got it," Sin said, already at the door. Opening it up, the usually totally confident Dom was confronted with two very imposing women, and not a pizza in sight.

"Is Dimitri Polst here?" Asked the older woman, and Dimitri, who had been heading back into the bedroom to get Shane out of the boxes and into the kitchen, stopped in shock at the sound of that voice. It seemed Peter heard the same thing, and poked his head around the kitchen wall and simply said, "Mom?" The fact that Peter sounded as shocked as Dimitri felt, wasn't much comfort.

"Hey babe, what's wrong," Shane came out of the bedroom, his bare chest glistening faintly with sweat. "Is the pizza here, I'm starving."

"Not yet, no." Turning and herding Shane down the hallway he pulled Shane under his arm and indicated the two women now standing in the lounge. "Shane, meet my mother, and grandmother, both known as Mrs. Polst. Mom, Gran, I don't know if you remember Shane West, my mate."

"I think I need to sit down," Dimitri's mother said, staring at Dimitri's arm around Shane and looking a little pale.

"Let me clear that for you ma'am," Sin said, jumping in to remove the boxes they had piled on the couch, filled with Shane's books and odds and ends. Once the couch was clear, Sin indicated that the two women were to sit down. "I'll go and put some coffee on," he said to Shane as he disappeared into the kitchen area.

Peter, clearly taking his cue from his older brother, stepped forward with a very nervous looking Kalel under his arm. "Hi Mom, Gran, this is Kalel. He's a cat shifter, and my mate."

"Both of you?" Dimitri's mother yelled, while for some reason Gran started laughing. Neither woman showed a hint of the intimidating persona they had at the door. The younger Mrs. Polst was in shock and the older one was in hysterics.

Dimitri's mother fixed both of her boys with a glare and said, "Neither of you were stupid enough to claim these young men, were you. Because that would involve," she broke off and shuddered. "If they are not claimed, we can fix this. You can come home and just forget this little interlude every happened."

"Excuse me, Mrs. Polst," Shane said, stepping out from Dimitri's embrace. "I don't think this is a conversation I want to be a part of."

"No, well, you wouldn't," Mrs. Polst said spitefully. "I do remember you from the pack Shane and you were a poor excuse for a man then, and a poor excuse for one now. You broke your mother's heart running off like you did. Trying to convince my poor Dimitri he's gay, when he was going to marry Angela. And now Peter as well? Have you got my boys on drugs or something?"

"Mom, you have no right to speak to Shane like that. This is his house, and he is a respected member of the Stockton Police Department. Shane has done really well for himself and..." Dimitri started.

"It's alright, D," Shane said softly. "Your mother has a right to come here and express her opinion. She has the right to try and convince you to go home with her. My mother never bothered and you should be glad she cares enough to try and help you stay with your pack and your family. Now, if you'll excuse me." Shane gave a half bow, and took off up to the bedroom. Dimitri didn't have to read Shane's mind to know his mate was really upset.

Turning to glare at his mother, Dimitri let every ounce of his anger show – something he had never done before. "You come down here with your narrow-minded attitude without being invited. You hurt my mate, who believe me, is well and truly claimed, just as I am, and the man you malign still treats you with respect. It devastated him to leave his family and his pack. He has lived alone down here for fucking years and no one cared. Well let me tell you something, Mrs. Polst, that man is my mate. I love him, I have claimed him and if that makes me fucking gay, then buy me a rainbow t-shirt. Now you can see yourself out, because I have an upset mate to appease."

Dimitri stormed off and heard his mother talking to Peter, trying to convince him to come home. He ran back into the living room, ripped Kalel's shirt from his neck and pointed to the scar. "Claimed, and Peter is old enough to make up his own mind. Peter, Ben, Shane and Sin are part of my pack, here, in Stockton, and we will look after each other. Now unless you can tell Peter how to get grease stains out of the paintwork in the kitchen, I suggest you leave. We've got pizza coming and a lot of work to be done before our move tomorrow."

"I know," Gran said suddenly. "How to get grease stains out of paintwork, I mean." She smiled at Peter and said, "Help me up, boy, and you and your pretty young man can show me the damage in the kitchen."

Dimitri shrugged, smiled at Sin and Ben who were studiously looking out of the living room window, probably for the pizza delivery man, and leaving his mother sitting on the couch, headed up to the bedroom. As he pushed open the door he found Shane examining a very unfortunate pair of purple leather pants.

"Throw away, or keep?" Shane asked, waving the pants at Dimitri.

"Definitely throw away, babe. I much prefer the black ones," Dimitri said suggestively as he came forward, tossed the hapless pants towards the black rubbish bags they were using and bent down to kiss his mate senseless. In his opinion it was the best way to stop the negativity he could see swimming in Shane's gorgeous green eyes.

"So," said Shane a little breathlessly when the two men came up for air, "I heard through the walls that you love me, you're gay and you have your own pack now. You have been a busy man. I don't recall you saying anything about any of this to me before."

Dimitri smirked. It probably wasn't the appropriate response but it was hard to think clearly when his mate's eyes were full of lust and so much love, and the man in question was running his hand across Dimitri's ass. Taking Shane's face in his hands, so they didn't go wandering themselves and cause a distraction, Dimitri said clearly, "I love you Shane West. I'm gay-for-you, and I think what we have here, or at least what we will have in our new house tomorrow, is the perfect foundation for our new pack. Not mine. Ours. What do you think?"

"You don't think Sin should be the Alpha? He's definitely more dominant than you or me." Shane said, teasing Dimitri with his words, and deliciously sinful fingers that were now running up the length of Dimitri's cock through his jeans.

"I seriously thought about it," Dimitri said as he let out a small groan and pushed into Shane's touch. "But I figured he might have a spot of trouble meeting any Alpha challenge, given that he doesn't have a wolf form."

"Hmmm, there is that," Shane agreed, as, somehow, he had Dimitri's jean zipper undone and was gently coaxing Dimitri's dick out to play. "And this gay-for-you business. You've been researching on the internet again, haven't you? You do know that there is no such thing as GFY? There's OFY, but not GFY."

"God, you are going to kill me with terminology," Dimitri groaned, and it wasn't because of Shane's fingers, that were now wrapped around his cock and stroking gently. "Okay. I'm gay. I told my mother I'm gay, for goodness sake. I just have never lusted after any other man except you."

"I actually think you are bi-sexual, because you clearly have had sex with women before, and you have had sex with me." Shane sped up his strokes, and Dimitri was finding it hard to concentrate. The feelings from Shane's fingers on his cock were resonating throughout his entire body.

"I thought it was important to you...fuck just a little bit harder, yeah, like that...that I be gay," Dimitri panted.

"I'm gay, babe. I have never been with a woman, and never wanted to be," Shane explained. "You're with me now, so the people around us will think that you are gay. I need you to accept that label, because trying to explain the truth to other people is just too damn time consuming." Shane was adding a twist with his strokes now, and Dimitri knew he was close.

"Shane, baby, hon, sweetheart, don't care. I just love you," Dimitri garbled out. Shane dropped to his knees just as Dimitri felt himself spurt and suddenly the head of his cock was deep in Shane's mouth. Dimitri rode out his climax with his hands on Shane's shoulders, keeping himself upright. God if this was the payment he got for telling his mother where he stood in life, then fuck it, he would do it every day.

Shane licked him clean, and then stood up, saying softly, "I love you too," before kissing Dimitri hard enough that Dimitri could taste his own spunk. After a long moment, the two men broke apart and Dimitri smiled. "Is it weird that I find it so hot that you tell me you love me with a mouthful of come?"

Smiling, Shane said, "Just another form of romance babe. Now where's my pizza, cos I'm still hungry."

/~/~/~/~/

Shane was surprised to see the two Mrs. Polsts were still in the house when he and Dimitri came out of the bedroom looking for food. However, he didn't say anything about it, especially as Mrs. Polst senior was in the kitchen helping Peter and Kalel clean the cupboards, and Mrs. Polst junior was showing Ben and Sin the right way to pack ornaments in the living room.

"Oh there you are," Dimitri's mother said. "The boys left you some pizza in the kitchen – it's in the oven, so it should still be hot."

"Thank you mom," Dimitri said automatically, leading Shane through to the kitchen, where sure enough, the pizza was waiting. Not bothering to look for a plate, especially when they were most likely packed, Shane grabbed a piece straight out of the box and sat on one of his kitchen stools, focusing on his food, rather than what was going on around him.

"I owe you an apology." Shane looked up to find Dimitri's mother looking at him, with a small smile on her face. Dimitri had inherited his dark hair, dark eyes and full lips from his mother, and the woman was still beautiful in a classical, full-bodied way. Like most shifters, Mrs. Polst was aging slowly and she could easily pass as Dimitri's sister, or heaven forbid, his wife.

"That's quite all right, Mrs. Polst," Shane said, remembering his manners. "I understand this must be quite a shock to you. It was to me, I can assure you."

"Yes," Mrs. Polst pursed her lips when she looked at Dimitri. "Peter told me that Dimitri knew you two were mates before you went through your first shift and that my apparently angel boy at school spent a lot of his time bullying you."

"It's all true, ma'am," Shane said throwing a smile at Dimitri. "But I don't blame him for anything – there's no point in dwelling on the past – not if we are to have a future together."

"Well that's a very mature attitude to take, Shane," Mrs. Polst said. "Look, I still see your mother at all of the pack meetings. Would you mind if I told her I had seen you, and that you were doing really well for yourself?"

Shane quickly took another bite of pizza to give himself time to think. He had been gutted when neither of his parents thought to check up on him when he had left the pack. They had been so upset about his coming out, that they hadn't thought about the logistical side of sending a seventeen year old out into the world on his own. And in Shane's opinion that equated with not caring. However, he had enjoyed a close relationship with his mother before he left home. Maybe she had mellowed a bit over time.

"As far as I know neither of my parents cared when I left the pack," he said quietly. "But if you think the news would be of comfort to her, then by all means let her know that I am doing okay. I'm a detective now, we have our own house and I have good friends around me."

"Good friends who will be humping all of your boxes and furniture first thing tomorrow morning," Sin said, coming through to the kitchen with Ben on his heels. "Me and the pup here are going to head off. Can we give you a lift back to your hotel, Mrs. Polst?"

"Call me Susan," Mrs. Polst junior said. "All of you, call me Susan, and yes, er, Sin, that would be lovely, thank you. Are you ready Elise?"

"I'm coming," Dimitri's gran said good naturedly. Passing by Shane, she surprised him with a huge hug. "You keep that Dimitri in line, okay Shane? Don't take any of his shit."

"I won't ma'am," Shane said, giving her an awkward hug in return. "You ladies stay safe now."

"Well, that went better than expected," Peter said with a sigh of relief, when Sin, Ben, Susan and Elise had all left the house.

"Yes," Shane said slowly, not sure what to think, but glad at least that if Susan did ring again, Dimitri wouldn't have to lie to her anymore. Then he looked at Kalel, who seemed to have a permanent place glued to Peter's side. "Mind you, if Mr. Polst comes knocking at the door, you and me boy, we're going run and let our mates deal with that situation."

Wide eyed, Kalel nodded, looking up at Peter with a worried look on his face. "Don't worry about it kitty," Peter said, stroking Kalel's face. "If Dad turns up me and Dimitri will be running right alongside of you. Isn't that right, bro?"

"So right," Dimitri agreed, putting his arm around Shane. "Now how about we all head off to bed. We've got a lot of work to do in the morning. And I don't plan on getting any sleep for quite some time," he added in a whisper in Shane's ear. "I still owe you an 'I love you' blow job."

"Always up for that, lover," Shane whispered back, feeling his cock harden in his jeans for the first time since Susan walked in the door.

"Maybe not yet, but you will be," Dimitri grinned as they headed off to the bedroom. And much, much later as he and Dimitri stepped into the shower together, Shane truly believed, for the first time since he saw Dimitri in the Captain's office, just a matter of a few weeks before, that his mate did love him, and was going to stay with him, no matter what. If they could survive men like Green, getting shot and Dimitri's mother – they could survive anything.

☐

## Epilogue

Shane sighed as he went through yet another stack of papers on his office desk. He and Dimitri had been back at work a month now, and things were really quiet, which was good when you were in the homicide business. But Shane couldn't shake the thought that something was wrong. Which was a really weird feeling, considering everything was going so well.

The new house, which Sin had found for them all, was brilliant. A huge six bed, six bathroom villa, with a gorgeous yard and plenty of garage parking was perfect for the six men who now lived there. Shane had been surprised that Sin had wanted to move in as well, because he figured his friend would be happier in his own place. But Sin had asked if he and Dimitri would mind, seeing as Ben now wore a solid gold chain in lieu of a collar. Shane secretly thought that Sin and Ben were mates, but as Sin was a permanent top, his neck was still free of any claiming mark.

Peter had managed to transfer colleges, and was now studying criminal justice at the local university, along with Ben, who hadn't been sure what he originally wanted to do. But so far he was enjoying the same courses as Peter, and Shane figured that it wouldn't be many years before Peter and Ben started working together in some area of law enforcement. The two men had been friends for far too long to separate now.

After long talks with Shane and Dimitri, Kalel had elected to stay at home, working online to get his GED. He had proven to have a really good eye for color and design, and was hoping after he had graduated high school, that he could do some kind of interior decorating course or similar. In the meantime he was learning cooking, with Peter's vocal encouragement. All of the men in the house were getting sick of take out for dinner, and Kalel was proving to be a remarkable cook.

As the three working men, Shane, Dimitri and Sin all shared the expenses involved in running the house. Shane found that even with the larger place, and higher utility bills, because he was now sharing those costs with the others, financially he was better off than he had ever been. He was putting money aside, hoping to surprise Dimitri with a cruise for the holidays. Shane knew Dimitri was helping Peter and Ben with their studying costs, and he thought a decadent luxury break away from everyone would be a nice change for them both.

The pack side of things was going well as well. Shane and Dimitri still went for their Sunday night runs, but now they were joined by Peter and Ben's wolves, and Kalel's cat. Kalel proved to be a cougar, and the cat could move surprisingly quickly when he had to. Sin often came with them, not so much for the run side of thing, although the man was super fit, but because he didn't like the idea of his young pup being naked around the others. For a confident Dom, Sin could be surprisingly old fashioned in some things, and accepting shifter's views on nudity was an issue he was having trouble with. Trent and Mace ran with Sin sometimes, if they weren't working and for the first time in his life Shane actually had a pack to run with – his wolf really enjoyed that.

Looking up and spotting Dimitri coming into the office, Shane was struck yet again with how fucking confident and good looking his mate was. Their sex life was awesome, they had so many things in common, and knowing that Dimitri was with him for life, gave Shane a sense of security he hadn't known he needed. But for the past week or more, Dimitri had been a bit nervous, almost as though he was hiding something and for the life of him, Shane couldn't work out what it was.

Shane's eyes lit up when he saw that Dimitri was wearing the near black suit that Shane had recommended to him when they were chasing down leads in the local menswear store. He knew he had made the right choice. The charcoal color set off the contrasts between Dimitri's hair and skin. The fit of the jacket and pants was near perfect, and the confidence that Dimitri showed as he strode towards their shared desks, was enough to set Shane's blood roaring.

"You're looking sharp there, partner," Shane said as Dimitri approached. "Very sharp."

"I had something special to do today," Dimitri said, coming around the desk and swinging Shane's chair around so that they were facing each other. Then to Shane's intense shock, Dimitri dropped to one knee and pulled a small jewelry box from his pocket. He wasn't...No surely he wasn't...He fucking was.

"Shane West, you make me happier than any other person alive. I love you with all that I am, and I want everyone to know how much you mean to me. Would you do me the honor of becoming my husband?"

His fingers shaking, Shane opened the box to find two large platinum bands. Dimitri plucked the smaller one from the box, and held it out to Shane, and praying that his hand wasn't visibly shaking, Shane let Dimitri slip the ring on the third finger of his left hand. Holding out the second ring, Dimitri indicated that he wanted Shane to put the second one on him. Taking a deep breath, Shane said, "You are the biggest idiot I know, Dimitri Polst, but I love you with all that I am and I will marry you anytime you like."

"I'm an idiot?" Dimitri asked as he leaned up to give Shane a wickedly debauched kiss.

"My lovely idiot," Shane said softly, ignoring the claps and cheers going on around the office. If anyone had a problem with Dimitri's proposal they weren't silly enough to say anything right at that moment. Especially not with Captain Reynolds in the room who was clapping as loudly as anyone else.

Shane's phone rang, and with a groan he pulled away and answered it.

"You've got a body," came the dispassionate voice of the call center. Jotting down the details, Shane clicked off the phone and looked over at Dimitri.

"You couldn't have done this over dinner? We've got to go to work," he said, although he really wasn't angry. He looked down at the ring on his finger. It felt so right.

"At a dinner, no one would have had the pleasure of seeing how cute you are when you blush," Dimitri said, leading them through the well-wishers and out to the car. "And besides," he said seriously, stopping Shane in his tracks for a moment. "I never want you, or anyone else, to doubt how much I love you and want you for life. Proposing to you at work seemed like the best way to go about it."

And as Shane started the car, and they headed out to another crime scene, he realized, not for the first time, that his wonderful mate was right.

# End

If you want to read more about the men in this story then keep an eye out for the next installment due out March 2015. In **"Copping a lot of Sin,"** Ben has some decisions to make when a new bear shifter comes to Stockton, and Dimitri and Shane are busy working on a new case that could threaten shifters everywhere.

## Other Wolf Shifter M/M Books By Lisa Oliver

## The Cloverleah Pack Series

### The Reluctant Wolf

(Book One)

Kane Matthews, Alpha of his small wolf pack in Cloverleah has been raised to believe that mates are not possible for gay men and has lived his life accordingly. Kicked out of his home pack years before because of his sexual orientation Kane has built a solid and comfortable life for himself in the small town of Cloverleah. Imagine his surprise when an unscheduled visit to the small town's diner unleashes a flood of emotions in the man he didn't think possible - not least of all, lust. But finding out it is possible for wolf shifters to have gay mates is just one of the things that Kane has to overcome if he is to have the forever future he has been hoping for.

Shawn Bailey never expected to find his mate. He is just too different - an "Other" who has the power to instill fear in any other shifter. After spending ten years on the run from his Alpha father he spends most days just trying to stay alive. When a chance encounter brings him face to face with his mate Shawn has to decide if the man in front of him is worth staying for.

But with hunters, Alpha challenges, Kane's parents and a smitten Alpha from another pack all interfering in Kane and Shawn's budding romance, not to mention some surprising answers about Shawn's own unique talents can these two true mates find the happily ever after they are looking for?

## The Runaway Cat

Book Two Cloverleah Pack Series

Griff Matthews knew he looked like trouble but for a wolf shifter mechanic he was fairly laid back most of the time. Pleased that his Alpha was finally settled with his new mate, Griff longs to meet the man of his dreams. Little did he know he would find it that same evening, when he was too drunk to realize that his good looking hook-up was actually his mate. Problem is when he woke up sober his bed was empty.

Derrick "Diablo" Franklin was just looking for a hook up with a like minded shifter. The sexy cat shifter was deep undercover for the FBI and although his case was coming to an end, he had hopes for his career that didn't involve finding a mate. However after meeting Griff Diablo realized his plans might have to change.

But nothing is easy for the two men as they battle the FBI, a crime lord from Baton Rouge and a host of contenders looking to take Diablo away from Griff. And just who is Angel Bandures?

## When No Doesn't Cut It

Book Three Cloverleah Pack Series

Scott Peterson, beta wolf in the Cloverleah Pack, has a good life. He loves his cars, riding his Harley, and going out with pack members and friends. But when an attack on his pack by a bear shifter, brings his mate into his world, from Texas of all places, Scott realizes he could lose everything he ever held dear.

Damien, Alpha wolf of the San Antonio Pack, didn't want to go to Cloverleah and definitely didn't want to be chasing a rogue bear shifter that was threatening the Alpha of the Cloverleah Pack. But he was in for a pleasant surprise when he finds his mate. Now, if he could just find the time to enjoy him.

Between murderous bears, deceptive wolves, two packs and a BDSM club, the road to HEA is anything but smooth for Scott and Damien. And then there's a fire, and an Alpha Challenge, and let's not forget Diablo and Griff's wedding. About the only thing Scott and Damien haven't got is time to be together, and it is that lack of time that could pull them apart.

Warning. This book is about gay wolf shifters. It contains m/m anal and oral sex, rimming and a spanking scene. There is also some violence, fighting wolves and a couple of deaths of minor characters. Child Sexual Abuse is also referred to. Please do not buy this book if these aspects offend you in any way.

## Never Go Back

Book 3.5 Cloverleah Pack Series

Damien, Alpha of the San Antonio pack had thought it was an awesome idea to take his mate, Scott, back to his ex-home pack to catch up with his parents and ex-Alpha. He had assumed that his power as a wolf, and the fact that he was from such a large pack would guarantee both men a good time.

A homophobic Alpha and a disgruntled mother are just two of the problems the men face. In fact if Damien isn't careful his mate might not make it back to Texas alive.

Included as a free read - **Malacai Finds His Mate**

Malacai, Second in the San Antonio Pack has waited over eighty years to find his true mate. When he and his Alpha Damien rescue a young shifter from a hole under a kitchen he never believed his search was finally over. Unfortunately life has a habit of intervening and the path to his HEA was going to take a lot more work than he had bargained on.

This is Book 3.5 of the Cloverleah Pack series and is based on the characters in Book 3 (When No Doesn't Cut It). While it contains enough back story to be read as a standalone, if you want to know more about the characters then please read Books 1 - 3.


## Calming the Enforcer
Book Four Cloverleah Pack Series
Troy Peterson has been waiting three long months for his true mate to return from his deployment in the US Army. But when Anton doesn't turn up as planned, Troy starts to second guess everything he knows about his mate - and that's before he has even met him.
Anton Sage fully intended on meeting Troy, the moment his ninety days service was up. But the Army had different ideas and now Anton is sitting in his wolf form, in a cage, wondering if he will ever get the chance to meet the man Fate intended for him.

Even after they meet, things do not go well. Between the Army, the mysterious Kylan, another wolf with the hots for Troy, an overbearing friend, and some old fashioned misunderstandings, Troy and Anton might never have the happily ever after they had dreamed of. Sometimes the mating gift can prove to be a curse.

Warning: This book is about two male wolf shifters. It includes fated mates, graphic gay sex, and references to BDSM, PTSD and cutting. Some foul language and violence.

## The Bound and Bonded Series

### Bound and Bonded Series - Book #1 - Don't Touch

Submissive wolf shifter Levi has met his mate, the one he wants to call Master. The problem is the Master concerned wants him for nothing more than a regular Saturday night scene and thanks to the rules the man has put in place there is nothing Levi can do about it.

Thanks to the war Steel is a damaged wolf. He knows Levi is his mate and wants nothing more than to claim him. But to do that means spilling more secrets than Steel has ever been willing to share with anyone. Does he have it in him to tell Levi what is going on, or should he release him to another Master at the club?

Two men who want each other - rules and secrets standing in their way.

Warning - this book is based on BDSM concepts and contains graphic scenes of M/M sex, strong language in places and a small amount of violence, plus an HEA.

28,000 words plus a sample chapter from the next book of the series.

## Bound and Bonded Series - Book 2 – Topping The Dom

Pearson, Alpha of the Bound and Bonded club and the pack it houses, has always wanted to find his true mate. But when the man turns up in the shape of wolf on the run he finds out the path to true love is not as easy as it seems, especially when Dante is as Dominant as he is.

Warning: This book is about male gay wolf shifters. Although set in a BDSM club there are no actual scenes of

BDSM in this particular title. However there are scenes of M/M sex. If this is not something you are into then this book is not for you

## Bound and Bonded Series – Book 3 – <u>Total Submission</u>

Kyle, one of the head enforcers of the Washington Pack, wants nothing more than to find the evidence he needs to convince his Alpha that the man he is following is gay, so he can head back home. Being in Iowa is doing his head in. But a fleeting encounter in a gay nightclub, has Kyle rethinking his priorities because out of nowhere, he had scented his true mate.

Teric is a cat-shifter with a job to do and more than a few secrets of his own. Scenting Kyle at a nightclub is the last thing he needed, but Fate intervenes.

When the two men meet, secrets come out and for the safety of his pack, Kyle has to let Teric do his job. But what happened to the total submission he had spent his life dreaming about?

Warning: This book contains graphic MM sex, violence and coarse language that may offend some readers.

## About the Author

Lisa Oliver had been writing non-fiction books for years when visions of half dressed, buff men started invading her dreams. Unable to resist the lure of her stories, Lisa decided to switch to fiction books, and now stories about her men clamor to get out from under her fingertips.

When Lisa is not writing, she is usually reading with a cup of tea always at hand. Her grown children and grandchildren sometimes try and pry her away from the computer and have found that the best way to do it, is to promise her chocolate. Lisa will do anything for chocolate.

Lisa loves to hear from her readers and other writers. You can friend her on Facebook here, or email her directly at yoursintuitively@gmail.com. If you want to chat with her on Skype, then email for contact details.

Made in the USA
Columbia, SC
07 August 2018